VERY
LeFREAK

VERY LeFREAK

RACHEL COHN

Alfred A. Knopf
New York

THIS IS A BORZOI BOOK PUBLISHED BY ALFRED A. KNOPF

All rights reserved. Published in the United States by Alfred A. Knopf, an imprint of Random House Children's Books, a division of Random House, Inc., New York. Originally published in hardcover in the United States by Alfred A. Knopf in 2010.

Knopf, Borzoi Books, and the colophon are registered trademarks of Random House, Inc.

Visit us on the Web! www.randomhouse.com/teens

Educators and librarians, for a variety of teaching tools, visit us at
www.randomhouse.com/teachers

The Library of Congress has cataloged the hardcover edition of this work as follows:
Cohn, Rachel.
Very LeFreak / Rachel Cohn.
p. cm.
Summary: Consumed with e-mailing, online video games, and the many distractions of her electronic gadgets, hyper-frenetic Columbia University freshman Veronica, known as Very LeFreak, enters a rehab facility for the technology-addicted after her professors and classmates stage an intervention.
ISBN 978-0-375-85758-4 (trade) — ISBN 978-0-375-95758-1 (lib. bdg.) —
ISBN 978-0-375-89552-4 (e-book)
[1. Self-realization—Fiction. 2. Technology—Psychological aspects—Fiction.
3. Electronics—Psychological aspects—Fiction. 4. Rehabilitation—Fiction.
5. Columbia University—Fiction. 6. Universities and colleges—Fiction.] I. Title.
PZ7.C6665Ve 2010
[Fic]—dc22
2009012305

ISBN 978-0-375-85096-7 (tr. pbk.)

Printed in the United States of America
January 2011
10 9 8 7 6 5 4 3 2 1

First Trade Paperback Edition

For Christobel Botten and Jaclyn Moriarty,
two great friends from Oz who so warmly cheered
on this book (and its author) in its original and final incarnations

VERY
LeFREAK

PART ONE

The Song Diaries

CHAPTER 1

Happy Birthday to You, Very LeFreak

It wasn't the fact that Starbucks did not—*would* not—serve Guinness with a raw egg followed by an espresso chaser that was ruining Very's hangover. Nor was Very concerned that she had stumbled into her campus Starbucks on the morning after an overnight "study session" with the beautiful engineering major from Ghana whose name eluded her, although Very knew there were many hard consonants involved. Hey, she wasn't even bothered that yesterday she'd been fired from her work-study "security" job checking student IDs—a feat that, contrary to her university career services advisor, was not, like, impossible to pull off—yet Very probably could be counted on later today to blow the remaining credit on her maxed-out card for primary wants like new headphones rather than for secondary needs such as food and tuition.

The fact was, Very wasn't even technically hungover, unless

a sugar coma from late-night Cap'n Crunch consumption, along with several rounds of Red Bull, qualified. It was the excessive inhale of birthday cake and cereal that had done Very in. Like the mild, fully clothed spooning session—rather, *study* session— with Ghana that had closed out the birthday party her dorm had thrown her, the sugar infusion had felt so comforting in the moment. It was the *after* that felt so empty, the Red Bulls 'n' Cap'n fallout headache, the *un*comfortable wake-up with Ghana, two strangers with stale morning breath gazing into one another's eyes, each silently begging the other: *Yo, let's pretend this never happened?*

Ghana had a girlfriend who was away for a semester abroad, and Very had no intention of getting in the way there. Her random act of intimacy hadn't been quite as dangerous, she assured herself. It wasn't like she'd cheated on either her real or her imagined boyfriend with Ghana. Bryan had been her best guy friend before becoming her real boyfriend, but, once their relationship had advanced to that level—when Very and Bryan were two of the only holdouts in their dorm not to go away for Spring Break—it had lasted only a day before she'd been forced to dump him. Bryan was just too good to be true: his own fault. El Virus, Very's imagined boyfriend, he of the passionate e-mails and IMs and text messages, he who taunted her every thought and feeling by existing in the electronic ether yet who refused to appear in live, physical form before her, had suddenly dropped out of the ether; she hadn't heard from him since what felt like an eternity (but technically, according to his last text message, since the week prior to Spring Break). The problem with an imaginary boyfriend was, if he chose not to answer her electronic missives,

Very had no idea where else to find him. She had no way of knowing whether the "facts" he'd given her about himself were, in fact, true. *Maybe* El Virus was an engineering student at MIT in Boston; *maybe* he was a CIA spy on a secret mission to ferret out Al Qaeda moles stashed away on whaling ships off the coast of Nova Scotia; *maybe* he was an insurance appraiser in Des Moines with a wife, two kids, and a kitten afflicted with cerebral palsy and that was why he could never sacrifice his home for his happiness and leave the family for Very; or *maybe* he was a bored and restless hacker up in Scarsdale, possibly within breathing distance of her. God, what if El Virus turned out to be some punk thirteen-year-old with a hard-on?

"Guinness with a raw egg?" the Starbucks counter person repeated back to Very. "I don't understand."

Very didn't understand, either. The concoction promised to be horrific, but her mother had sworn by this hangover remedy, and while Very had no intention of, like Cat, losing her life to chemical effects, she had to believe that her mother would most reliably have known the best chemistry for curing the after-coma.

"Just please may I have a latte." Very sighed. "*Triple* shot. *Whole* milk." What could ruin her kind-of hangover, she realized as she pulled her wallet from her jeans pocket, was that . . . fuck, she had no cash, and her credit card and Starbucks birthday gift cards were tucked away in her dorm room.

"Broke again?" a familiar voice from behind her in line piped in.

Very turned around. Lavinia. Very had never been so happy to see her roommate's disapproving gaze.

"Got a fiver you can loan me, Lavinia?" Very asked Lavinia.

"Jennifer," Lavinia said. "My name is *Jennifer.* Here, borrow five dollars. Again. Happy birthday to you, Very LeFreak."

That was it! Today's primary playlist, Very decided, would be called, simply, "Happy Birthday to You, Very LeFreak." Very's top personal goal, beyond mythic goals like eating more protein and vegetables or volunteering to teach mobile-electronic-communication skills to the elderly, was to make a music mix to commemorate each and every mood that should strike her. To seek spiritual enlightenment and physical well-being in life was challenging enough, but to exist within one's soul without proper musical inspiration for each day's quest was just plain pathetic, an existence not worth living. While some chose to write in journals or blogs to record the loves, losses, obsessions, and miscellaneous musings of their daily lives, Very chose to remember hers via music mixes, her form of daily diary.

When she died, the future biographer(s) of her Very Unextraordinary Life would only have to unarchive and research her playlists to unearth the everyday secrets of her heart and mind. Very decided this year's commemorative b-day list would include "The Ballad of Cap'n Crunch" by Pirates R Us, covers of "Happy Birthday" by Loretta Lynn, New Kids on the Block, and "Weird Al" Yankovic, plus an assortment of moody boy-trouble songs TBD and some Irish-pub drinking songs, and conclude with Stevie Wonder's "Happy Birthday" (obviously).

Or, instead of the birthday mix, she could show her appreciation for Lavinia's fiver and title today's list "What Is Jennifer's Aneurysm?" in tribute to her roommate. Very didn't know what that girl's problem was. "Lavinia" was so a better name. A Lavinia might be descended from Eurotrash celebrities; a Lavinia probably went to boarding school in Switzerland, where she had a mad lesbian affair with the headmistress who wrote the glowing recommendation letter that got Lavinia accepted into the Ivy League; a Lavinia would write her roommate's freshman University Writing course term paper—Very wouldn't even mind if Lavinia chose depressed ol' Virginia Woolf—and it would be *brilliant*. A Jennifer was just a girl who shared a name with so many other girls. This particular Jennifer was a typical one from suburban New Jersey, a girl who maintained a respectable GPA and dressed straight out of the J.Crew catalog. But despite her uncalled-for resistance to being called Lavinia, this Jennifer was a rather endearing one, whose earnest good-girl-ness was almost exotic to Very. Unfortunately for Very's sleep clock, she was also a Jennifer who woke up at five every morning to row on the crew team and to consequently, unfailingly, disturb her roommate's first hour of sleep.

A Very LeFreak was a girl who probably needed a "room of one's own." But she could peacefully coexist with a Lavinia as a freshman roommate. "If I don't mind being a LeFreak, why should you mind being a Lavinia?" Very said. She gratefully plucked the five-dollar bill from Lavinia's hand. "Thanks!"

"With logic like that, and you wonder why you can't finish your Age of Reason assignment," Lavinia said. She was so feisty—it was what Very loved about her, despite Lavinia's refusal to write term papers for her. And Lavinia never failed to take on impossible tasks—like waking up at dawn to *exercise*—as she did now, reaching over to attempt to mat down Very's tangled strands of fire-hair. "Please let me buy you a blowout at a salon for your birthday present instead of the balance board to play *Ultimate Cheer Squad* that you not-so-subtly text-blasted that everyone could chip in to get you. I really need to see what that wild hair looks like if it's tamed, *Veronica*."

Her birth certificate would show that Very had indeed originally been a Veronica—named, according to Cat, after Cat's favorite old movie star, Veronica Lake, with the gorgeous drape of long blond hair, but it wasn't until her early teens that Very, whose head spouted a very un-Lake-like mass of curly red hair, had discovered her mother's secret stash of *Archie* comics and figured out her true namesake. No matter, Very had never been a good Veronica. She was, as Cat used to say, *so very Very*. She was a Very who, on the first day of kindergarten, when the other kids were dancing the hokeypokey, shimmied with abandon to the song inside her head instead, the one on constant replay from the old disco mix given to Cat by a long-gone DJ boyfriend. While the other kids were shaking it all about, Very copied her mother's center-aisle *Soul Train* moves, singing out, "Aaahh, freak out! Le freak! Say chic!" Veronica had been Very LeFreak ever since.

Very didn't mind the name. Who'd want *not* to be a freak? Was such an existence possible?

Very swatted Lavinia's hand away from her hair. "Now that I'm so rich, can I buy you a scone or something?" she asked.

"Buy our room some peace from Bryan," Lavinia answered. "The boy called the room line about twenty times after the party last night looking for you. And he trolled the hall all morning waiting for you to show back up at our room. Could you find him already and put the rest of us out of our misery?"

"Poor Bryan." Very felt genuinely bad for him. But he'd asked for it.

Very hadn't meant to break his heart. That was what she did

to boys—she had a long history in this sport. She'd warned Bryan of this in advance, so he really had only himself to blame. Very had fended him off for months, since freshman orientation last semester, pleased to grow with him as friend rather than lose him as fuck. Why'd he have to finally go and proclaim his love for her just as El Virus mysteriously disappeared from Very's online wonderland?

"Poor Bryan's ex-girlfriend's roommate," Lavinia corrected Very.

Coffees in hand, Very and Lavinia seated themselves at a corner window table—prime viewing area for watching Morningside Heights students and professors, professionals and psychotics, stroll by. "So did you meet any guys you like at the party last night?" Very asked Lavinia.

Lavinia shook her head.

"Girls?" Very asked.

"How many times do I have to tell you?" Lavinia snapped. "I am *not* a lesbian."

"You seem awfully defensive about the suggestion, crew girl," Very chastised.

"Softball players are typically the lesbians, Very. Not rowers!"

"You just keep telling yourself that, sweetie."

"I think I might like Bryan," Lavinia blurted out, suddenly red-faced.

"Oh," Very said, jolted awake. "Wow. Why didn't you say something earlier?"

"I don't know. I don't think I realized it until recently. I sort of missed him when I was away over Spring Break. Bryan's just so . . . *there* all the time. And then when he wasn't, I wished he was. But the whole idea is stupid, probably. How could I compete with"—Lavinia stood up and shook out strands of her disciplined brown hair, then ran her hands in a curvy silhouette shape alongside her slim hips as she tried to imitate Very's party-girl dance moves—"*you?*"

"Why would you want to?" Very asked. *That* was the reasonable question. Very embraced her inner freak because it was who she was—no use denying it—but why would a nice girl from West Orange, New Jersey, who had two stable parents and a solid B+ average and every potential to one day have the house, the car, the career, the kids, try to compete with a LeFreak? Very was spawned from freaks; it was in her blood. The biological father Very had never known had been a 'shroomer and a mosher, her mother's one-night tent stand the year Cat had opted to drop out of college and follow some roving music festival instead. Cat had been the queen of free-spirited freaks, but look what happened to her, the victim of her own excesses: one too many geographic moves gone awry, one bad trip down memory lane, dead before age thirty-five. Very felt sure her path was the same as her mother's. But while Very might not save her own self from the inevitable crash and burn, surely Very could block dear Lavinia's curiosity from veering toward that destructive path.

Lavinia shrugged. "You just . . . Everyone likes you, wants to be you. Guys fall at your feet."

Very said, "People like me because they want someone to show them a good time, to break them out of their own shells. They have no interest in who I really am. They like what I can bring out in them, in a particular moment. Where are they when I need help with the courses I'm failing? When I can't afford breakfast? Where are those guys when I'm puking my guts out in the bathroom stall the next morning?"

"I'll always hold your hair back for you," Lavinia promised.

That meant so very much to Very. It was settled. "If you like Bryan, I think you should have Bryan. He should be so lucky. But, honey?"

"Yes?" Lavinia said.

"Please don't let me get together with a boy you like. You have to let me know these things first. I'm sorry enough for that momentary brain freeze with Bryan to begin with; but really really really retroactively sorry if he's someone you were interested in. I might be a freak and a slut and a very bad student, but I really want not to be a bad friend. Deal?"

"Deal," Lavinia said, smiling in her suburban-girl splendor of perfect teeth and sensible ChapStick'd lips. Girl so needed the right cosmetics consultation with the next available cross-dressing MAC counter boy-girl. Very vowed to invest her last scraps of funds toward her roommate's fabulousness makeover rather than blow the dough on the new sound devices she really, really wanted. This would be her birthday present to herself.

CHAPTER 2

Tragically, Even a LeFreak Cannot Resist ABBA
(Esp. on Her B-day)

Very slept in fits lately, an hour or two here and there: restless, dreamless, hopeless. She could attribute the sleep deficit to any number of stresses. There had been her inability to effectively balance her course load with her recently-fired-from work-study job (phew!), which she'd needed to help finance the college education she had no parents to provide for her. The dorm parties she occasionally organized—from which Very occasionally skimmed funds off the beer money to finance the audio player(s), laptop(s), and rotating cell phone habits her college lifestyle necessitated—required a substantial per capita investment of Very's late-night time and energy. But mostly it was the simple noise that kept her awake, the chronic chime of technology, messaging her with IMs and e-mails and voice mails, ringing in news of batteries needing charging, songs to be heard, overdue papers, negligible grades, study groups to be scheduled, some guy who thought she was hot and wanted to meet her at the Hungarian Pastry Shop to discuss Kant, some girl-crush inviting Very to a coffeehouse poetry slam, or poor dear Bryan, who would (used to) want Very's undivided attention to work on The Grid, the online platform the two of them had developed for their freshman dorm. Mute button? As if. Off button? Never.

Very could blame any of these noises for her lack of restful sleep.

Very chose to blame ABBA, her mother's musical remedy for any heartache situation.

> *The love you gave me, nothing else can save me*
> *S.O.S.*

The song had Very in a trance. If she hadn't slept for more than four continuous hours since El Virus's disappearance (if the sudden silence from a stranger she'd never met counted as a "disappearance"), it was because she had listened to the song "S.O.S." by ABBA so many times lately that it was almost as if no other song had ever mattered, as if the infinite hours she'd invested in building her epic song library had never happened. "S.O.S." was not only Very's song of the moment. It was the sound track to her life, defining it, the message inside her brain playing over and over, seemingly beyond Very's ability to, simply, hit the Stop button.

> *When you're gone*
> *How can I even try to go on?* . . .

S.O.S., Very thought.

Exactly.

Who could sleep when a heart longed so badly and only ABBA understood?

The other primary obstacle to sleep was sleep's unreasonable requirement that a body lie still. Very had been moving moving moving her whole life. From a childhood with a mother who loved to wander the world, Very had learned never to settle comfortably into a "home" that could be taken away at any random moment. Why bother to unpack her meager belongings when they'd be moving to the next town, state, or continent, seemingly at the drop of a hat—or of a lover—with no means to support themselves other than Cat's sheer will that they'd survive, or that a new and improved man would save them? (Never happened.)

Never get comfortable. That was supposed to be the rule. Even if the dorm room Very had shared with Lavinia for barely seven months felt like the first real home Very had ever allowed herself to settle into. That is, dorm life had felt cozy until lately, until some indefinable *what-the-fuck* had caused a shift in Very's body chemistry. She couldn't pinpoint the cause, but Very felt as if Pandora's box had recently been opened and had yet to reveal its contents. Until that happened, chaos—mind/body/soul variety— would prevail.

Tranquility? What was that? The only time Very could remain completely still was when her body collapsed from exhaustion.

Very tried lying on her bed for a birthday nap—surely she was so entitled? She'd promised Lavinia, who didn't like the red burn inside Very's eyes, that she would try to rest. But Very tossed and turned, fully aware that one bad turn and she could easily asphyxiate herself.

Cables coiled around her body. Wires from her new premium headphones dangled from her ears to the floor, where her iPod was lodged, while inside her left ear, underneath the large headphones, she'd slipped a small earpiece for her iPhone in case birthday calls should ring through. (Very believed in separation of church and state, and in the sanctity of music collections, which deserved their own independent electronic storage devices separate from cell phones—thereby requiring separate but equal, and concurrent, use of both her iPod and her iPhone.) A laptop charger cord extended from Very's stomach, where her computer rested, to an outlet below her nightstand. Most dangerously, perhaps, a feather boa strung with chili lights dangled from her neck, a birthday gift from the Sylvia Plath Society two floors down, but it was too cute for a birthday girl not to wear all day long, even if the accessory did require nearness to an electrical outlet to achieve its best visual effect. Completely worth it.

To uncoil was not an option. What if El Virus chose her "sleep" time to strike? Her laptop and phone needed to be locked, loaded, and ready.

Very was not unaware that she could have her choice of guys (or girls, if the moment, or the right Ani DiFranco song, called). She certainly didn't lack for time spent taking advantage of her own appeal. A whole university, a whole city, of crushes—Very was fond of every last one of them. But they were playthings.

The One Not Seen owned her heart. If only he'd come a-callin' again.

She'd "met" El Virus in an online poker room that had quickly turned into a marathon IM session during her first term at Columbia, when she was still in the adapting-to-a-roommate phase of the freshman transition. The roommate part wasn't hard; Very had shared a van or a tent or a motel room or, some years, an actual bedroom with her mother for most of her life, so sharing a small space wasn't a problem. Lavinia's snores versus Very's night-crawling body clock was the real challenge. Wide awake while Lavinia snored, Very tapped away on her laptop from her side of their dorm room, entwined with her online soulmate. Everything she'd ever tell nobody, she told him.

What Very knew about El Virus, the reliable facts: nothing. What she liked about him, anyway: He made her laugh. He pined for her without the benefit of ever having feasted on her red curl-tresses or the voluptuous breasts and hips that sent the boys into trance states when seated near Very—and her boob-spillage blouses—during lecture courses. The thought that Very and El Virus's in-person chemistry might not match their electronic chemistry was of course considered—and discarded. Very and El Virus had promised: When the time was right, they would meet. They would not force it. She had college—she hadn't lied about that fact. (Lied about being a spirited farm girl from Nebraska? Maybe.) Their fated meeting would happen when it happened. He had "issues" to work out first. Who didn't, buddy?

So why the sudden hush? El Virus had been her secret man, a loud girl's silent comfort. She might not have been faithful to him in body, but in her heart, she was all his.

Whatever happened to our love?
I wish I understood. . . .

S.O.S., *El Virus. Come back*, Very willed her laptop as she finally started to drift into sleep. *I don't need just anybody. I need YOU.*
The person she electronically received instead was her elderly

16

great-aunt, whose voice announced itself through Very's cell phone earpiece, inside Very's ABBA-trance: "So. You're nineteen today." The voice might well have sung *Happy fucking birthday to you, you silly, silly niece*, for all the enthusiasm Aunt Esther's voice conjured.

"Yessiree," Very answered. "Nineteen." She moved the laptop from her stomach up to her chest so she could play online Chinese checkers with a stranger somewhere in the universe during the birthday call with her only known relative.

Sure, today Veronica turned nineteen, but it was an occasion Very LeFreak found laughable rather than exciting. How could she only be nineteen? Very felt ninety, practically as old as Aunt Esther, for all the lifetimes she felt she'd already experienced. Mostly in Manhattan, but also in Baja, on Haight Street, in Goa, in Seattle—Cat and she had lived in all these places, depending on the climate that time of the year, or depending on that year's Cat-man. So much living already—it was why Very had to keep on moving, wherever the whim should lead her. Get it all in now.

"Did you receive the sweater?" Aunt Esther asked in a tone implying irritation that the five-day turnaround time on a thank-you note she expected from Very for the birthday sweater had not been met.

"I received the sweater," Very mumbled. Since Aunt Esther didn't seem to have the words "Happy birthday" in the repertoire of her birthday-phone-call etiquette, Very decided she'd save the words "thank you" for the note to Aunt E. that she'd have Lavinia scribble and mail on her behalf tomorrow. It was like her aunt made the sweaters just to receive the thank-you notes.

Aunt Esther was a retired, widowed schoolteacher who passed her days watching television and knitting sweaters. Very had hated being deposited in her aunt's home to ride out her teen years after Cat died, but the premium satellite TV hookup and the handmade sweaters had almost made the creaky-old-Connecticut-house-with-a-batty-old-lady experience worthwhile. As she was extremely ancient, nearsighted, and color-blind, with hands that often shook, Aunt Esther's sweaters looked like they'd been created by a geriatric stylist tripping on acid. Sewn together with psychedelic knit patterns that were sometimes stitched with random pieces of fabric—often from Goodwill military shirts or items once worn by the son Aunt Esther had buried many sad wars ago—the sweaters were lopsided, often patchworked together with yarn rather than thread (easier to see), with arms typically made from two completely different patterns. Each sweater had a label—attached to the back of it by glue gun—that proclaimed, in shaky ballpoint handwriting: *This sweater has been knit for you by* ESTHER. As fashion, the sweaters fell somewhere between butt-ugly and absolutely brilliant. Very adored them. One day, when she had the time, she'd try to sell the product line to Bergdorf or Bendel.

"Should I expect to see you soon, dear?" Aunt Esther asked.

Why? Very thought. Very was an orphan. She didn't owe visits to anyone, not even to her only known relative. She and Aunt Esther had been victims of circumstance.

So when you're near me, darling can't you hear me?

Very hit the Stop button on ABBA and let herself lose at online checkers so she could give full attention to her aunt on the phone—and eavesdrop on the conversation taking place outside her dorm-room door. Very heard Lavinia's voice assuring their resident advisor that Very was sick in bed and no, now wouldn't be a good time for Very to discuss the keg (empty, but still) that had been found in an underage student's dorm room down the hall after Very's birthday party last night.

"Should I expect you for Passover dinner later this week, dear?" Aunt Esther asked.

Very considered the question. Maybe a little time-out was in order. A breather from school and parties, from El Virus–pining, from Bryan-dodging. And, bonus: Aunt Esther made truly great soup, and cookies. And further, admittedly, the lady was pretty decent company to watch TV with, in no small part due to her 50-inch plasma TV, best use of a tax refund ever. That TV had consistently proven itself Very's most qualified nonhuman babysitter during her high school years, soothingly keeping Very company at a low surround-sound hum so she could focus on her schoolwork. But that had been back in Very's youth, when she used to focus on silly things like schoolwork.

Yes. Very would take haven in New Haven—a brilliant plan. And a religious excursion could let her beg off the talk with the RA for at least a few more days. Their last talk had been the "Final Warning" one to Very. The next talk's edict would be . . . Never mind, it just wouldn't happen.

"Sure," Very told her aunt. "I'll come. But I can never remember how this Passover thing works. I don't have to fast or anything, right?"

As if the shock of losing her independent life with her mother wasn't enough, there had been Very's deliverance upon Aunt Esther's doorstep in New Haven after Cat's death, seeing the mezuzah inserted outside Aunt Esther's front door, and only then realizing . . . *We're Jewish?!*

CHAPTER 3

There's Got to Be a Morning After
(Your Birthday / Your Mistakes)

If she was Jewish(ish), Very might have had a bat mitzvah when she turned thirteen. Instead, she and Cat had been living in a re-mote beach-resort town on the Arabian Sea in India, where her mother was "homeschooling" her via the Internet (basically, Wikipedia-ing the Important Facts from the History of the World, and ordering appropriate-level math textbooks from Amazon) and where there probably weren't other Judaic tribe members available to celebrate Very's passage into womanhood. Not that there had been much cause for celebration at the time. Very had prematurely ushered herself into womanhood just prior to her thirteenth birthday, which had elicited no proud moments of maternal joy from Cat.

So later, at the age of nineteen, Very asked one of these tribe members—Ruth Goldberg, who walked into the study lounge on their dorm floor at ten in the morning on the day after Very's birthday—what the experience had been like. "Hey, Ruth. Was your bat mitzvah, like, the best day ever in your life?"

Ruth observed Very lying on the lounge sofa with a blanket over her body, a laptop visibly tucked under it. "Did you sleep in here last night, Very?"

"Kinda."

"Why? Did you throw a loud party, so Jennifer kicked you out?"

"Hardly!" In fact, Very had spent the night in the study lounge out of respect for Lavinia, who'd had trouble falling asleep while sleepless Very had been typing too aggressively on her laptop. Also, Lavinia often giggled in her sleep, along with snoring loudly, and since it was too tempting to wake her to say *What's so funny and am I involved?* Very had decided to be a good roommate and give Lavinia some peace. Somebody ought to get a decent night's sleep. Very said, "So this bat mitzvah thing. Was it great?"

Ruth Goldberg said, "The memorization part was hard. The party after was pretty great, though, and having all my family there from all over was really special. The only bad part was when my cousin Jonathan decided to try to get my best girlfriend alone in a supply closet at the temple during my service, and her very loud shriek of '*Ewww!*' was heard by everybody there, including my great-grandma with the hearing aid."

"But . . . did you feel closer to God?"

"Who?"

"G-o-d."

"Oh yeah, Him. Sure, I guess. I also felt closer to getting the really cute dress I'd been eyeing at Bloomingdale's because of all the gift cards I received."

"Thank you, Ruth. You've been so helpful."

"If you really want to know about the experience, why not send out a meme? Get a broader perspective."

"Exactly!" Very said. She reached for her laptop, which had been resting on her stomach while she'd been resting her eyes, and typed her query into The Grid: "My Jewish sisters and brothers. Please, tell me your tales of mitzvah-ing circa your thirteenth year." Very closed the laptop, covered it with the blanket, and moved her sleep mask down from her forehead to cover her eyes. She hoped to get a few moments of shut-eye before returning to the laptop to read the sure-to-have-accumulated responses that would fill the gap in her Judaic knowledge, and do so in a warm, anecdotal way rather than through some sterile textbook accounting of the details.

"Very," Ruth said.

"Hmm?"

"Are you really trying to sleep in here? This is a study lounge. I came in here to study. Other people will come in here to study."

Very's hand gave Ruth the thumbs-up. "Okay by me."

Ruth Goldberg said, "It's hard to talk in here if you're trying to sleep. A friend was going to meet me in here to review for a Biology quiz."

"You won't bother me," Very chirped, completely unaware that it was she who'd be bothering Ruth, and not the other way around. "Thanks, though!"

Amanda Yamaguchi arrived in the study lounge next. "Very!

I'd recognize that hair even with the sleep mask over your eyes. Sorry I missed your b-day party over the weekend. Is there going to be a makeup party?"

"Possibly a Thursday party this week," Very said. "Lavinia is doing some research study for her Psychology class—you know, one of those deals where participants get, like, five dollars to fill out a survey about their masturbation habits or something. But it's surprisingly hard to get people to show up for these things even when they've signed up in advance, so I might throw a party for anyone who does it, and then everyone can pool their five bucks, and one person—say, the best karaoke-er of the night—will win the loot. Like a lottery, but with beer. I haven't quite worked out the details, but check The Grid. I'll post there as soon as it's finalized."

"Cool, I'll be there!" Amanda said. "And can I borrow your Lit Hum notes from last week?"

"You can, but they probably won't make sense, since I zoned out during class and ended up just drawing slightly porno cartoons about Aristotle and Plato."

"Oh."

Very reached into her pocket for her credit card. She held it out for Amanda. "But if you'll run over to Tom's Restaurant and pick me up an order of eggs and home fries, your breakfast is on me."

Amanda took the card from Very. "I'm there! Well-done or over easy?"

"Over easy, 'course."

"Meet you back here in twenty."

"Awesome. And if you can find someone with decent Lit Hum notes from last week who'll loan them to us, even better."

A male voice Very knew all too well responded, "You can borrow my notes."

Very rolled over onto her side so her backside was facing the latest person to arrive in the study lounge. "That's okay, Bryan. But thanks anyway."

What, was he trying to be nice since he hadn't bothered to give her a birthday present?

The previous Halloween, Very had gone all out for Bryan's birthday. She and Lavinia had thrown a Halloween-night birthday party for Bryan and his roommate, Jean-Wayne, who lived one floor below their own dorm room. It was the party after which Very and Bryan had stayed up all night creating The Grid, the online social hub that had solidified their friendship, and their campus celebrity.

Neither Bryan's nor Jean-Wayne's birthday fell on Halloween. In fact, their birthdays weren't even close. Bryan's was in early September, Jean-Wayne's in late November, but Halloween fell in between and therefore was excuse enough for a party.

At the beginning of their first semester, the two sets of roommates—Very and Lavinia, Bryan and Jean-Wayne—had evolved into a tight circle at Columbia's John Jay Residence Hall, an all-freshman dorm made up mostly of single rooms, with a few doubles scattered among the various floors. Very and Lavinia lived in room 745, Bryan and Jean-Wayne in room 645. Conveniently, both rooms were situated at a most choice social location—next to the kitchen lounge, home to the all-important microwave allowed on each floor. (Some people harbored private microwaves illegally in their rooms, but most students just used the permitted one in the kitchen.) Soon after freshman orientation, Very and Lavinia had learned a most important lesson in luring cute boys—or anybody, for that matter—to their room for socializing: No one could resist the smell of microwaved Chewy Chips Ahoy! cookies. They tasted better than homemade Toll House cookies straight out of the oven, required way less work, and tasted better still when topped off with the spliff that the boys one floor down sometimes procured somewhere in the stairwell—where the dorm's petty dealer dealt—on their jaunts to follow the trail of the upstairs girls' yummy freshly baked chocolate chip cookie smell. (Lavinia abstained from the weed but was always willing to pop the cookies back into the 'wave for an extra twenty seconds upon the burnouts' request. A real sport.)

Not that it was hard to make friends in Jay, cookies or no cookies. Their particular residence hall was known as one of the more social dorms on campus, where students typically left their doors open for passersby to drop in at any whim to hang out or— doors sometimes closed and sometimes not—make out. Also, the building was home to John Jay Dining Hall, which due to its central location on campus could always be counted on as a prime meeting-and-greeting place, convenient as well since one could find an assortment of great breakfast cereals available for consumption at any time of the day or night. Cap'n Crunch = Primary Food Group, in Very's optimal food pyramid.

Very and Lavinia, soon after moving in and discovering they weren't of the I-hate-the-very-sight-of-you roommate variety, had organized the furniture in their room to maximize its socializing potential. They crammed their beds side by side in the far corner of the room to leave open the rest of the space for cheap throw pillows and beanbags tossed on the floor for visitors. Very kept the Chewy Chips Ahoy! cookies in stock at all times, despite Lavinia's responsible concern that SnackWell's was a healthier option (true—but also not so tasty), and Very kept her laptop's tunes set to Shuffle for listeners to enjoy the manic mixes that grooved from soul to punk to funk to space opera to honky-tonk twang. Lavinia took care of keeping the room stocked with napkins and drinks for guests, and Clorox wipes for spills, to keep their room as tidy as it could possibly be for a near way station.

The Halloween party the girls had thrown for the boys was a surprise party, though not in the sense of people jumping out from behind closet doors and from underneath beds to yell "Surprise!" Their dorm room was too small for such surprising, although Very, who often fantasized about transmogrifying herself into a feral jungle cat who lunged in surprise attack on her prey and then smothered her victims in tender, lickful kisses as compensation for peeling off parts of their flesh, wouldn't have minded such a dramatic surprise-party option for greeting Bryan and Jean-Wayne when they arrived at their b-day extravaganza.

Instead, the boys' surprise had been the roommate clique's first flash mob, of sorts.

Very had organized the campaign online to include many of the residents at Jay. The plan was that at exactly 11 p.m. on the night of the party, participants should return to their rooms, and those who had the forbidden microwaves should turn them on, and those who didn't should turn on their highest-voltage electrical appliances—hair dryers, TVs, etc. Just before 11 p.m., Lavinia went downstairs to do her part, while Very led Bryan and Jean-Wayne to the window of her room, which overlooked West 114th Street. Then, at exactly 11 p.m., the lights in the dorm room—no, in the whole building—flickered off and on, then went off entirely, as did all the other appliances in the building. Total building power outage.

"What the hell?" Bryan said. His kinky brown hair appeared kinkier still in the glow from the outside streetlamps. That hair, so ungoopy on such a goop, was one of the more endearing features on his boyish face.

"Look out there," Very said, pointing out the window. She didn't bother to check out Jean-Wayne's hair. That boy knew his way around some serious product and always looked good. Nothing goopy about him, despite the gelled goop often spiking up some of the short black pieces of hair at the front of his head.

A row of fellow students stood on the sidewalk on West 114th Street (their hair difficult to discern at such a distance). As the power went out, everyone assembled on the street suddenly flicked on a lighter and waved it in the air, concert-style. At Lavinia's cue, the group yelled from the street, "HAPPY BIRTHDAY, BRYAN AND JEAN-WAYNE!" Because it was Halloween, the assembled crowd included several superheroes, some movie stars, some cartoon characters, some monsters and zombies, a vampire here and there, a few princesses and French maids, a couple gangsta boys, and several "commuter" people chained together as if they were holding on to an overhead rail on the 1 train. The view from the dorm room was that of a complete freak show—just the way Very liked it.

The power turned back on in the building soon enough, and the party moved down the hall from Very and Lavinia's room to the student lounge, which could accommodate more people, but already folks were buzzing about the success of the endeavor, wanting more. Very, dressed up as Lara Croft, had a dance with anyone of any species who'd have one with her, while Lavinia, dressed up as a sexy tennis champion, obligingly kept folks' cups filled and kept the watchful sober eye on the group to make sure no superhero-daredevil's drunken antics inspired any jumping from Jay balconies (which had an unfortunate, and tragic, history at Columbia).

Very had tried not to feel omnipotent about what she'd pulled off. She'd created a moment of complete darkness in an entire building in New York City, after all. Take that, Lord Voldemort. But it was hard not to ignore the requests from fellow students at the party as they danced the night away with her:

"Hey, Very, you should organize more stuff like tonight's. I was thinking about a flash mob at one of the cupcake places the tourists go to. You know, everyone just shows up at once, talks loudly about how the cupcakes at another place are better, then abruptly leaves."

"Very, you know that Chinese restaurant you always order from when people are in your room? I think we should all go there in person, and everyone scream 'VEGETABLE LO MEIN!' at the same time, then leave."

"Tomorrow night, Very, everyone gathers in your room and puts flash mob ideas into a hat, and we choose the best one."

"Hanukkah *gelt* equals guilt, girl. We lead a group of prospective students on a campus tour to Mondel Chocolates on Broadway, then we all assemble inside to talk in old-lady voices to the prospects about buying Hanukkah candy and 'Call your mother already!'"

Very hadn't liked this last suggestion.

She didn't have a mother to call.

Some people took things so for granted.

Very had turned away and pulled Bryan, dressed as Larry of the Three Stooges (to Jean-Wayne's Moe), for a slow dance rather than hear more about the Hanukkah plan.

"You do Lara Croft nicely," said Bryan, who'd inspired Very's costume by once telling Very she reminded him of what Lara Croft would look like if Lara were a freaky-haired redhead who replaced her hot pants with Very's long, flowing hippie skirts and bare feet, and if Lara swapped her machete for an iPhone. (The slutty, tight-fitting tops remained the same.) "And thanks for the party."

"I have another present for you," Very said. "For Jean-Wayne, too. Where'd he go?" She looked around but did not see J.-W.

Bryan said, "Dude disappears at random times. Don't bother looking for him. Once he disappears, usually late at night, he'll be gone for hours."

"Does he have a girlfriend? Or boyfriend?" J.-W. was a fey one—hard to pinpoint on the sexuality meter.

"Not that I know of."

"Curious," Very said. "Maybe he's a secret go-go boy at a gay club."

"The guy has a terrible sense of rhythm. Doubt it."

"Damn." Very would very much have liked to have a friend who was a secret go-go boy. "He probably won't appreciate the mix I made him, either, then. If he indeed has such a bad sense of rhythm."

The party had thinned out, as these things did at three in the morning, and Very and Bryan returned to her dorm room so she could give him his birthday present.

Lavinia, already asleep on her bed, did not stir as Very and

Bryan curled up next to each other on Very's bed to listen to the birthday mix she had made for Bryan: "*Mwah* Hah Hah Scary Scary: Angry-Girl Bitch Tunes (A Happy B-day Tribute)."

"It's the requisite angry A-girl name bitch songs, like from Alanis and Avril and Ani," Very explained. "Along with some bhangra and soca for alone-in-your-room danceability. And 'The Monster Mash' song so you remember this is your Halloween-not-birthday birthday mix."

"Why the angry-girl songs?" Bryan asked, placing his hand on Very's hip in what Very hoped was a platonic way.

Very placed her hand on his hip in a most definitely platonic way. "To prepare you for the future bitches that might break your heart. Listen to this stuff and it's like ammo. You'll be equipped to deal 'cause you'll know what to expect."

Bryan asked, "You know how college friends are, like, incestuous? How come we're not?"

"Because we're cuddle buddies," Very said. "And because I've been known to make mincemeat of kind boys' hearts." She wanted to add, *So don't let me.* "Do you like your mix?"

"*Like?* Try *love.* It's awesomeness. Every guy's dream for Lara Croft to make him one. How did you learn about all these different styles of music?"

Very shrugged. "The usual, I guess. The Internet. Plus, I grew up all over."

"Where was your favorite place? Musically, I mean."

"India," Very answered. "The music there, it's so sweet, and yet really passionate. Highly danceable and fashion-inspiring."

"Worst place?"

"San Francisco, for sure. At least according to my mom. All

those music-poseur snobs who think they know better than everyone else. Can't just relax and enjoy a fucking song for what it is. She'd say."

Bryan, in his cuddling, sometimes made Very feel too safe. She felt a cry coming on. Too close for comfort. She squirmed out of Bryan's embrace, stepped out of bed, and walked to her desk. She powered on her laptop.

"The flash-mob thing?" Very said to Bryan. "I think we should formalize it."

He, too, got out of bed. He sat down in Lavinia's desk chair, next to Very's.

"Yeah!" Bryan said. "I've been thinking we ought to make an online group for our friends at Jay, anyway."

"Like, our own private networking site, for people here," Very said, nodding.

Bryan's hand touched Very's on her keyboard. "A hot girl who can program," he teased. "You're kind of like the Holy Grail. Let's do it. Stay up till we've finished."

Total, total turn-on. But of the programming variety.

And so they consummated the dance of finger-tapping into the night.

But that had been months ago. The Grid, the site they'd created that night, had become an unqualified success, but Very and Bryan's friendship, lately, since Spring Break . . . not so much. Obviously he'd learned nothing from the angry A-girl b-day mix she'd made him.

They must have been alone in the study lounge now, because Bryan leaned down to whisper in her ear. "I didn't know what to get you for your birthday. I was going to organize something for you on The Grid, but then . . . you know. Feels weird. Is that okay?"

The iPhone lodged beneath Very's thigh vibrated. She instinctively grabbed for it—was El Virus back? But no, it was just a text message from Lavinia. *R U awake?*

Very's thumbs went into action. *Study lounge. Bryan alert. Bryan alert.*

Bryan said, "Very, I'm trying to talk to you."

She didn't look up from her iPhone. "What?" If only it would vibrate again and be El Virus. Very typically slept with the iPhone lodged underneath her thigh so she could be instantly alerted to new text messages. Prior to his disappearance, she'd received enough messages from El Virus in the middle of the night that now any mere electronic buzz against her flesh got her hot and bothered.

Why had El Virus turned off? He was the technological pusher who'd awakened the electronic beast inside her. And wasn't the pusher supposed to keep the user using? Very needed El Virus to feed the beast. She'd go mad if he didn't pimp himself back online, where he belonged.

"Very," Bryan repeated. "Are you even listening to me?"

Big big big mistake, sleeping with a dear friend as substitution for an AWOL El Virus. *Never never never do that again*, Very resolved.

"Pay Lavinia some attention," Very muttered. "I'll take that as my birthday present."

She considered texting Bryan the real message she wanted to convey to him: *Please go away now. And return El Virus to me.* Instead, she sat up on the sofa, giving up on the idea of more sleep, and placed her computer on her lap. She turned up the

volume on the machine, which announced that her online handle, Very LeFreak, had joined an online poker round of Texas
Hold 'Em.

Bryan left the study lounge.

He got the message.

CHAPTER 4

End-of-March Madness, or,
Men Who Frequent the Library
When They Should Be Watching College Basketball

Great. Now another awesomely cheesy song owned Very's soul.

> *Since you been gone*
> *I can breathe for the first time*

Very kept her head down low as she passed through the majestic marble entrance to Butler Library, but she couldn't fail to notice the many students passing her and flashing her the thumbs-up signal and *Hello* waves. Very smiled in regal acknowledgment but spoke to no one as she approached the back elevator. She needed to study and not be distracted by friend or flirt prospects. Seriously. She dodged the hormone-racing enclave of the Main Reading Room, headed straight to her secret hiding spot in the remotest corner on the top floor of the library, and sat herself down in her favorite musty cubicle. It was the one campus sanctuary where she could truly hide, and finally get some studying accomplished. Sweetly, since March Madness had reached the Sweet Sixteen round, the library was relatively empty, and Very had her choice of quiet spots.

> *Out of the darkness and into the sun . . .*
> *And breakaway . . . lalalalalalala.*

Truly. *How* had people survived before the iPod?

Very was an hour into studying before she was aware that another soul lurked in the darkest crevice at the back of the sixth-floor stacks in Butler Library. Startled to feel a tap on her shoulder, Very looked up to see a pissed-off guy standing in the library aisle. He banged his hands against his ears, the universal code for *Turn the Fucking Music Down*.

Very hit the Stop button on her music, but did not take off her headphones. "Sorry, dude," she whispered to Angry Man. "I didn't realize the music was so loud. I'll turn it down."

She hit the Play button again and returned to staring at the book on her desk. She hated postmodern art. She wanted her art in the form of sly smiles and bare buttocks and heaving bosoms, please. Geez. She could paint splotches just as easily as that Jackson Pollock guy. Where was *her* exhibition at the Met?

Concentrate, Very, she told herself. She needed a 3.0 grade point average to maintain the New Haven Benevolence Society scholarship that was the primary source, after student loans and part-time jobs, funding her Columbia education. Very teetered at 2.7, based on midterm grades. But one mind-blowingly good Art History term paper, and Very could get to 3.0. She could.

Loud cough. Louder than the pop song's guilty-pleasure wail.

Very looked up from her book again. Why was Angry Man still standing there?

Very turned the volume down and took the headphones off. "What?" she asked him.

"You were singing very loudly, too," he said.

She inspected him more closely. He looked grad student age—ruffled hair, bewildered expression, Ivy League tweedy. Totally, legitimately old enough to buy the kegs for future parties Very might be commissioned to throw.

"And you're complaining because of my taste in music or because I was making too much noise?" Very asked.

"Both," he said.

"I take requests," she advised.

He laughed. "I'll take early Britney Spears, please?"

"Song or dance moves?"

"Wow, hadn't thought about it in those advanced terms. How 'bout both?"

Jackson Pollock was so very boring. Time for a study break.

Very spun the wheel on her music player to the appropriate song, then spun the chair she'd been sitting on out from under her. She didn't have the outfit or, quite frankly, the body, but she could still perform a damn impressive rendition of Britney's "Oops! . . . I Did It Again" dance routine. "I played with your heart, got lost in the game," Very sang, but in a polite whisper so as not to disturb any other potential study-lurkers in the back cavern of the library.

The stranger applauded her act.

Oh baby, baby.

This was the problem. Very could recite song lyrics at whim, remember the step-by-step dance moves from bubblegum music videos she hadn't watched since she was a kid, but her brain was no longer cooperating with the *useful* part of its usefulness. Despite a lifetime of moving from school to school, city to city, country to country, Very's ability to excel at academics, to achieve near-perfect scores on standardized tests, had always been her one stabilizing reward; that is, until lately, until her brain had decided to care *only* about song lyrics in sync with any buzz that announced the sexy siren call of an e-mail or IM.

The stranger glanced at the book on her desk and asked, "Art History class?"

"Yeah," Very said. "I'm calling my term paper 'Jackson Pollock: A Window into the Modern Psyche, or Just a Contemporary Psychotic?' "

"He was both. I'm doing my master's thesis on postmodern art in America."

"Love you," Very said. She'd have to hide out in the library more often—and call upon the cute-guy-summoning powers of fallen pop princesses more often, too.

It was only four hours later, mid-make-out-session, long after the lights had gone out and neither Very nor Not Such an Angry Man Anymore had bothered resetting the timer to turn the lighting back on, that Very discovered how not hidden her hidden spot was.

Deafening-*Ah-choo*-wrist-slash-inducing-squeak noise.

Very could recognize that sneeze anywhere—it sounded like

a hyena had ferreted her out in the stacks. How could that un-sexiest of sneezes *not* cut short her otherwise extremely satisfying kiss-a-thon with the guy who'd just beautifully written the conclusion statement on Very's term paper? No, *written* her term paper was not what the cute grad student had done. That would be plagiarism. Cute Grad Student had whispered suggestive sentences into her ear as she'd sat on his lap and typed the words herself. Very totally wrote the paper herself. She had a broken fingernail from tapping the keys to prove it. (Should the nail be saved in a Baggie as forensic evidence in case she was ever called to a Disciplinary Committee plagiarism adjudication? No, no. *Worrying is for schmucks*, as Cat used to say. Usually Cat said this the day or two before rent was due, the day or two before Very knew she and Cat would be moving again.)

A-hem.

Bryan. Poor Bryan. Hung up on the wrong girl, and allergies that always announced his presence.

Sex—just that one time—had changed everything between them. Herewith, Very vowed to stay the course on her newfound path—strictly making out and above-the-waist fondling à la Ghana and Tweedy Grad Student, until the time came when Very and her true love, El Virus, could be together.

"Very!" Bryan said, not bothering with the library-etiquette whisper. "I need to talk to you." He looked up at the ceiling while he spoke, to give the vixen and her victim time to disentangle.

"Text me," Very whispered in the grad student's ear. She admired his lovely rear view as he disappeared into the library stacks. Another one bites the dust.

Very turned her attention to Bryan. "Do we not think your approach is somewhat stalker-worthy?"

She didn't mean to be so cruel. But she wanted to go back to being friends with Bryan, and the brutal route seemed the optimal way to return him to the platonic-without-any-false-hopes friendship track. And the crueler Very cut him loose, the more appealing Lavinia could appear to him.

Bryan said, "I'm over you. Don't flatter yourself." When he was so cruel in return, he could turn tempting again. *Careful, Very.* "Not going to make that mistake again."

Bryan slapped a copy of the *Columbia Spectator*, the student newspaper, down onto her cubicle desk. A headline on the bottom of page two read: "University Vows Crackdown on Freshman 'Grid' Crowd."

"Uh-oh," Very muttered.

The narcs were closing in. Very could feel it. What to do, what to do? Someone at her work-study job—*former* work-study job, the one she'd been fired from for using the office photocopy machine to make two hundred copies of The Grid's old-school-style paper newsletter—could easily have tipped off the *Spec*. Why, oh why, hadn't she replaced the toner cartridge herself, or cleared up the paper jam that finally killed the ancient machine?

She was so close to that 3.0, and to the end of semester. If she could only make it through the next six weeks, she'd have the summer to get her shit together, to lie low, to give the university and her dorm's resident advisor the chance to forget any of the minor troubles she might have contributed to in her freshman-wilding stage. A summer was all she needed; it would give her time to figure out a new income source, to close the wounds with

Bryan, to seek out El Virus and find the peace and contentment that would guide her, uneventfully and without threat of university probation or scholarship loss, through the remainder of her university years. Easy.

"They don't know," Very told Bryan, not really believing her own words. "They can't trace it to us."

"They can," Bryan said. "They will. We've created a monster. We need to summon a meeting. You, me, Lavinia, and Jean-Wayne. Find a remote place, and figure out our escape plan."

"Passover dinner in Safe Haven, New Haven?" Very said.

CHAPTER 5

Passover for Beginners

"You smoke?" Lavinia said upon bursting unannounced into Very's room at Aunt Esther's.

Very sat hugging her knees in a window seat, her bare feet and legs under her loose skirt, seemingly not bothered by the cold air coming in through the open window as she smoothly exhaled her cigarette smoke out it. She rested a cheek against her knee as she took another drag and blew out a smoke ring.

"Only when I'm here," Very said. No matter how welcoming Aunt Esther was, being at her house, in this attic room, was stressful. Very's casual smoking habit became a necessity here. Returning to this home that was not her own brought up sad, unsettling memories of the displacement, loss, and heartache that had been Very's high school years. All that angst was supposed to have gone away when she moved to New York to go to Columbia, like magic.

It had not.

Very looked around the attic bedroom that had been her high school sanctuary in the period after Cat died, when she'd been taken in by Aunt Esther. Very had remembered meeting her aunt a few times as a child—mostly remembered those meetings taking place soon after eviction notices or the expiration date on one of her mother's boyfriends came due, necessitating a cash infusion from Aunt Esther—but those meetings were always in the city, at one of Aunt Esther's choice urban destinations: Saks Fifth Avenue, Zabar's, the Georgette Klinger or Elizabeth Arden salon. It had been almost surprising to discover Aunt Esther's home dwelling in New Haven for the first time and to realize that the lady lived in an actual house and not within a grand store. Her house was a nice one, too, a beautiful old Victorian with secret rooms and closets and nooks to explore throughout, smelling like a custom old-lady blend of freshly brewed coffee, lemons, and BenGay. But neither of the two bedrooms available for Very's choice had been to her liking; she'd begged for the attic, then spent weeks clearing and cleaning it out to make it suitable as her own bedroom. She'd liked the privacy and spookiness up there. If she was going to be a motherless teenager stranded at a great-aunt's house in New Haven, Very wanted her room to reflect her circumstances. To live in the attic was to be the damsel in distress, the prisoner in the tower.

Also, Aunt Esther, frugal spawn of the Great Depression that she was, refused to pay for an Internet connection, and the attic was the only place where Very could reliably pick up the neighbor's wireless.

"I can't believe I've lived with you all this time and not

known you smoke." Lavinia grabbed the half-burned hand-rolled cigarette from Very and deposited it in Very's soda glass. "And if you can make your own cigarettes and blow smoke rings that efficiently, you're obviously way too experienced with this vice."

"Great," Very said. "Now you've wasted my cigarette and my Coke. You owe me five dollars." Cigarettes were like IMs from El Virus, Very thought. Once you started, you just wanted more more more, a physical craving embedded into your internal code whether you realized it was happening or not. But there it was: a wanting, that grew into a hunger, that grew into a burning need. Never deflating or dissipating.

"You owe *me* five dollars," Lavinia reminded Very.

"Then we're even." The instant nicotine surge from the half cigarette she'd smoked now made Very wish she could pass the rest of this Passover thingie chain-smoking in the attic. More nicotine. More badness. More *Please, El Virus, where the fuck are you?*

Longing. Why did it never stop?

"And your reward is that you now have that much less chance of cancer and obesity. You're welcome." Lavinia turned off the small desk fan that Very used to help blow the smoke directly out the window. Advancing age might have caused Aunt Esther to lose many of her physical abilities, like climbing the stairs to the attic, but the woman could smell cigarette smoke probably even from the basement. Two things Aunt Esther would not tolerate: cigarettes and the f-word.

She also wasn't fond of female newscasters who broadcast their cleavage along with the death and despair of the world, or weathermen generally, and more specifically weathermen with highlights in their hair. But who could blame Aunt Esther, really?

"And I didn't hand-roll this cigarette," Very said. "I bummed it off Hector. He makes his own."

"Hector?"

"The janitor." In response to Lavinia's blank stare, Very added, "At our dorm."

"You mean Hector the Janitor who hates all of us overprivileged college kids and says the girls on campus dress like *putanas*?"

"Yup, that Hector. *Hombre* rolls some tiiiight shit."

Lavinia shook her head. "You still owe me five dollars."

"Fuck fuck fuck fuck fuck," Very sighed.

"Don't drama-queen," Lavinia said. "The sacrifice of a cigarette and a Coke is not that tragic. And we both know I'll never see that five bucks again, so don't sweat it."

"I wasn't planning to. I just needed to let the f-word out a few times before we go back downstairs with Aunt Esther. Get it out of my system. You brought the boys with you?"

Very had taken the early-morning train out to New Haven, ahead of her dorm friends, and ahead of the meeting with her resident advisor she'd conveniently forgotten. She told Lavinia she was heading out early to help Aunt Esther prepare dinner, but really she wanted some alone time to hunt for El Virus online. Not that Very couldn't hunt for him online in their dorm room while students flowed in and out of it regularly; certainly no one would be the wiser. But this El Virus disappearance was getting dire. Very wanted to hunt for her private man in private. She felt like desperation might be starting to show on her face, or in the aggressive taps of her fingers on her keyboard.

MIA.

Still.

Was it possible to sue an online paramour for loss of electronic affection? Very had grown used to "seeing" El Virus on a regular basis—his status updates, his IMs, his virtual-world avatar (a monk), his naughty photos depicting him in various stages of icon fetish. To take that away from her so callously was an act of cruelty and desertion conceivably at the level of litigation.

His photos never showed his full face. He often wore a mask, so she'd seen him as a Teletubby, as Darth Vader, as Madonna (cone-breast era), as disgraced former president Richard Nixon (her personal favorite—it was E.V. holding up his peace-sign fingers that clinched it). Inspired by the Madonna shot, she'd responded in kind, sending him only cleavage shots of herself: Very in Elizabethan costume; Very in a too-small, too-tight Gap T-shirt; Very introducing her sister cupcakes, Blossom (red velvet) and Round (straight-up choc on choc). No, no, make that: boobs in Elizabethan costume; boobs in too-tight tee; delicious Blossom and Round, waiting to be monk-devoured.

Another thing. How had civilization existed before the camera phone? How did one even pass time before instant electronic gratification became imprinted into human evolution?

So many questions, for El Virus, for the universe. So few answers. None, to be precise.

While Very had twittered at Aunt Esther's, Lavinia had gone out to New Jersey to borrow her parents' car and driven back into the city to pick up the boys to bring them all to New Haven for the seder with Very and Aunt Esther. Rare possession of a vehicle, all agreed, mandated a shopping trip to Target on the way home, and this almost made the excursion to New Haven seem exciting. So many dangerous experiences could be on the horizon in New Haven, outside the cozy confines of their Manhattan college campus. Target could happen. Maybe even IKEA. And, of course, the escape-route master plan—to be plotted after dinner—which would swallow The Grid and make possible the rest of their undergraduate academic careers.

Passover would also mark the first time since before Spring Break that the two sets of roommates had been together, this foursome who'd seemed inseparable until recently. Very suspected they all hoped the time together would pass over quickly. She'd commemorate the awkward feeling by programming the Passover dinner playlist with songs by famous Jews like Sammy Davis Jr. and Bob Dylan (even if she wasn't a fan) and a bevy of Spring Break–themed beach songs cut in with forlorn "You've Lost That Lovin' Feelin' "–type songs.

Lavinia said, "Bryan and Jean-Wayne are present and accounted for. Your aunt asked them to go to the basement for a ladder and then go outside to replace some lightbulbs in the garage. That lady is impressive. We were barely in the door two minutes and she'd put the boys to work. What have you been cooking all day? The kitchen smells great."

Very had been cooking a plot to skywrite the world with messages to El Virus until he showed himself back online, where he belonged. Instead, while Aunt Esther fussed in the kitchen, Very, unable to forage El Virus, had passed the day blasting heavy-metal music along with Aunt Esther–inspired Mel Tormé croon tunes while logged in to her favorite virtual otherworld, the one where her avatar was way skinnier than she'd ever be, had glorious curly red hair that never spazzed when it rained, and, most important, could fly like a superhero and ride a motorcycle like a badass. Very wouldn't waste her energy feeling bad about not helping her aunt cook the Passover meal. Aunt Esther was a kitchen tyrant, and they'd discovered long ago that they coexisted best when the aunt cooked and the niece did the dishes after the meal.

Very grabbed Lavinia's hand and led her down the creaky attic stairway. She sprayed air freshener along their path, then deposited the bottle at the foot of the stairs, where a prominent ring stain in the wood marked the spot upon which Very had been depositing the air freshener bottle since she'd started secretly semi-smoking (only bumming cigs, never buying, therefore not truly a smoker) at age sixteen.

Lavinia coughed. "I really don't think your aunt can smell the cigarette smoke up here. Gosh, choke me much?"

"I just wanted to bathe you in the seducing scent of Tropical Rain Forest."

"Bathe me in the scent of smoke-free air, please. I'll settle for that."

"You want to bathe with me?" Very teased. "I thought you saved that for your locker-room crew girls."

"Only in your fantasies."

"So if it's not a crew girl . . . what kind of fantasies are you harboring about Bryan right now? Heh-heh."

"I'm meh on Bryan now. Not heh-heh. Before, his shy

awkward was kind of cute. Now, since he's so obviously weird with you because of the Spring Break thing, he's awkward with me, too, by extension. He doesn't look me in the eye anymore. Doesn't come find me for lunch. It's not fun to try having a crush on him. My like-like liking moment for him passed, I think. Oh well."

Lavinia's *Easy come, easy go* sigh indicated no heartache whatsoever at the loss of Bryan from her crush list. Very wished her own crushes could be so nonobsessive. She wished she didn't agonize day and night, moment to moment, about where the hell El Virus had gone. Life stuff that Very was supposed to be getting done in the meantime was not getting done because of said obsessing. Very wished she had even one iota of Lavinia's common sense.

Lavinia added, "At least we won't have to stock up so heavy on the Chewy Chips Ahoy! if Bryan's not coming around so often. He was the prime abuser of those."

Amazing. Even fiscally, Lavinia could turn what seemed like a sad situation into a happy one.

Very said, "Eh. The 'meh,' I understand." As sex went, Bryan had been a disappointment. His potent sensual power was that he was an awesome cuddle buddy. It was so gay and endearing about him.

The girls rounded the stairs to the second level of the house, where they found Jean-Wayne, whose potent sensual power was that he wouldn't turn down an elderly hostess who asked him to perform a chore before dinner. He was standing on a ladder in Aunt Esther's bedroom, changing a lightbulb.

"How many multilingual Canadian-Chinese engineering majors does it take to screw in a lightbulb?" Jean-Wayne asked them.

"How many?" Lavinia and Very replied.

"*Je ne sais pas,* I can't decide. But if you find another one, could you send him or her my way, because I am highly in need of a doppelganger. *Ni-hao.*" He paused. "And some help, please! Hand me that bulb on the bed, will you?"

Jean-Wayne's parents, a French-Canadian artist mother and Vancouver-based Chinese businessman father, were both Franco-philes and cowboy movie aficionados; they'd met in a Montreal patisserie next door to a revival house cinema where they'd both been to see a matinee showing of *Stagecoach,* starring John Wayne. They'd named their hybrid boy in tribute to their hybrid passions.

Bryan, whose name, alas, stood for nothing other than "Bryan," bounded up the stairs and stood in the doorway to Aunt Esther's bedroom. "How many Gridkeepers does it take to screw in a lightbulb?" he asked the assembled team.

"How many?" Very, Lavinia, and Jean-Wayne responded in unison.

"Three, apparently," Bryan said.

"Was that supposed to be funny?" Jean-Wayne asked.

Bryan said, "No. Just logical. Very, Lavinia, you. One-two-three. It takes all of you, apparently, to screw in the lightbulb. Jean-Wayne on the ladder, Lavinia holding the ladder still, and Very to sit on the bed, compulsively fixated on her iPhone while you two do the work."

No one laughed.

Bryan's unfunny-isms used to be hilarious. Or maybe they'd been too stoned.

"Logic is overrated," Very said. She wanted to add, *As are your tongue-kissing abilities, Bryan-boy. Learn the art of flutter and not of slobber, will you?* She started to Google "better kissing methods" on her iPhone to pass the information over to Bryan, then decided such information gathering would not be in the best interests of keeping the group happily assembled for their religious observation. In all fairness, though, while Bryan's kissing abilities left something to be desired, the boy knew how to work his hands. He'd probably be pleased to know that Very rated him an A-for-effort student, with a B— in ability, but with potential to improve, given the right mentor-girl. A less fickle one.

The lightbulb in place, Jean-Wayne stepped off the ladder as the group gathered around Very on Aunt Esther's bed.

"So what are we going to do?" Lavinia asked.

"We have to take down The Grid," Bryan said.

Problem: The Grid had gotten out of hand. What had started out as the two sets of roommates' online diversion for John Jay Hall had spread across campus. Everyone wanted in. The Grid's platform had gone largely unnoticed or uncared about by the university administration until the great Valentine's Day flashmob massacre, when approximately a hundred students—many of them not even freshmen, most not from John Jay, and some, reportedly, drop-ins from NYU and Hunter College—had chosen the university president's speech to Wall Street recruiters and a large segment of the Columbia Business School population to spontaneously start singing "U Can't Touch This" every time the president gestured with his microphone. The phallic symbolism had not been lost on the crowd, nor had the flash mob's breakdancing, which, while not offensive, had just been plain bad. Very had noted for future flash-mob events: Leave the dancing to the MC Hammer professionals of the world and just stick

50

with song. It was only because the mob had dispersed after the second round of gesturing that the event had not gotten totally out of hand (so to speak).

"I agree with Bryan," Lavinia said. "The Grid has gotten too big and it's taking away from our schoolwork." She glanced in Very's direction. "Yours in particular, Very."

"Disagree," Jean-Wayne said. "I support freedom of expression. Can't let the tyrants shut us down."

The group paused, waiting for Very to weigh in with an opinion. But instead of Googling "better kissing methods" for Bryan, she'd done an image search of the word "fickle," and the search results had popped up some hilarious cartoons, pornographic art, and bird-flipping angry-bitch photos, all of which were most entertainingly occupying her attention. She was aware of the conversation going on, but as background noise.

Lavinia grabbed Very's iPhone and placed it in her jeans pocket. She told Very, "That's time-out number one. Don't make me have to take this away from you all night. You'll get it back when we finish this discussion. We're waiting to hear your opinion about what to do with The Grid."

"Agree with Jean-Wayne's disagree," Very said. She loved it when Lavinia played rough. "We've invested way too much in developing it to let it go under now."

"So why'd you have to go and print a newsletter advertising what's supposed to be a covert online thing?" Bryan said to Very.

"Yin-yang," Very said. "Every movement requires a counter-movement."

"We're a movement?" Lavinia said.

Jean-Wayne said, "Not a political movement. I think Very

means that any flash-mob movement of cool needs a counter-movement of uncool."

Bryan added, "So any flash mob organized on The Grid must be counterprogrammed by a flash mob organized by a *freaking printed newsletter* randomly distributed by Very and not authorized by the rest of the group?"

"Exactly!" Very said.

Bryan said, "The B-school event last month went off without a hitch. So why did you have to take it one step too far for the J-school flash mob and send out a newsletter, Very?"

Lavinia said, "It would have been nice if you'd talked to us about it first. I mean, everyone knows The Grid is ours, even if it is a private site. We did utilize university bandwidth to build it."

Jean-Wayne said to Very, "Even if you are awesome at diverting ISPs to nonsense locations like in Kuala Lumpur and shit. You could have, like, a career in corporate espionage or something."

Bryan said, "Or she can have a career behind bars when I testify that I had nothing to do with the newsletter and I'd like to not be expelled, thank you very much."

Very pointed at Bryan. "It was *your* idea for the flash mob to convene outside the Pulitzer Prize nominations press conference on campus, Bryan." She pointed to Lavinia. "And *your* idea to boost attendance by promising homemade pies afterward." Lastly, she pointed to Jean-Wayne. "And *your* idea to chime the *High School Musical* sound track into the public-address system."

Bryan pointed to Very. "But, alas, *your* idea to publicly out the group on a printed newsletter illegally photocopied in your work-study office."

Aunt Esther stood at the entrance to her bedroom. "Who smells like smoke?"

Three fingers pointed at Very. "She does."

Very knew all too well: *Where there's smoke, there's often fire.*

CHAPTER 6

Remembrance Songs:
"Passovers Past," "Spring Break," "Planet SexyTime"

The first Passover that Very experienced was also her mother's first full-scale fire. Cat had caused minor fires before, as would any diligent pyro. But Very would always remember the Passover fire of her tenth year as the one that officially kicked off Cat's descent.

Technically, they hadn't been invited to the seder at the New Rochelle home of Mortimer and Felicity Steinberg. What Morty had said to Cat, allegedly, was "Hey, you, me, and your kid, we oughta go out to dinner one night Passover week. Teach the kid about religion." What Cat had taken from this conversation was *Hey, now oughta be the time for my wife to meet my girlfriend. We'll break matzo together, have us a grand old time.*

Not surprisingly, Mrs. Felicity Steinberg had been less than pleased by Cat and Very's arrival on her doorstep. She'd said,

"My parents and children are inside the house! You couldn't possibly be serious about coming in for Passover, could you?" (There may have been stronger language involved, but Very had repressed the exact dialogue in light of the events that followed. In fact, only expletives may have been involved.)

Tugging on her mother's skirt, Very had begged, "Please, Mommy, let's go home." This was when they lived in the tiny studio apartment in the East Village, pre–yuppie gentrification, paid for by Morty, an insurance appraiser for whom Cat had temped as a secretary. Very had loved that apartment. It was the first home where they'd stayed for at least a year. She had friends at school. Real ones, not the kind you didn't get attached to because you knew you'd be moving within a month. The neighborhood was vibrant with graffiti-art-grunge; Very felt exactly at home there. She didn't understand why she and her mother had to ride a train to New Rochelle for some event called "Passover," surely a celebration that should have been passed over when anything they could possibly want was already within a five-block radius of their East Village studio.

At Felicity's denial of their passage into Passover, Cat had grabbed Very's hand and stormed away from Felicity's doorstep. But Cat and Very didn't go far. Cat had watched as Felicity inspected them walking away from behind her sheer-curtained window, but once Felicity returned to her guests, Cat turned back around. She led Very to Felicity and Morty's yard. Only this time, they approached the garden shed in the back of the house rather than seek admittance again at the front door.

Inside the shed, Cat lit a joint while Very sat on the ground and opened the latest Baby-sitters Club book she kept in her backpack for occasions like this. But Cat's agitated lighter-flicking was more persistent this time. On/off, on/off, on/off, each flick a step closer to imminent disaster, Very knew. "Stop it, Mommy," Very whispered. Cat was not listening. Cat flicked the ember from her joint onto a piece of newspaper lying on a wooden worktable. To save the joint for a later time, she extinguished it between her two fingers, then slipped it into her pocket. Cat watched as the discarded ember, fed by the piece of newspaper underneath, turned into a small flame.

"Wait outside," Cat told Very.

Later, back in their East Village apartment, when the police came, Cat said the fire, which had burned down Morty's shed and seared away much of Felicity Steinberg's adjoining rose garden, had been an accident. No charges would be filed. Arson could not be proved, or maybe Morty, who knew from arson, just did not want it proved, as he had enough trouble to deal with in the form of a very angry wife, who may have been more outraged over the loss of her rosebushes than over the desecration of her marriage on a holy day.

Very and Cat were evicted from the apartment the following month.

What Very remembered most about the Passover day was not the fire, though, but the rosebushes. How beautifully tended they were, growing on trellises outside the gingerbread house and garden shed of Morty and Felicity Steinberg. Like that family must live in a perfect dream, to be surrounded by so much pretty yumminess. How mean it had been of Cat to destroy even one of those bushes. What had Felicity Steinberg done to her to deserve that?

Very made the sign of the cross at her chest in remembrance of Felicity Steinberg's rosebushes as she stared out at the yellow rosebushes not yet in bloom outside the Passover dining room at Aunt Esther's. Very wondered what Cat would have made of this scene, Very breaking matzo with "the old biddy," as Cat had referred to Aunt Esther, rather unkindly in Very's opinion. She quite enjoyed this matzo-ball-soup concoction that Aunt Esther had prepared. If religion could always be so dependably delicious, Very might get on board with the program.

"Did you fast today?" Lavinia asked Aunt Esther. Lavinia, a Unitarian, had indeed fasted for the day. Her widowed grandfather had recently fallen in love with a Jewish widow, and so Lavinia felt compelled to go along with the fasting in solidarity with her future *bubbe*.

Very was grateful to Aunt Esther not only for the delicious meal but also because her presence allowed for safe, unthreatening conversation. If the four students were alone, they'd still be bickering over whether to dismantle The Grid. Or if they were having dinner at school, they'd be accosted constantly in the dining hall with flash-mob proposals, when obviously that whole idea was so used up. Very wouldn't have minded a silent Passover, with the only conversation to occur by text messaging. Human evolution was headed in that direction anyway—why not start at the High Holy Days?

"Oh my, no," said Aunt Esther. "I don't fast anymore. Too old for that. God gives exemptions to seniors."

"What kind of exemptions?" asked Jean-Wayne.

"Coffee-nip candies. I've been eating them all day." Esther smiled in satisfaction at the group assembled around her Passover table. "I rather enjoy having all you young people here!"

The weird thing about Aunt Esther, Very knew, was that as warm and gracious as she was to her guests, in private she would probably be on Very's case, like a legal guardian or something. *How are your grades, dear? Will you be able to maintain the New Haven Benevolence Society scholarship? Mrs. Lee at mah-jongg keeps asking me what your GPA is. She has her eye on that scholarship going to her grandson, let me tell you. I can only advocate the scholarship going to you so long as you do as well at Columbia as you did in high school. Veronica, why is your hair always in your face? I can't see you! And you were smoking? What, do you want to turn out like your mother? It's not enough that you look just like her—you want to ruin your life with reckless behavior like her, too?*

Very was about to bite into one of Aunt Esther's amazing matzo balls when the iPhone in her pocket vibrated. She took the phone from her pocket for inspection. Just a message from her resident advisor. *Please see me ASAP.* Once again, not El Virus.

"You shouldn't have your phone on at Passover dinner!" Lavinia scolded.

"How do you know, shiksa?" Very said. "We probably also shouldn't have a post-Passover bonfire in the backyard and make s'mores for dessert, but that's totally what I'm going to propose anyway."

S'mores looked like her sacrilegious El Virus, Very imagined. He'd never shown her his full face in any of their many photo exchanges, but she'd seen glimpses of his skin under that monk's hood. He was dark, but not African and probably not Latin (just a feeling, she didn't know for sure). His skin appeared to her to be a possibly (passably?) milky South Asian, a honey-graham-cracker tone. She imagined him to have dark-chocolate eyebrows and marshmallow-white teeth, like a film star.

She'd asked him once, *What is your race?* His response had

been *Haji Jew-boy*, which had made her so happy, picturing him as a turbaned bar mitzvah mensch.

They'd never exchanged Real World real names, only first-name initials. They were both Vs, which obviously solidified their true-love destiny. How many other Vs could there be in the world, ones who found one another? When they married and got their own ranch house with monogrammed towels, they'd be "the Double V."

V., V., who could he be? Vincent? Victor? Did he wonder about her V?

"Very, your marshmallow fell into the fire," Bryan grumbled.

She'd been so deep into her V-trance she hadn't noticed the sacrifice of an innocent marshmallow as it crackled in the flames of the backyard campfire she and the boys had made after dinner. Very shrugged. She was more concerned about the joint Jean-Wayne was passing back her way than the loss of a sugar treat. Only a big fat one could keep her from abandoning her guests to return to full-time El Virus e-scan. The joint's buzz helped Very stay determinedly mellow while, across the fire, Bryan stared at her accusingly, angrily. She was well aware Bryan wasn't so much concerned with her s'more carelessness as with the fact that she'd carelessly taken his V and then tossed him back into the fire without so much as a tender hug.

Tender hugs, that's where Very and Bryan's problems started. Bryan came from granola stock in Portland, Oregon. He'd been raised on yoga and hugs. He was good at them. It had seemed strange to Very that a boy who was such a prize cuddle buddy had not managed to do the actual deed with an actual girl once during his high school years, but Bryan was a true geek, more concerned with academics and computing than with the horny babe-hunting one might have expected of his demographic.

That one time between them, the sex that had seemed so much less intimate and satisfying than the cuddling Very and Bryan had previously shared, had happened when El Virus first went missing. With most everyone away for Spring Break, Very had been obsessing on him hard alone in her room. His profile page(s) said only "El Virus has been a very bad boy and is being threatened with reform school if he doesn't mend his wicked ways. Farewell for now, kids!" And that was it. No personal e-mails or IMs or naughty photos to Very, just a broad announcement that he was temporarily out of commission. Rude!

And his phone was not only not taking messages—the number was no longer even in service. What had happened to him?

Lavinia had been in Florida visiting family, and so Very, unleashed to spend all her time alone looking online for El Virus, had quickly turned to spending all her time lying in bed, pining for El Virus, playacting with him in rich sexual fantasies that Go Ask Alice!, the Columbia online health Q&A service, had assured her were a completely safe and appropriate outlet. Bryan just happened to walk into her dorm room at the peak moment of Very's fantasy delirium.

"Whatcha up to tonight?" Bryan asked. "Want to go see a movie?"

Very opened her bed blanket to Bryan. "Don't wanna go out," she said. "You come in." She needed a warm body to go along with the El Virus fantasy–induced fire raging across her loins.

Poor Bryan couldn't have known that when Very invited him into her bed for a cuddle, she was already hot hot hot on him

him Himbo. In that moment, she had been deep inside her favorite fantasy, the one where El Virus was a haji Jew-boy version of a space-age captain. "Captain Himbo," Very called him—he was her El Virus–meets–Captain Picard from one of those *Star Trek Enterprises*. Very had always loved TV shows about outer space, where even the chaos seemed orderly and where, most important, everyone understood the technology.

With a quick snap close of her laptop, she could lie down in bed and bring it:

Very is the social director at a posh resort on Planet SexyTime. Captain Himbo, who commands a, like, rilly rilly superhuge intergalactic fleet, arrives for some R&R. To Very, he seems different from the other shore-leave horndogs. He knows history; while she is leading him to his guest quarters, they discuss the Microsoft-Google alliance that brought about the fall of Western civilization back on 001 (aka Earth). He knows archaeology; while she is showing him the tropical splendor of Planet SexyTime's oceans, they discuss ancient Vulcan ruins and mystical Cylon baths. (They do not concern themselves with the unlikelihood of Vulcan/Cylon crossover mythology.)

One night, she slips into Captain Himbo's bedroom, wearing a flimsy silk teddy under a silk robe demurely tied at the waist. Too much cleavage so suddenly, especially cleavage such as hers, might intimidate the grave, graham-cracker-colored captain.

Captain Himbo is lying in bed reading, drinking chai tea, hot. He drops his tea on the floor, startled when she enters his chambers unannounced.

"I thought you might need someone to talk to," she says, leaning down to caress his jowled cheek. "Your job, it's so . . . big. You have so many responsibilities, so many people under your . . . command.

So much firepower." Soon, if she plays it cool, she'll have her dirty way with that smooth haji-head. She sits down on the chair next to his bed. "Here," she says, extracting a Venusian joint from the pocket of her green silk robe, "this will help you relax."

"Really, Ms. . . . ," he protests, but Very lights up anyway, and immediately the potent smell intoxicates him. No one can resist pure Venus weed. Captain H. acquiesces. "Just don't tell anybody," he says, inhaling a furtive hit.

"Computer," Very says. "Marvin Gaye." Her seduction playlist immediately fires up on unseen speakers.

> I've been really tryin', baby
> Tryin' to hold back this feelin' for so long

"I wonder if this is a bit unprofessional, Ms.—" he starts.

"Very," she interrupts.

"Very," he sighs. "I just knew you'd be an awesome V."

She climbs into bed alongside him, running her hands along his captain's uniform, over his sturdy chest, then around his neck and ears.

"You," he says, moving toward her, his resistance broken down by the herb and the sensual song. "You are so beautiful." Hearing her cue to move in for the kill, she kisses his bald head, then runs her hands slowly across it. He feels so good.

"Kiss me, El Virus—I mean, Captain," she says. "Kiss me as if it were the last time."

The power is hers. She straddles him, then leans down to take his mouth into hers. She can taste the chai from his tongue, and it's hot, baby, it's hot. Their mouths disentangle, and he leans up, pulling his many-medaled uniform off his chest. Triumphant, she sits across his waist, waiting for him to take off her camisole. She leans in for another *long, hot kiss, and feels his sturdy hands running through her hair. She waits, rubbing her thighs against him. His hands reach for her voluptuous hips, caressing them, moving upward under her silk garment, over her full, taut breasts. She thinks she might die from desire if he doesn't remove the teddy now. She reaches for his hands and lifts them over her head, flinging the garment to the floor. Breasts exposed, she knows her power.*

"Take me!" she cries out.

"Make it so!" he gasps, then heaves her onto her back, where she lies panting, waiting for him.

Bryan made it so by bursting into her dorm room. She'd held her arms out to him. She didn't want to let go of the dream. She'd maybe pretend Bryan was her real-time Captain Himbo. Just the one time.

Bryan shut her dorm room door and crawled into bed with her like they'd done so many times. He spooned her, letting her nestle her head into his neck. His arms around her felt so comforting and tender. They'd playacted this cuddle scene so many times since the beginning of freshman year; so why did this time feel different? Was it that Bryan sensed her horniness at that moment, almost like he'd walked in on her when she was drugged with longing? Or that this time she'd decided not to ignore his boner pressing into her backside?

Perhaps emboldened that she hadn't shoved him away, but rather had pressed closer to that thing sprung between them, Bryan had whispered in her ear: "Don't hate me for saying this, but I think I'm in love with you." Surely words like that were the kiss of death. Bad hippie parents, bad bad, raising their son to be so open with his emotions. Preferable to kiss him on the mouth than to let Bryan spout more of that nonsense. Very turned to him and did just that.

Very knew better than to play with the affection of someone whose heart yearned so true. It wasn't nice. Well, certainly it had been nice for Bryan when she allowed him full access, and then when he collapsed on top of her with the biggest grin Very had ever seen on a boy's face. His noises, however . . . that squeal. Not so sexy. She'd felt nothing other than relief when he finished. The sooner he got off her, the sooner she could return to fantasizing about El Virus. Bryan had not proved an adequate substitute, after all.

Very wanted to be nice, she really did. She did not want to be a reckless girl who toyed with others' feelings. She knew the intimacy had been meaningful to Bryan, and not just as sex. *Idiotgirl,* she smacked herself. It was his first time, so now her careless acquiescence would be imprinted into his erotic memory for the rest of his life.

Very knew he desired more from her than physical intimacy. He wanted a real relationship. Gross.

"So are we, like, together now?" Bryan said after.

She'd said yes, already knowing she'd give him a mere twenty-four-hour grace period before she dumped him. Very was nice enough to know that she didn't want her dear friend to remember his first time ending with some bitch shoving him out of bed and telling him she preferred him as a cuddle buddy rather than a lover. This way, he could retain the afterglow, with hopes of more to come, for at least a day.

She'd done Bryan a favor, really.

So why did he continue to scowl at her?

CHAPTER 7

Meanwhile, Back at Campfire Sucks-to-Be-Here

Bryan's scowl threatened to burn a hole through Very's very guilty soul.

She had to redirect that scowl he burned her way over the backyard fire into a lustful gaze in favor of Lavinia, who was in the house, happily knitting away with Aunt Esther. Lavinia and Aunt E. had discovered they didn't both just love knitting, they also shared a delight in passing the needle time watching old episodes of *The Golden Girls*. A match made in heaven, except Very needed to redirect that match, also, by prying the knitting biddies apart and getting Bryan and Lavinia together. Turn that "meh" into "heh-heh!"

Commonsense Lavinia had already figured out the pairing with Bryan would never work; not-so-commonsense Very thought the experiment should be pursued anyway (if only to find out whom Lavinia really could like). Very loved no challenge more than an impossible one, like fitting a square into a circle.

There was no way out except through. Through some quagmire of illicit sexual shenanigans, Very speculated.

"You know what would be hot?" Very said to Bryan and Jean-Wayne, who were seated side by side on a log at their dying campfire.

Jean-Wayne, content and stoned, said, "If you got me a sleeping bag and a pillow and peed for me so I could just fall asleep right here and not have to break my nice buzz by moving at all? *That* would be hot."

Bryan, who hadn't drunk as much of the stale Manischewitz wine as Jean-Wayne and Very, and who'd barely shared in their post-Passover-meal campfire joint, was not in the mood for games. He said, "Very, we still haven't resolved what we're going to do about our problem."

This was why she could never fall for Bryan. She'd been about to propose a threesome—her, Bryan, and Lavinia—from which Very would tactfully sneak out at the right moment so Bryan and Lavinia could join bodies and souls and thereby relieve Very of her guilty conscience. (Jean-Wayne would have to be excused from the naughtiness on account of being so baked he'd likely fall asleep right when it got good.) Bryan had no sensual imagination. He couldn't fathom that she was about to propose making every straight boy's fantasy come true. Very snapped, "Don't worry about it. It's my problem, not yours. The Grid can stay up, and I'll turn myself in. Absolve you all of responsibility. That's what you want to hear, right?"

"It's what I want to hear," Bryan said. "But not necessarily something I actually believe you'll do."

"I will. Don't worry. When we get back. I've been summoned for a meeting with the dean anyway. I'll take care of it then."

"You promise?"

"Swear."

Bryan's scowl downshifted a few notches. He also had a scholarship to protect. And he actually cared about school. Yes, Very would do him this favor; it was only fair. She'd explain everything to the dean, be appropriately contrite, make sure the other administrators of The Grid were not held accountable, and they could all move on. No prob.

"So what would be hot, then?" Bryan asked.

As with anyone with whom intimacy has been shared, it was impossible not to look at Bryan and think: *We did it. You have been inside me.* Very knew he thought the same. The thought hovered over all their interactions now, and it was a shame, because she missed the Bryan she'd known before. The Bryan who let her cornrow (badly) his mass of electric hair; the Bryan who programmed and laughed with her through so many late nights in the Jay study lounge; the Bryan who grabbed her hand so she could hold steady on a crowded subway train; the Bryan who tried to teach her cleansing breaths; the Bryan who always let her use the oregano shaker first when they went out for a midnight slice. And, of course, she missed the cuddling most. How he held her with no expectation of more, how he just let Very *be*. She'd felt safe and happy in his arms, like it was okay if a stray tear slipped down her cheek when she missed her mom, it was okay if maybe she had a reputation as a slut, because Bryan understood the good heart underneath. (Her slut reputation notwithstanding, the truth was she'd only ever been with, *really* been with, four men. Or boys—whatever you wanted to call

67

them. And one and a half girls, if you wanted to be technical, and if it counted when hands between legs caused one party to reach orgasm but not the other.)

"I think it would be hot if you two kissed," Very said, pointing at Jean-Wayne and Bryan. She was no longer willing to offer up girl-on-girl, even if she already knew from experience that Lavinia's response to that proposition would have been *If I was going to go that route, it wouldn't be with* you, *fickle wench.*

"Do you ever think about anything even reasonably worthwhile?" Bryan asked Very. "I mean, if you're not on your laptop or your iPhone or playing a video game, you're flirting with anyone who comes your way. Are you really that shallow? Do important issues even concern you?"

"I probably am that shallow," Very said quietly.

But was she?

Very considered What She Wanted from Life, Circa Now, as Determinant of Potential Shallowness. She wanted:

- For El Virus to reappear, but live and in the flesh this time, and to make all her Double V fantasies come true; a life of great companionship and sensuality and kinky role-playing, all settled for her without her having to go on any further quest to seek this life for herself. If he was independently wealthy, that would be a nice bonus, as Very was getting weary of a life skating by. If he wanted her to be his "con girl" and go to sci-fi and comics conventions with him, she'd be up for that, and she'd wear costumes, too. A beautiful partnership.

• For Aunt Esther to die a peaceful death, not, like, right now—she should have a few good years left, but Very knew it was in the cards; Aunt Esther frequently proclaimed she was eager to move on and up, to return to her husband and son, and to her own parents. But Very had gotten used to her, and she didn't want her aunt to go quite yet. Cat's death had been sudden, and tawdry. No one deserved to go like that, especially a benefactress lady who made bitchin' sweaters and matzo-ball soup, and who'd taken in a traumatized orphan once upon a time. Aunt Esther should live at least long enough to see Very graduate from Columbia, maybe longer if her sweaters turned out to be big sellers. It had been Cat's dream for her daughter to get into and graduate from an Ivy League school. At least Very's aunt should see that happen. Mostly, though, Very would like for her one known relative to experience a way out that was peaceful, with the satisfaction of having lived a full and loving life. See? Very had potential for depth. She did.

• For premium cable or satellite TV she didn't have to pay for to be hers, streaming through her iPhone (she'd also like not to pay for that). Also, a lifetime of free downloadable songs with online connections that never hung during download thus causing the need to reboot and other malfunctions. Key.

• For Lavinia to switch presumed majors from

English Lit to Premed. Lavinia was so smart and science-y, compassionate and caring, it would be a shame to waste that talent on finding meaning in boring novels that had no meaning anyway. Also, if Lavinia became a doctor, Very wouldn't have to worry about paying for health insurance. Lavinia would be a truly selfless and noble physician, totally Doctors Without Borders–ish, relieving Very of the need to worry about the problems of the world, because why should she if her closest confidante and much more competent friend was already on the case? Very could stick with setting random Google News Alerts to learn about the great issues of the world while Lavinia went out and tackled them in 3-D. Awesome.

• For mobile devices like phones and laptops to dispense chocolate and condoms. Not dispense them together, obviously—though chocolate-dipped condoms presented some enticing possibilities—but no, Very wanted her machines to provide not only for her instant information gratification but also for her physical satisfaction.

Yes, she really was that shallow.

Bryan knew her too well.

Perhaps it was the mental haze from the joint, but suddenly Very figured it out: *Aw, hell. It's Bryan who's Pandora's box.* Somehow, in allowing herself to be intimate with a friend as opposed to a casual acquaintance, she'd caused something in her body chemistry to trip out of whack. Because this one had repercussions. This mistake she got reminded of every time she logged in to The Grid.

El Virus going missing had only added to the reminder. What if El Virus was dead? What if—cue horror-movie background sounds—he had another online girl on the side? Or boy? Or what if—cue sad song of desperate woe—he had a Real Person in Real Time in the Real World?

This Pandora's-box schiz had to be temporary, right? Whatever dysfunctional imbalance it was causing Very, she knew she had to figure it out on her own and take care of it on her own. She couldn't count on anyone to help her through. Could she?

There had to be an iPhone application to address this problem. If there wasn't, Very could make her fortune creating it. An application into which a user could stuff those *what-the-fuck* indefinable feelings of dread deep inside their own personal iBox of demons, and the goal of the game would be to teach the user how to keep that box shut tight instead of allowing it to open and let the demons run rampant.

Very couldn't deal with the sight of the Bryan demon any longer. She sought out Lavinia instead.

Very left Jean-Wayne and Bryan sitting on the log, not K-I-S-S-I-N-G, and found Lavinia in Aunt Esther's TV room, perched on a rocking chair. Aunt Esther sat on a sofa nearby, slumped asleep, knitting needles still in hand.

Very told Lavinia, "I tried to propose an orgy but the boys weren't interested."

"I miss *everything*," Lavinia pouted, holding up her night's work for Very's inspection. "But look! I finished a scarf!"

71

Very couldn't help but admire Lavinia. Not only did Lavinia take on tasks—like schoolwork, and exercise, and knitting—but she *completed* them. Very could never finish anything she started. Too many distractions. She couldn't get through a university lecture without IM-ing half the room to beg them to send her their notes so she could sneak out early and play *Guitar Hero*. She couldn't jog a Wii block without having to return to her laptop to reprogram her workout playlist. And *knitting*? WTF? Fingers were meant to tap tunes and keystrokes and joysticks, not tap knitting needles to make things that were actually useful, like sweaters and scarves and blankets. At least, useful in colder climates.

"Why do we like Bryan?" Very asked Lavinia, sitting down on the floor at her feet.

Lavinia said, "Basic stuff, I guess. He's good people. He's cute, but in that geeky, not-obvious way. He has no idea he's cute—bonus points. He's smart. He's kind."

"Not lately."

"Would you be kind to you if you were him right now?"

"I would, actually."

"That's true, you probably would. Maybe that's part of the problem. You're so busy being free-spirited with everybody that you don't see yourself hurting one special person who really wants to be close to you."

Lavinia was right, as always. Why had Very been so mean to Bryan? Very cared about him. She shouldn't have hurt someone who cared about her. She needed to make it up to Bryan. She needed to give him a consolation prize. She owed him that much.

"Bryan is birkensex, you know," Very informed Lavinia.

"He's what?"

"Earnest sex with granola people. You know."

"I *don't* know." The most lovable part of Lavinia? She was a virgin. Not a "Jesus wants me to save myself for marriage" and all that bullshit kind of abstainer. Lavinia was just quietly, and firmly, resolute not to do the deed unless she genuinely cared for the person and the feeling was mutual. Lavinia didn't seem to feel that horny rush to do it that so many college coeds whom Very had encountered so far seemed to have, herself included. It was called self-respect, or something. Bizarre.

"Have you ever tried a vibrator?" Very asked Lavinia.

Lavinia put down her needles. "I may be a Unitarian, but I really feel like that's not an appropriate question to ask me. Crossing a line."

"Why?"

"It's just none of your business."

"That means you have."

"I haven't. The thought never even occurred to me until you just suggested it. Satisfied?"

"Consider yourself suggested. You should try it sometime. It's a bit satisfying. Until the right person for you comes along." Very didn't add: *The technology is satisfying only technically, for the briefest moment. Then it just feels sort of sad and lonely.*

Very didn't know this piece of useful health information from her own experience. But she had read enough customers' reviews of vibrator products on drugstore.com (as instructed by the *Go Ask Alice!* health people online) to feel educated on the topic.

"Very? Seriously? I don't know anyone who knows so much about this stuff by your age. You just turned *nineteen*, for goodness' sake. How old were you when you first had sex, anyway?"

Just in case Aunt Esther was a teensy bit awake, Very whispered: "Thirteen." The answer was a lie. Very had been a month shy of her thirteenth birthday.

"That's terrible," Lavinia said, looking at Very pityingly. Lavinia placed her knitting on the floor and stood up. "I need to go to sleep. I suggest you do the same before you stir up more trouble." She wagged her finger at Very, teasing. "No orgies out there tonight, okay, young lady?"

"All right," Very groaned.

Lavinia stepped over to Aunt Esther to lay her down properly from her hunched position. Aunt Esther barely stirred as Lavinia guided her legs onto the sofa and moved her head onto a pillow, then took the afghan hanging on the back of the sofa and placed it over her.

Lavinia placed a kiss on top of Very's head. "Good night," she said, then headed upstairs to bed.

Very was not tired. The night was still so young.

How could she pass this time trapped in New Haven without imploding? She was too buzzed from the meal and the weed to study. She could go onto The Grid and see what everyone back at school was up to. But no, she wasn't finished with the Grid people here in New Haven yet. She should return outside, where she and Bryan had unfinished business that Very knew exactly how to handle.

Very walked into the kitchen en route to doing exactly that, but the dishwasher seemed to call to her: *Unload me, Very! You know that would be the smarter option.* Wow, now even the dishwasher was talking to her. She'd thought her psychic intuition with appliances only happened with machines that could go online.

But if she unloaded the dishwasher, Aunt Esther would only complain in the morning that she'd put everything back in the wrong place. She thought to alphabetize Aunt Esther's cookbooks instead, but that would only fill Very with disdain for that old-fashioned way of cooking, when there were perfectly fine recipes to Google and cooking demonstrations to YouTube.

Very returned to the TV room and plopped herself onto the armchair. She could watch TV. Yes, that was the safest option. But before Very could tap into the remote, her iPhone vibrated. *Please*, Very willed the phone, *let it be El Virus, at last!*

But no . . . it was Amanda Yamaguchi, who wanted to know if there was going to be another party this weekend.

Party on her iPhone, of course. That's how Very could pass the time tonight.

Very played with the vibrate feature, setting it on and off to make it buzz on her hand, on her stomach, on her thigh, and, oh my, she was turned on for real now. If she'd developed that Pandora's-box app for her iPhone by now, for sure the demons in it would be telling her, *Very, Very, don't be contrary. Close the box on Bryan already. We know you know how. Go on out there, girl.*

They were tricky, those demons. Could they be trusted?

Of course they could be trusted. She'd created them. She owned them. They wouldn't lead her astray.

Very still had to give Bryan his consolation prize. Because wasn't the flu staved off by a vaccine of . . . more flu? That's what Very had to do. Inoculate Bryan against Very by giving him a last dose of Very. That's what the demons in the box meant she should do. That's how she could shut the box finally.

Very returned to the backyard, where Bryan sat alone, finishing off their joint from earlier.

"Where's Jean-Wayne?" Very asked Bryan. The hardest part about dealing with Bryan since the Spring Break incident was the looks he gave her now, underneath the angry look he put on for pride's show. Underneath the anger, hurt and longing shone too forcefully through.

Very's conscience was glad for the dark now that the fire had burned out. Darkness didn't require thinking.

"Jean-Wayne went inside to bed."

"Well. Good, then." Very dropped to her knees in front of Bryan. "There's something I want to give you."

CHAPTER 8

The Long and Winding Road
(Back to Columbia)

As life changed, playlists evolved, updated/deleted/added on to every day, like a prayer (which was an awesome song, by the way, despite Madonna's faux religious angst, and it deserved inclusion on many a booty-shaking-themed mix). Very did not identify herself as belonging to any particular group of music-obsessed persons. She was not an indie-label DIY hipster, not a grunge girl, not a death-metal monster, not a gangsta hip-hop girl, nor any other stereotype that could be pinned on a person's musical identification. She simply loved music. She loved soul, rock, punk, hip-hop, even loved classical and some opera (Aunt Esther's influence). She loved vinyl, too, of course, loved the records' scratchiness and how they required so much more listening concentration—which she had little of, so therefore did not listen to vinyl as much as, for instance, her mother had.

Musically, Very did not discriminate against the uncool or champion the overly beloved. She didn't classify herself as "eclectic," knowing that the mere self-classification of "eclectic" musical tastes meant one's tastes were, in fact, anything but. Mostly, she loved any song she could sing, dance, laugh, or cry to. She loved being able to listen to any radio station beaming from anywhere in the world through an Internet stream; a lifetime of Internet radio was the method by which she'd received much of her musical education (with a bonus shout-out to that French disco radio station, Hot Mix Disco Radio Hot Hot Hot, or, in the French DJ's parlance, *Hawt Meex Deeeescooo RahhDeeOhhh Hawt Hawt Hawt*, so brilliantly awful one almost never needed to change the station).

Yet, musically, as with everything else in her life lately, Very was experiencing information overload. Too many song possibilities. Accordingly, she couldn't make herself *stop* making mix lists. She already had two going for today: "The Long and Winding Road (Back to Columbia)," songs of boredom for the awkward car ride back to NYC, tunage that was completely overshadowed by the day's more radical playlist, "BJs Don't Count, Despite What Lavinia Says," a pleasant Fugazi / Bad Brains–fest. But neither of which complemented tomorrow's list, which Very was already calling "Songs to Slash Your Wrists To" in anticipation of her meetings with the dean and her RA, and since apparently Lavinia had decided to stop speaking to her.

"Merritt Parkway is faster than I-95 for getting back to the city," Very said from the passenger seat next to Lavinia, who was driving them back from Aunt Esther's. "It's more windy, but it's lots quicker. I can tell you how to go if you want."

Lavinia shrugged. Silent.

From the backseat, Jean-Wayne said, "She doesn't like the narrow lanes on the Merritt. Makes her nervous."

Oh, so now Jean-Wayne was speaking *for* Lavinia?

Very hadn't realized Lavinia could be so passive-aggressive. Or maybe it wasn't that Lavinia was being passive-aggressive so much as that, true to her word, she really wanted not to deal with Very for a while. That, and Jean-Wayne sincerely loved to be helpful.

The previous night, when Very had finally gone to her attic room to sleep, she'd found Lavinia, still awake, on her king-sized bed, which had once belonged to Aunt Esther's son. "I saw you," Lavinia said.

"Huh?" Very said. Lavinia couldn't have seen what she seemed to be implying she'd seen. Very had glanced toward the open attic window. That window faced directly down to the backyard. There was indeed enough light from the moon and a nearby streetlamp for Lavinia conceivably to have seen. But still. No way. Lavinia was not a voyeur like that. She slept through everything.

"I heard some weird sounds from the window, so I got up to see what was going on. I saw you. With Bryan. Doing . . . you know."

Way.

Why did Bryan have to be so noisy?

Instantly, Very went on the defensive. "Really, that was nothing."

"It was something to him, probably."

"Are you mad because you liked him?" Why had Very assumed Lavinia wouldn't care? Or had Very known Lavinia would indeed care, but chosen to disregard that by assuming

79

Lavinia would simply never find out about the minor indiscretion?

"I'm not mad," Lavinia said. "Just disappointed in you. For mind-fucking us all, especially Bryan, so regularly. What you do with your 'skill set,' as you call it, is your business."

"Listen to me," Very said, feeling a tinge of desperation. Why she needed Lavinia's absolution, she didn't know. "It doesn't count. It was just a thing. To close the box. To help him let go."

"To help *you* let go," Lavinia said. "Now he's only going to be more confused."

Lavinia was so precociously ignorant. Very wanted to explain to her virgin friend the logic behind pleasing a boy in that certain way, which Very considered to be one of her master crafts (at least, based on former conquests' reviews) after JavaScript, HTML, and site-hacking. Sex, *real* sex, not oral sex, should only happen with someone special. Getting a boy off the not-real way was actually a method to stave him off, even if it might seem the opposite. It was a way for the giver to maintain control over the receiver's pleasure while simultaneously allowing the receiver to feel satisfied and grateful, but not attached. At least, that's what Very told herself at the time. She hoped for Bryan not to be the one exception to this rule that had proved scientifically solid in her experience to date. (She knew if anybody would be the exception, it would be Bryan. Damn.) *Real* intimacy, at least according to rumor, though not necessarily what Very knew from her own experience, was the kind that made your heart explode in shimmers and glows along with every precious, beautiful inch of your flesh, and that experience should be reserved for those with whom a person felt a mighty connection, for the El Viruses of the world. A mouth on someone's genitalia? That was *nothing.*

Still, it was possible that *nothing* hadn't been Very's wisest move. She couldn't deny it. Those tricky demons shouldn't have been trusted. But it wasn't like she hadn't given Bryan *something* quite sweet in return. Right?

Lavinia turned over on her side on the giant attic bed, so as not to look at Very any longer. "You can have Bryan. I wouldn't want him now, anyway. I feel sorry for him, though, being so completely whipped."

"He's not whipped! He understands there's nothing between us. If you decided you liked him again, I know he'd totally like you, like, come around to *like*-like you. I'm totally out of the way now. For sure!"

Lavinia put her hand up behind her back for Very to see the Stop signal. "Really. Don't do me any favors. Let's not talk. I want to sleep."

She'd assumed Lavinia was just PMS-ing and it would all "blow" over the next day, but Very couldn't believe it: Lavinia's silence was indeed lasting into the next day. Very couldn't stand it. She'd seated herself next to Lavinia in the car so Lavinia would know she didn't harbor bad feelings. Bryan had seemed to want to crawl into the backseat and not be noticed, anyway.

"So are we going to stop at Target or IKEA?" Very asked cheerfully.

Not cheerfully, Bryan finally found his voice in the back. "No! Let's just get back to the city as quickly as possible, okay?"

"Agreed," Lavinia said.

So unfair. Very had been counting on a shopping expedition. She'd spent all night after Lavinia fell into her snore-sleep searching online for the cutest pair of Target pj's. If she went to the store instead of purchasing them online, she could avoid shipping charges. Also, Very really wanted to eat those meatballs at IKEA. Now she would have to be quelled by the several jumbo bags of M&M's residing in her Hello Kitty backpack (purchased online through SuperCuteHandbagsOrSomething.com, free shipping, and free Dora the Explorer fanny pack with any purchase over fifty dollars).

Jean-Wayne, who like Very could not bear the silence in the car, spoke up. "Your aunt gives good Passover. She made me a fabulous sweater, too." Very turned around to inspect the sweater Jean-Wayne displayed beneath his unbuttoned jacket. It had the words "Tutti Frutti" sewn across the chest.

Very informed Jean-Wayne, "She must like you. She gave you one of her Collector's Edition catch-phrase sweaters. Usually Aunt Esther emblazons Yiddish expressions like *Bupkes* or *Oy Vey!* on her sweaters."

"Oy, let us get home and out of this car already," Bryan muttered.

Talk about ungrateful.

Amazingly, Lavinia's silence continued through the duration of the return journey back to Columbia, and even after Lavinia had brought her parents' car back to New Jersey and returned to their dorm room. But by that time, Very had a plan in motion to counteract Lavinia's silence. It was called "Songs to Alienate Your Roommate By," a playlist she'd made during Lavinia's New Jersey run, consisting of songs that Lavinia would hate—but that would also make her speak up.

Lavinia had to wake up early for crew practice. She always fell asleep by ten. At eleven, Very unplugged her headphones for the music to blast forth.

"Turn it off, Very!" Lavinia screeched.

The Spice Girls had never, ever let Very down.

"Let's talk," Very said.

"I have to get up at five tomorrow morning for crew practice. Let's not!"

She left Very no choice but to queue the next song. The angelic voice of Karen Carpenter sang out: *Johnny Angel, Johnny Angel*. Lavinia placed her pillow over her ears.

No choice left but to play dirty. *Chiquita, tell me what's wrong,* ABBA crooned. Lavinia tossed her pillow at Very.

The two roommates looked at each other, smiling.

"You make it difficult to turn you off, Very."

"Thank you. Love you too. So we're over this?"

Lavinia sat up in bed. She said, "I'm not trying to be mean to you. But I need to back off for a while. You have a million friends. You won't miss anything by not hanging out with me for a while."

"B-but," Very stammered, "I mostly like hanging out with you, Lavinia."

"*Jennifer.* J-e-n-n-i-f-e-r." L/J lay back down in bed and rolled onto her side again, so as not to look at Very. "And it's not me you need to apologize to. It's Bryan."

Very still didn't understand. The B/J *had* been her apology to Bryan.

CHAPTER 9

April Fool's Day:
Joke's on Your Wallet, Fool

Very suspected that the rapidly worsening cost-benefit ratio would catch up with her soon enough. How could it not?

Consider: Her undergraduate education, assuming she completed it, would cost her a minimum of fifty thousand dollars in school loans. (How the hell would she ever earn that much money to pay it back? Really. *How?*) Already, in her freshman year, she'd rung up five thousand dollars on her first credit card—an amount expended on school necessities like electronic "research" paraphernalia, Chinese food delivery (so easy to treat everybody and be a good tipper when signing instead of handing over cashola), cultural-awareness expeditions (late-night music shows downtown), Thai food delivery, cabs, Mexican food delivery, frequently rotating but extremely important hair-care products (she couldn't have her curly 'do riding so frizz-high she blocked the view of students sitting behind her in class), and, oh yeah, those stupid useless textbooks. And pizza delivery.

So financially this school thing wasn't working out so great so far. The New Haven Benevolence Society scholarship only applied toward tuition. Otherwise, it seemed to Very that this education so far was just a sinkhole of debt surrounded by (mostly) attractive coeds. Where exactly was the *benefit* part of the cost-benefit ratio?

Cost: Bazillion-dollar education, not to mention the ridiculously expensive Manhattan lifestyle that came along with her school choice. Very couldn't possibly live long enough to pay it all back. Why hadn't she opted for affordable UConn instead? Maybe she should set up a PayPal account for Columbia tuition donations, or just to cover cab fares. Or, she could set it up to only cover a monthly unlimited MetroCard, so she didn't appear too greedy? Perhaps she could auction her soul on eBay in exchange for a debt-free existence, so long as fully loaded, fully paid-for iPhone/iTunes accounts were included?

Benefit: Very's mother had dropped out of college after her freshman year and spent the rest of her life regretting that choice. Cat had been determined that, if nothing else, her daughter would not make the same mistake. Cat hadn't cared if Very ate ice cream and Doritos for dinner every night or if she didn't take a bath for a week, but homework and study time had been her mother's number one (and perhaps only) mandated priority for her. If for no other reason, Very needed to complete her college education for her mother. What else would Very ever be able to do for Cat? Nothing. She had to live out her mother's one dream for her, no matter the cost, and even if its only benefit was to a dead person.

Computing this equation cost Very more class time than, you know, actual class time listening to the professor drone on and on. What class was she even in?

Very looked down the rows of lecture seats ahead of her to the teacher at the podium. It was the shaggy professor: hippie-long, ponytailed, salt-and-pepper hair, unkempt beard. Vegan shoes = macrobiotics = macro-something-or-other = voilá, Intro to Econ, that's where she was. Very knew her prescient cost-benefit analysis hadn't come from nowhere, even if she wasn't paying much mind to Professor Shaggy.

Very scanned the lecture hall seats. She knew at least two dozen of the fifty or so students in the room. Of those two dozen, sixteen were favorite'd on her IM list. Of those sixteen, ten had their laptops open and operating for supposed lecture note taking. Time to send out a meme. She'd make it an easy one, so as not to appear too obviously ironic on April Fool's Day.

Make-out or make-up?
Foo (fighters) or pho (soup)?
Dining hall or delivery dining (specify why)?
Purple or orange (alerts)?
Weed or beer?
Fantasy homo love match: Harry Potter / Draco Malfoy or Hermione Granger / Ginny Weasley (I know, that last pair's practically incest . . . get over it and have fun speculating)?
Macro or micro economics (LOL! Who cares!)?

Very hit Send and turned to her webcam to make bored-in-class faces at her Skype friends hanging out on the beach in

Costa Rica while she waited for the meme responses from her friends in the seats surrounding her.

From two rows ahead of her, Bryan flipped her the bird behind his back, then shut his iBook and opened a real notebook for note taking.

Bryan used to love her memes.

Bryan was probably, fairly, still sore over this morning, when Very had sat down next to him in the dining hall and dipped her spoon into his bowl of oatmeal. She'd said, "Lavinia says I am supposed to apologize to you. So . . . sorry. And . . . maybe add some brown sugar to this oatmeal? Makes it tastier."

He had moved his oatmeal bowl out of her reach, then pressed his hand to his heart. "I find myself overwhelmed by both your sincerity and your gastronomic superiority."

" 'Gastronomic superiority'? Good one!"

"Please get your own breakfast and leave mine alone."

Very's stomach always led her own heart, so she left Bryan to step over to the hot-food line, fully anticipating returning to Bryan's table to finish off the apology already. But she was intercepted by the dreaded drab Debbie, senior girl resident advisor who might as well be advising a senior center. Debbie's idea of fun dorm social activities usually involved Scrabble marathons and Make Your Own Chop't Salad refreshments. *Dreabbie*, Very privately called her.

"We need to talk, Veronica," Dreabbie said. "Are you free now?"

Very snatched an apple from the fruit table. "Apple's all I have time for. On my way to an exam."

Exam: fool-proof Dreabbie-dodge excuse. Hopefully Miss

Resident Advisor "Beware the Freshman Ten" Food Police would also take note of the wholesome, healthy food choice Very had made in picking up an apple instead of the apple danish, as had been her intention. Freshman Ten, indeed. She dared not step on a scale, but Very knew her number was closer to Fifteen. Luckily, ninety percent of the weight gain had gone to her breasts. Gazoombas!

"What time does your exam end?"

"A couple hours from now." Very bit into the apple. *Act casual. Like getting tossed from student housing is not even a possibility. Don't stick your boobs out to distract. Dreabbie-type chicks don't like that. Save that for Bryan.*

"Please find me in my room immediately after. You know why."

"I've been summoned to the dean's office after class." *Double Dreabbie dodge! Score!*

Very tried, unsuccessfully, not to make a sour-green-apple face as she bit into the fruit. It probably looked like gloating.

Dreabbie stared at her angrily, gloated-at. "Five p.m. Be there. No excuses!"

If she concentrated hard enough, Very knew, she could not only *will* the meeting with Dreabbie to never happen, she could *will* a return to her laptop screen from El Virus during Econ class. No one was responding to her meme. Rude! Was the April Fool's silence the joke on her?

She'd rather do anything than listen in class. Why had she bothered to show up today? She could have slept in. Oh right, she'd shown up to avoid Dreabbie and because of a note from the professor's teaching assistant indicating Very's truancy issues needed to be remedied or would result in automatic failure, regardless of whether she passed the final exam.

If she couldn't will El Virus into physically being live and direct with her now, she could open his picture file instead. She had to do *something* to pass this class time. If she didn't open the folder that contained the secrets to her heart, she'd start online shopping again to pass the time, and really, she needed only so many cute handbags or so much hypoallergenic bedding (Very didn't even have allergies, it was just that Lavinia said it was a good precaution to take with dorm mattresses that went through so many users). Her credit card was maxed out anyway. Online shopping during class could quell only so much suppressed energy without the sweet buzz that came from clicking on Purchase.

Very opened the El Virus photo file on her laptop. How was it that two people as passionately devoted to their electronic attachments as they were had maintained the agreement never to speak on the phone—to only exchange e-mail and text messages, with the occasional cryptic photo, full frontal face never allowed? It had been like a ridiculous chastity pact, designed to save the purity of their relationship for the first time they actually . . . met. In person.

She loved his turbaned photos best, the ones that allowed a peek at black hair and beard stubble. She loved how cozy it made her feel to imagine herself as his sari goddess, flying through an auburn sky with him. They'd be love deities who sprinkled iPhones to their disciples on the ground, like when those World War II planes sent packages of Spam and smokes and Hershey bars to suffering people in war-torn Europe. Yes, Very and El Virus would operate some kind of modern-day airlift program, only without the unpleasant issues of postwar ravages, and without the Spam, of course. They'd be nice just for nice's sake.

Very concentrated on her IM list, willing Him to appear. El Virus could pop up . . . *now* . . . or *now* . . . or . . . *WHEN?!* WTF already? Why didn't her deity fantasy extend to IM-summoning superpowers?

Very might as well turn her attention to Professor Shaggy. No IM from E.V., and no one in class had bothered to answer her meme. If no one was responding, was it possible the professor was saying something worthwhile to the lecture hall after all? Very momentarily tuned him in:

"No single factor will affect the global economy—and your personal future—more importantly than . . ."

Nah, not interesting.

Very slipped the earbuds hiding underneath her shirt onto her ears, then draped her hair over the earbuds to keep them out of sight of the TA. She tuned her browser to Google. She could spend the rest of the class time watching David Bowie trans-sexualness glam. Or just observing traffic patterns in downtown Helsinki at this very moment. Either one would adequately pass the time.

Google, her favorite boyfriend.

Free 'n' easy.

Just like Very.

CHAPTER 10

"Jean Genie" in the Office of the Dean Deanie

Very needed a father to flank her. That was her problem. She'd settle even for a father *figure*. Someone to reassure her, to pay her bills, to care about her unconditionally. Someone to accompany her to the dean's office and stand up for her in stern indignation and In the Name of My Hard-Earned Tuition Money, Sir, I Will Not Stand By and Allow This Slander Against My Darling Veronica.

Certainly she'd had a mother, and a mother figure in Aunt Esther, but how exotic and cool and provided-for would it feel to have a Mighty Manly Man standing up for her, looking out for her. Why couldn't Very get anything right?

As it was, Very arrived in the Dean of Students' office twenty minutes late. She'd stopped by the Alma Mater statue on the walk over, hung out with some Jay folk there, and been recruited to host a karaoke marathon later that night. Shit just took up time.

Very didn't use those exact words with the dean. What she said was "I lost track of time. Sorry."

Luckily, the dean was one laid-back kind of dude. He almost had to be, with a name like Robert Dean. Which made him, in his academic capacity, Dean Dean. Very was clearly destined to program a "Jean Genie" / David Bowie mix out of this meeting experience.

Dean Dean tilted back in his chair, put his feet up on his desk, and did that chin-stroking thing that, well, a good father figure would completely do for her if he were here now. "Veronica," he said, almost comfortingly, "tell me about what's going on."

"Like how?" Very said.

"I think you know what I'm talking about," Dean Dean said.

"I don't," Very said.

She did.

"Songs for the Fatherless"—that could be an alternate playlist for the day. Songs reflecting all the Dad moments she'd missed in her life. If she found that mosher her mother had one-night-standed so many years ago, Very felt sure he'd be the grunge grown-up variety, all yuppified but still glorifying his old Kurt Cobain wannabe days. Father. Daddy. Papa. Pop. Old Man. Sigh.

Songs to cue for fatherlessness-sob-story mix: "What's Going On" by Marvin Gaye, "Come as You Are" by Nirvana, "Papa Don't Preach" by Madonna, "Daddy Could Swear, I Declare" by Gladys Knight and the Pips, "Family Affair" by Sly & the Family Stone, "Papa's Got a Brand New Bag" by James Brown, "Daddy I'm Fine" by Sinéad O'Connor, "Rescue Me" by . . .

Dean Dean cleared his throat. "Veronica? I'm asking you a question. Why do you think you're here today?"

"Someone's nominated me for student council president but you're worried I'd be taking on too much, what with my heavy course load and all?"

"That's quite funny. But indeed. Let's talk about your course load." Dean Dean whipped a term paper out from a file folder and placed it on his desk for Very to inspect. It was one of her own papers.

Damn, this dean guy was looking *right at her*, waiting for an answer. When he was looking right at her like that, oozing genuine concern, she couldn't possibly pull out her phone and start texting classmates to see if anybody wanted to start a jihad, could she? Very's hand touched her handbag, where she could feel her phone vibrating this very second. Someone was calling her!

"Don't you dare answer that," Dean Dean said.

Very placed her handbag on the floor and kicked it a few inches away so she wouldn't feel any vibrations forthcoming from it.

Okay, whatever, she'd give in. Uncle.

Very glanced at the term paper, then picked it up from the dean's desk. It had a large D marked across the top, written in thick red marker and circled all fancy to highlight its D-eity. It was her last Lit Hum paper. What did the dean care if she got a suck grade on a paper?

"I didn't plagiarize that, if that's what this is all about," Very said.

"Believe me, no one is accusing you of plagiarizing this paper."

"Good."

"Because when one writes one's Literature Humanities paper not on Plato's thoughts on life, but instead chooses to focus it exclusively on speculation of exactly what type of homoerotic space-age Guitar Heroes that Plato 'and his dudes,' as you refer to the Great Thinkers, would have made, one does not necessarily get accused of plagiarism. The professor gave you the D rather than an outright F solely for your paper's original content."

"Cool."

"It's not cool, Veronica. It's an offensive attack on your professor's time and energy. You seem to be making a habit of turning academic essays into work that's essentially glorified fan fiction, which is fine for your private time, but in pursuit of your Columbia degree? No. What were you thinking?"

I didn't give it any thought at the time. But wouldn't you agree, Dean Dean, that fan fiction is way easier to write, and far more entertaining, than a real term paper?

Very shrugged. "Dunno."

"You need to figure it out, young lady, if you're to progress in this school. This isn't the only academic work of yours that's been called to my attention. There seems to be a growing concern that you appear to think you can fake your way through your course work by avoiding the actual texts and focusing on cleverly inane nonsense. . . ."

Cleverly inane. So close to cleverly insane. Or cleverly in-anal. Hah-hah-hah-hah-hah! Next stop, Sodom and Gomorrah fan fic, fuh sho'.

Dean Dean said, "I can see I'm not getting through to you on this level. Let's move on, for now, to the next topic. This Grid business."

"Can't be traced." Why had she said that? If ever there was an admission of guilt, there it was. Then Very remembered. She'd promised Bryan she'd stand up and take responsibility.

"Don't be ridiculous. Of course it can."

"You're right. It's me. Me me me, and only me."

Dean Dean perhaps had decided to take on a new interrogation tactic, because he took his feet off his desk and leaned over to open a mini-refrigerator. He pulled out two bottles of flavored water. "Would you like one?" he asked her.

"Do you have raspberry?"

"Goji berry."

Not as good, but the goji factor might be refreshing in her mouth. "Okay. Thanks." Very took the bottle the dean extended to her and opened it for a sip. Indeed. Refreshing.

Dean Dean would really make some lucky progeny an awesome father or father figure. He totally knew the vitamin tricks to put a girl at ease. He'd probably let his kids chew Flintstones for their daily vitamins.

"The Grid," Very said. "All me. Blame me. Sorry. Won't do it again."

"Here's my problem with these flash mobs organized on The Grid."

Very clasped her hands together and tilted her head to the side, adopting a sincerely Sincere face. "I'm listening," she said.

"This disorderly conduct. What's it about? *Nothing*. You're not even protesting anything meaningful. I mean, this particular university was the beacon of student protest in the sixties. For better or worse, to the university administration, student protest is one of Columbia's proudest legacies. But these flash mobs? They're merely disruption for the sake of disruption, emptily occupying time and space, with no viable social or political message."

"So you're saying if The Grid can swing some protests

against, like, racism or homophobia or war-mongering or some-thing, then it would be all right with you?"

"No, that's not what I'm saying. I'm saying, Find a meaning-ful path for yourself at this university, and stick to it. Stop blocking others' paths here for no reason other than your own amusement."

Very nodded. Still sincere. "Got it. Cool. Okay."

Daddy-O Dean, I won't let you down. Flash mobs. So over. Fan fiction: Will save for the online Hogwarts covens only.

"That's too easy a response. I don't think you're getting it. Your academic career is in jeopardy. You're at risk of expulsion. We haven't even addressed the concerns from your resident ad-visor. Let me ask you something, Veronica. I want you to think about this seriously. Do you even want to go to this university? Because your academic performance and social antics would in-dicate otherwise."

Did Aladdin Sane Dean Dean just say "expulsion"? Harsh judgment for a few minor indiscretions!

But because he'd offered her a bottle of vitamin-rich water, and so unconditionally, and a really tasty flavor it turned out, too, Very pondered his question seriously.

Did she want to go to this university?

Because, Very had to admit, she spent more class time send-ing memes, texts, and e-mails than paying attention to lectures. It wasn't like Very cared about Columbia's esteemed Core Cur-riculum schooling students in the classics of Art, Literature, and Humanities. She spent more time Googling speculation about Plato's sodomite tendencies than trying to break down the dude's thoughts on life. (*Obviously*, the D-marked paper winked at her.) She couldn't sit through an easy class of Art History slides without losing focus to her stylus pen instead, doodling onto her laptop nasty cartoons of the Great Thinkers in various states of . . . thought. Naked thought.

"I don't know why I'm bothering," Very said to Dean Dean quietly. "You're right."

" 'Bothering'? That's how you think of the privilege of an Ivy League education?"

"No. Yes. No. I mean, I don't know what I'm doing here."

"Then I'd suggest that you figure it out, and quickly. You've got until finals to get your act together. If you expect to return here next year, I'll need evidence of rapidly improved academic attendance and performance, and a recommendation from your resident advisor. Who is expecting you in her dorm suite immediately after you are excused from this meeting. I'll be calling the RA to let her know you're on your way."

Very placed her half-consumed water bottle on the dean's desk. She wouldn't finish the drink, as a form of silent protest. It was one thing to drop the word "expulsion" on her. Totally another to send her into the vulture's lair of Dreabbie's dorm suite.

So not cool, Dean Dean. And just when she was getting comfortable with him, opening up to him.

That's what dads did. Let daughters down.

Flintstones vitamins were essentially sugar cubes. Nothing healthy about them. Everyone knew that.

Very hadn't missed anything not having one of those bothersome creatures.

CHAPTER 11

Die, Grid, Die Die

Very should have known when she entered Dreabbie's suite and was ushered to a tattered couch in the communal living room area rather than summoned directly into Dreabbie's bedroom for a private talk that she was being set up for something. But Very had been so pleased that if she was being forced by Dean Dean to have this discussion in the first place, then in the second place, mercifully, there was a TV on the table behind where Dreabbie sat. The TV had been left on, muted, but Very didn't mind. Dreabbie could talk all she wanted while Very watched QVC behind Dreabbie's head.

Was Dreabbie accusing Very of piloting a keg of beer into the freshman dorm at a recent party, even if she had no tangible proof that Very was the organizer? Check.

Did Very want that thigh-buster machine behind Dreabbie's head Fed Ex'd to her stat? Check to the hells yeah.

Dreabbie whined, "I need to know that you won't be giving me any more cause for suspicion the rest of the school year, Very. Or I'm afraid I'll have to recommend that you not be allowed back into student housing next year. Do you realize what the cost of rent would be in Manhattan if you had to get housing on your own? Do you realize the gravity of this situation?"

"Exercise is very important," Very said. Stay on message. That was Dreabbie's message, right? Freshman Ten. Blah blah blah. Dreabbie should be pleased by Very's acknowledgment of the importance of exercise. She needed more of it, needed that natural high. Those endorphins that Lavinia lived off so wholesomely—yes, Very would like some of those, please. Check. She'd start by taking a run as soon as she could escape this Dreabbie session. She'd perhaps start by bolting out of this room any second.

Except.

Lavinia, Bryan, and Jean-Wayne arrived in the common area in Dreabbie's suite. Bryan took a guard post at the door, like he anticipated Very's sudden need to colt-bolt, while Lavinia and Jean-Wayne sat down on either side of Very on the couch.

"What the . . . ?" Very said.

Something was extremely not right.

Lavinia started with "We love you very much, Very. But we're worried about you."

Jean-Wayne picked up with "Debbie asked us to join her today so we could talk about our concerns together."

No fucking way. Very said, "Is this an . . ."

". . . intervention," Bryan finished. "Yes, it is." He didn't sound concerned. He sounded triumphant. Certainly there'd be nothing coming his way involving the letters B or J from VLeF ever again.

This. Was. Outrageous. This had to be an April Fool's Day joke. A flash-mob intervention that would spontaneously disperse within seconds.

But Very could see by the serious look on her friends' faces that this meeting was no joke and that they intended it to last longer than a flash.

Very wanted to explode in anger at the intrusion into her privacy, but felt even more frustration about her inability to completely combust. Dean Dean had specifically sent her into this situation by instructing her to talk with Dreabbie. He was keeping tabs on her. Clearly, this was an intervention not just among "friends," but one with a direct antenna to the dean's office, that unfortunate higher power that could control her scholarship and her destiny, too. Very couldn't squirm her way out of this one. (Yet.) She had no choice but to sit through this treasonous bullshit.

Indignantly, Very proclaimed, "I don't have substance-abuse issues. A little weed here and there does not an addict make." She looked in Bryan's direction. "I bet your *parents* smoke more weed than me!"

"They know how to maintain," Bryan said. "You don't."

Lavinia said, "And it's not your substance abuse we're worried about."

This was perhaps the worst slap of all—that they'd recruited Lavinia to this hateful cause. Very didn't know if she could sleep next to this girl for the rest of the semester, knowing Lavinia could so easily swing against her.

Dreabbie clicked off the TV and snatched the vibrating iPhone right out of Very's hand. "It's sort of the general consensus in John Jay Hall, as well as, apparently, among all of your professors and peers, that you have a technology problem."

"That's bullshit," Very said. "A *technology* problem? Give me a break. That's not even a real problem."

Dreabbie shook her head sadly. "Denial. The first wave. My advisor said you might respond that way."

Lavinia said, "Very, for real? I think it *is* a real problem. You can't make it through an hour without being online or attached to your phone or playing a video game."

Bryan added, "Your relationships are suffering."

Jean-Wayne said, "Your school performance is at risk." He sounded scripted, but unconvinced. He had to be the weak link in the consortium. Very would remember that.

Betrayal. Very said, "I thought we were comrades! The Grid! *Stolichnaya* and whatever!"

Bryan said, "*Stolichnaya?* That's a vodka, not a propaganda slogan. And for your information, most of the people who come to this school had to work their asses off to get here. So you test well and did well in high school. But since then, have you truly *earned* your place here? We're comrades only so long as you earn your place within the collective."

Lavinia took on a good-cop tone. "Of course Very *deserves* to be here. We wouldn't want to be here without her, right? She's our girl. But, girl"—Lavinia turned to Very—"you are seriously worrying me. Something's got to change. We don't want to lose you."

How could they *lose* Very to a so-called technology problem? Which wasn't even a real problem? Preposterous.

And yet. A tear ran down Lavinia's face, bisecting a drop of snot falling from her allergy nasal drip. The earnest worry of that snot-tear caused Very to at least entertain the notion they were presenting her. The sight was just so pathetic. Maybe Lavinia wasn't one hundred percent a traitor. Maybe she was genuinely worried.

Very allowed, "So let's say, hypothetically, that I have this 'technology' problem, which isn't even a real problem, but since you're so gung-ho on the idea I'll go along with it, just to humor you. So I have this 'problem.' " Gawd, they'd incited her to gesture finger quotes around "technology" and "problem." What kind of friends were these people, anyway? "What do you propose I do about it?"

Dreabbie said, "For one thing, in consultation with the dean's office, it's been decided that your iPhone should be confiscated for the time being. We can't force you to surrender it, of course, but we're hoping you'll do so voluntarily, for your own good. Agreeing to this measure will look good for you when your housing case comes up for review soon. If you give your phone to me, you will be allowed to check in with me twice a day to listen to your messages. In the interim, you may use the land line in your room if you need to make calls."

"What if I need to call long distance?" Very spat. "The room line is only good for local numbers."

Jean-Wayne fished a crumpled phone card printed in Spanish from his pocket and handed it to Very. "We got this for you at a bodega by Morningside Park. The most *muy excelente* rates we could find. You can kick it old school. If you need to talk to anyone long distance, particularly in El Salvador, you can use the land line and talk for a very long time with this card."

"Not helping," Lavinia muttered to him. She nodded toward Bryan, who approached them with a backpack and handed it over to her. Lavinia fished out a ginormous laptop from the backpack. "I got this from my parents' basement. It's a really old computer with no Internet connection. You can use it to write your papers and stuff, but without all the online distraction."

"You're joking," Very said. "That's, like, the size of a toddler." She lifted the relic. "It's heavier than one, too."

Bryan said, "We've gone ahead and removed your own laptop from your room. For the time being."

WHAAAAAAAAAT?!?!?!?!?!?

It was like Bryan had taken a saw and brutally carved a limb from Very's body, completely indifferent to the blood and cartilage splattering onto all of them, while Very sat passively on the couch, shocked and too pained to even acknowledge the horrendous crime.

Jean-Wayne said softly, "I know it's totally not cool to do that. It's only because we care about you so much."

Lavinia said, "We want you to come back to school next year. We can choose a suite together when we're sophomores. That'd be awesome, right?"

Dreabbie added, "Your friends are doing this because they *care*. We all *care*."

At this point, the shock of the assault was so great that Very would have agreed to anything just to get out of the suffocating room.

"I'll try," Very said.

To herself she added, *I'll try to make it through these last few weeks of the semester and then fuck you all and this place and everything about it. I'm going to find El Virus and never come back.*

CHAPTER 12

Hello Hello Hello, Is There Anybody in There?

That Richard Chamberlain had been onto something. Appease-ment could maybe possibly work.

Wait a minute. Neville Chamberlain had been the appease-ment dude. Richard Chamberlain was the gay priest? Or had that been Richard Simmons?

Whatever. Neville Chamberlain. Was the World War II ap-peasement dude. Very was sure of it.

And she'd figured this out without a Google query!

Very was, indeed, kickin' it old school in the natural world. One whole comfortably numb week in April, without the con-stant techno blast surging through her bloodstream, and she was accomplishing things. At the behest of Dean Dean, she'd rewrit-ten that Lit Hum paper, actually reading the texts instead of merely Googling relevant passages. She hadn't skipped a class since the electronic purge, which meant she also hadn't sent or answered an IM or a meme, which meant she'd somewhat absorbed the lectures she'd been supposed to be listening to all along. (That Econ shit . . . Whoa. Important.) She'd also completed two shifts at the Morningside Avenue Food Co-op, and was now the proud owner of two bushels of organic, fiber-rich Empire apples that could substitute for the nutrient-poor, credit-card-delivery meals Very couldn't afford for at least a week. Best of all, her joystick-induced carpal tunnel syndrome had eased, the chronic tension in her hand happily giving over to pain-free textbook-page flipping rather than video-game playing.

The music thing was kind of killing her, and she was going to find where Lavinia had hidden her emergency spare iPod even if she had to do a body search on the girl, but, Very had to admit, this taking away of her gadgets, this *allowing* her treasonous friends to think they were helping her, wasn't entirely a bad idea. For the time being.

Clean for a week now, Very felt an epic shift occurring in her body chemistry, rather like the sudden temporal rift that happened from long-distance airplane travel, from falling asleep on takeoff and then landing to awake in a completely different environment. The intervention was a joke, Very reminded herself, but she could prove to the world, and to herself, that SHE COULD DO IT.

SHE COULD DO IT by pretending the whole experience was a virtual science experiment she was being forced to act out in the Real World.

Very missed her gadgets, surely, but the emotional weight of them might indeed have been a burden. With no laptop or phone on which to scan for messages from El Virus (now MIA for almost a month, which was like a quarter century in online romance time) and without the immediate means through which to send or answer a meme or play a video game, Very had to acknowledge she felt suddenly free, like that delicious feeling of going to a foreign country and not speaking the language or knowing the customs but randomly setting out into the culture to see what would happen. Could acclimation happen?

Well, no, acclimation couldn't really happen. Very would get her stuff back eventually, and the sooner the better. And the sooner she appeared to have relaxed into it, the better the traitors would determine her mental well-being to be, and return her fucking stuff to her already. Appeasement was just that: appeasement. Everyone knew it didn't last. (Sorry, Neville.)

For now, Very would play the game. She only had to survive a few more weeks, until classes ended in early May. While most of her classmates had internships and far-flung adventures lined up for their summer breaks, Very had yet to figure out a plan, having decided long ago that El Virus would appear just as final exams concluded to whisk her away for a summer of frolic and fun. So this No Techno experiment might help and not hinder the reality check Very's summer planning needed, since Real World El Virus was apparently nowhere on the horizon.

Very had refused to speak to Lavinia in the first couple days after the intervention. But the silent treatment had quickly grown old, and boring, too, with no online adventures or music to distract Very in their room. All it had taken was one batch of microwaved Chewy Chips Ahoy! that Lavinia had brought in just for Very, and Very fell out of Mad and into Yum with her Chum in an instant. Very wished she had higher standards for holding a grudge, but, at least where Lavinia was concerned, she didn't, apparently.

For pragmatism's sake, Lavinia put Very on a thirty-minutes-per-day Internet allowance regimen specifically for the purpose of researching a summer job and abode. The addendum to that allowance, however, was that the research would be done on Lavinia's laptop, by Lavinia. Which meant Lavinia had to do the thinking for Very, which Very minded not at all. Bonus all around.

"So which is it?" Lavinia said, tapping away. "We've only got three weeks of school left before finals, and you need to figure this out already. Do you want to spend the summer in New Haven and find a job there, or try to stay in Manhattan? It's possible to sublet graduate student apartments over the summer. But pricey."

Very, sitting next to Lavinia on Lavinia's bed, dropped her head onto Lavinia's shoulder. "Why can't I just live with you?" she asked.

Lavinia said, "A summer in Vermont would be so exciting for you, I'm sure."

"Better than a summer in New Haven," Very whined.

"You'd want to be a camp counselor to a bunch of tyrannical tween girls with me?"

"No," Very said. Hang out with Lavinia all summer—sure, why not? Work, at a job—no way, ick[dot]yuck[dot]horrible. Very wondered why she couldn't be the offspring of independently wealthy people and do, like, nothing all summer, but in a really posh apartment paid for by someone else, and with an unlimited food-delivery line of credit? (Also, as always, the optimal situation would include cable and other assorted hookups on someone else's dollah.)

Lavinia pointed to some Web site hits on her laptop. "Look,

I've found a few job possibilities for you in New Haven. Just temp stuff, but good leads. Do you have a résumé prepared?"

Very had to incite Lavinia to stop dropping that douchey "résumé" word already. Her head still relaxed on Lavinia's shoulder, Very moved her arm from behind Lavinia's back to Lavinia's behind. She then slipped her hand underneath her roommate's shirt. Her hand was barely an inch up the warm, soft skin of Lavinia's back before Lavinia jumped off the bed.

"Don't think you can molest me to find your spare iPod," Lavinia said. "I know your tricks."

How was it that Lavinia knew Very's every predatory thought?

"Please," Very pleaded. "I just want my music. Where's the spare 'Pod? You know my primary music library is on my spare and not on the iPhone. Please. Don't make me beg. Or I'll have to tickle the location out of you."

Lavinia rolled her eyes. "I'm not ticklish."

"That's not what your crew girlfriend told me."

Lavinia would not rise to the bait. "Sorry. No 'Pod for you. I will not be your enabler." Lavinia took her CD case from her desk and handed it to Very. "If you want to listen to music, here's my collection. You can listen to it on my Internet-less and radio-less CD player."

"But . . . ," Very sputtered. "Your music sucks." Lavinia's taste was so predictably college-radio alternative music. Absolutely not. Unacceptable. Too earnest. Very needed her groovefire.

"Deal with it," Lavinia said. "Hum to yourself if you need a tune."

Very singsonged, "Please let Very have her iPod, darlingest, most beautiful Lavinia."

"Will not enable you will not enable you will not enable you," Lavinia said. She retrieved her laptop from her bed, away from nearness to Very. "Stop this nonsense already. I'm going out."

"Where?" Very said. Lavinia had *better* not say . . .

"Study break with some friends from crew."

That.

Very hated Lavinia's crew friends. They were all like Lavinia, so smart and sporty and together, without being super special like Lavinia. They had names like Amanda and . . . a few more Jennifers, Very was pretty sure. She'd only met, like, five of them, but she'd hated them on sight for diverting Lavinia's attention. She hated Lavinia having fun without her. True, Very socialized plenty without need of Lavinia, but that didn't mean Lavinia should also be so entitled.

Very said, "You mean you guys will be meeting in some Amanda's room and pretend to study but really watch her collection of *The L Word* episodes?"

"*Queer as Folk*," Lavinia retorted.

Very loved it when Lavinia played back. "How butch of you."

Lavinia pointed at the dinosaur computer that Very had been relegated to. "Stop dodging the subject. I'm assuming you have no résumé. Prepare one. I expect you to have a rough draft finished by the time I get back tonight."

Very shrugged, indifferent.

Lavinia softened. "Okay. You're killing me with that sad face. One song when I get home. I'll give you one song."

"We'll have a spontaneous dance party?" Very asked, brightening.

"One song. Dance party. If your résumé is drafted by the time I get back. Affirmative."

"Spice Girls?" Very said.

"Pussycat Dolls!" Lavinia called out as she left the room.

"Poseurs," Very muttered.

Dreabbie stood in the doorway Lavinia had just abandoned, holding Very's iPhone. "Are you ready for your ten-minute-allowance message check?" Dreabbie asked.

Was she!

Very snatched the phone from Dreabbie's hand and popped open her messages.

And there it was, at last.

Contact.

From El Virus.

His message said: *Find me, dearest. Monsignor needs rescuing.*

Catch him if she could.

She would.

CHAPTER 13

April Showers Bring . . . Full-on Freaks

She was a LeFreak who was a freak magnet.

Very would never have imagined Jean-Wayne Chang was *this* much of a freak, however.

Dy-no-mite!

First, he wore deep-sea-green eyeliner. No big, right? Right. Lots of guys wore eyeliner. But. Jean-Wayne only wore eyeliner when going online to engage in a certain fetish involving fishes that Very might normally have dismissed as cool-but-not-her-thing, but that, in this case, she'd embrace wholeheartedly.

She had to, because J.-W. was the master leading her back to her domain.

Meaning, second, J.-W. was a source, a hustler, a kingpin, within his secret world.

His secret world consisted of a posse of engineering-major dudes who also wore green eyeliner but who couldn't trace their inner lids with the same suave flair that Jean-Wayne pulled off. The posse met for after-midnight rituals in a basement cove in the East Asian Library, where they immersed themselves in all-night marathons playing a hypnotic, postmodern Dungeons & Dragons–esque game called *Dream with the Fishes*. It was a cult game, played online between various teams around the world, an elite who could join only by invitation. The Columbia team's gaming station was in an unused, unmarked room, which one could enter only by pressing a thumb into an unseen finger-scan machine behind a peeling hallway wall. The room was set up with an enormous plasma screen that took up the length of one of the room's four walls. Chairs that looked hijacked from the first-class section of an airliner were set up with video consoles attached to the arms. The chairs were assembled in neat rows for prime viewing position opposite the wall screen.

If she hadn't known better, Very might have guessed the room was decorated in tribute to the bridge on any given *Enterprise / Battlestar Galactica* starship. (She would never suggest to the guys that their decorating scheme was so space-age-crossover deriva-tive, however. She valued her own life too much.) She also might have guessed that Jean-Wayne had allowed her secret entry into the cove because what the group needed most was not necessarily a token girl, but a sixties-era stewardess figure who could bring them cocktails while they gamed, and whose Fresh-woman Ten-, er, Fifteen-induced cleavage could offer them up the fantasy of mile-high (or mile-low, in their case) adventures while they cavorted/hunted/massacred/algae'd their way through their oceanic underworld game.

Very's instinct had been right that Jean-Wayne was the weak link in her friends' stand against her technology habit. She'd found him straightaway after reading the first message from El Virus. She'd gone to his and Bryan's room. She was actually looking for Bryan, knowing he was the one really holding the grudge, ergo, he must be the one who'd hidden her laptop. And she needed her baby back. NOW. No more games. No more appeasement. She couldn't go online on any of the university computer terminals because they required a university log-on—and Dean Dean had arranged for Very's unsupervised online privileges to be turned off until she could be approved for good-behavior repatriation by Dreabbie. Lavinia took her laptop with her at all times now, so as not to tempt Very, and sure, Very could ask any number of fellow students if she could use their laptops, but she wanted to think she had her situation under control. She hadn't stooped so low as to beg others for Internet time or to go to some Internet kiosk— How ghetto. She wasn't that cheap or far gone. Not yet, anyway. She *would* stoop so low as to sneak into Bryan and Jean-Wayne's room, however, and she would damn well find her own machine therein even if she had to uncover untold amounts of dirty socks and porn in their room in order to do so.

When Very got her machine back, her first playlist would be called "Gimme Back My Machine, Bitches," and it would shuffle songs by Public Enemy, Run-DMC, Cat Power, The Smiths, Eminem, Kanye, Janis, and Erykah Badu, and she might throw in "Jenifa" by De La Soul for Lavinia, depending on how angry she felt at the moment of compiling the musical diary entry.

There turned out to be no need to sneak into Bryan and Jean-Wayne's room. The boys' door was open when Very arrived. Jean-Wayne was inside the room, applying eyeliner in the mirror.

"Where's Bryan?" Very asked him, standing in the doorway.

"Dunno where he went," Jean-Wayne said. "He's out with a girl."

"Shut up."

"Not a real date. Just someone Debbie thought she could set him up with."

"Ew."

"Kinda."

Very stepped inside the room and sat down on Bryan's bed. Best just to get right to it. "I want my laptop back," Very demanded of Jean-Wayne. "Do you know where he's hidden it?"

"No."

"But it is Bryan who has hidden it. Yes?"

"Yes."

"Are you going to give me the speech about not enabling me?"

"No."

Cool. Trust established.

"So why are you putting on eyeliner?" Very asked.

"Want to find out?"

She jumped back up from Bryan's bed. "Yup." Very pulled one of Bryan's light jackets, the geeky newspaper delivery boy jacket that she used to love, from his closet to go out with Jean-Wayne.

She'd work the laptop situation later. The eyeliner mystery beckoned first.

See, Very could walk away from her so-called problem anytime. She just had.

Jean-Wayne placed a pair of sunglasses over his eyes, and together they headed out. "I was going to come find you now anyway. Something special has been arranged for you, by my secret society." His tone sounded ominous, and what with him dropping the words "secret society," and his green eyeliner, sunglasses, and overall great fashion sense, Very imagined him to be taking her to a Skull and Bones–type tribunal, but like one of the Ray-Banned Leprechauns, as fashioned by Calvin Klein.

It was 2 a.m. as they walked toward the East Asian Library, on the kind of April night Very loved, drizzly and brisk, with the promise of a dewy, warm morning ahead. Straggles of students milled along College Walk and on the steps at *Alma Mater,* but the campus was empty of its hordes of daytime people. Very loved this serene time on campus, seeing the stately university buildings framed in nightlights, hearing the hum of buses and taxis going up and down Broadway nearby, with only shadow figures dotting the landscape, smoking and talking and passing beers in brown bags. This must be the cozy campus fantasy her mother had wanted for her.

"You need it badly," Jean-Wayne said to Very as they walked up the steps toward the library.

"Excuse me?" she asked, mildly insulted. Her slutty reputation aside, his comment seemed a crude suggestion from such a gentleman.

"Not *that,*" Jean-Wayne said.

"Because I can get *that* if I want it," she said.

"No one would dispute that. I mean, you need a fix. I can see it in your eyes. They've gone all hollow since you were turned off. It's hurting me, that empty look of yours since your goods were taken away."

Could it be that Jean-Wayne understood her predicament? And knew that appeasement was obviously a big fat fake that needed to end?

Very said, "So you're going to help me? Give me back my machine?"

"No. I don't know where Bryan put it, to be honest. But I am taking you to a special place for a fix. Think of it as like a flophouse, for people like us."

"What do you mean, 'people like us'?"

"People who need uninterrupted, nonjudgmental tech time."

She was people like Jean-Wayne, indeed.

There were more messages awaiting her from El Virus. Very knew it. Her great love never sent only one message; he always sent one starter followed by a blitz of many. But she'd need unlimited, unsupervised online access in order to find the messages. She didn't want to beg for it. But here Jean-Wayne was, her newest bestest friend ever, intuiting her need, prepared to give her what she craved, with seemingly no strings attached.

"Outsiders are forbidden here," Jean-Wayne said as they approached a side door to the library. They entered a long, narrow hallway that was dimly lit. Jean-Wayne tapped twice on a janitor's closet door, then kicked it. The door opened to a dark staircase leading downward. Jean-Wayne retrieved a flashlight from his coat pocket and ushered Very down the stairs. They had reached the peeling wall, against which Jean-Wayne placed his index finger for scanning. As the unseen machine processed his fingerprint, Jean-Wayne told Very, "The group has made an exception for you. You're sort of like a rogue hero to them. Guys here, on the inside, they feel for your situation. Want to help you out."

They entered the dark room. Very couldn't believe what she saw. The sheer green of it all overwhelmed the space. The walls were painted a bluish green, and ceiling track lights emitted soft pastel shades of green. A massive plasma screen dwarfed the room, with the oceanic game on majestic display. The background sea green color against which the game was set was so vibrant and mesmerizing that Very could see how playing the game could be like smoking crack—instant narcotic, instant addiction. It was like you looked at that screen and were immediately transported down under to a private deep-sea adventure, surrounded by lush plant life and schools of tropical fish, each player an eco-warrior up against fish, whales, sharks, pirate ships, coral reefs, tsunamis, icebergs—all the waves of ocean life from around the world. The noises emanating from the game— waves crashing, water lapping, dolphins squealing, boat engines churning—somehow all these even sounded green, if it was possible to apply a color to a sound.

"You play *Dream with the Fishes!*" Very said to Jean-Wayne, dazzled. "How did I not know this about you before?"

"What happens in *Dreams* stays in *Dreams*," Jean-Wayne said. He took off his sunglasses and guided her around to the front side of the chairs to introduce her to the assembled players. There were seven other dudes already assembled, all with tribal forms of green stripes splashed across their faces. They were already deep inside the game—their eyes had that glassy look Very knew so well—but they acknowledged her presence with nods and grunts.

Very recognized a few of the grunts from their profiles on the now-defunct Grid site. Yes, defunct. But who de-functing cared? Not Very, that was certain. What Grid?

Bryan, at the "encouragement" of Dean Dean and Dreabbie, had announced he'd shut down The Grid immediately after the intervention, but who'd even notice? A replacement site of one sort or another would undoubtedly pop up soon, if it hadn't already. It wasn't like people weren't already connected by a million other sites, anyway. It wasn't like Very couldn't put up another site *like that*, whenever she wanted to, and next time without stupid Bryan knowing all the passwords and programming code.

She could shrug off The Grid as easily as she'd shrugged off Bryan. No problem.

Of the *Dreams* players assembled, two were boys Very was pretty sure she'd made out with at freshman orientation so many months ago, or maybe she'd asked them to make out with each other at that first party she'd thrown—not entirely a clear memory so many kegs ago. One player she recognized as her definitely post–b-day party make-out partner formerly known as Ghana, and she was clear on that memory (nice), and one player she recognized as a fellow Canadian friend of J.-W.'s (they traveled in packs, those Canucks on campus). The remaining players Very recognized from around campus but didn't know—but she'd like to, she could tell already.

Jean-Wayne said to the group, "Everyone, this is Very. Very, everyone."

Aargh! she wanted to say, pirate-voice, to the boys in their captain's chairs. Instead, she said, "Hey."

"Hey," they mumbled back.

"So do I get to play *Dreams* also?" Very asked Jean-Wayne.

"No way. There's a whole initiation ritual you'd have to go through. And sorry to be all sexist pig on you, but girls suck at this game. Total downer. But see that empty chair over there? Hector the Janitor delivered it here for you. Big fan of yours, apparently. There's a laptop on the chair, donated for your personal use in this room. Obviously, all necessary hardware and software are on the machine already. So go to it. Return to the mother ship."

Jean-Wayne sat himself down in the empty chair in the middle of the group—he was clearly the team leader—and picked up his console to enter the game. And instantly, he was Inside, and Very knew she was on her own here. The boys had their feed, and she should step aside to go to hers.

There was a moment's hesitation—perhaps she'd been better off restricted from all this? But the moment was only that: a moment.

Of course she wanted to hit the juice. She stepped out of the boys' game vision and over to her queen's chair behind their rows. She saw the laptop, shiny and beautiful, calling to her.

She'd answer.

CHAPTER 14

28 Messages, 21 Days till Finals, 99 Problems
(Actually, Quite a Bit More)

She is Ensign Bella de la Mermaid on starship USSR Galactica Titanica. She is Venezuelan for this episode, just because. (Technically, she is Venezuelexican, since the Northern South Americas' hostile takeover of Central America back on 001, so many moons ago.) She doesn't so much look native Venezuelan, but who cares? Her long, curly red hair is up-do'd, with soft tendrils caressing the sides of her alabaster face and sheer-pink-lipsticked mouth, and she wears a minidress Federation uniform with bitch-ass black go-go boots.

It feels good to be a Venezuelan hurtling through space.

"Mi Enseñita Sirena," he calls her, using his best conquistador accent. He is El Capitán. Her loco virus himbo. He is the hot-headed, brilliant leader of their rogue starship, which has renounced the Federation and gone on a pirate mission to explore strange new worlds populated entirely by fairies and gnomes. Their journey has been long and arduous, and it turns out there aren't a lot of fairy/gnome planets waiting to be discovered, and trying to outrun the Federation or Cylon or whoever-the-hell-they-are bounty hunters has gotten to be exhausting. Luckily they have taken solace in each other and their marathon lovemaking sessions on the lido deck, closed-circuit-filmed and available for downloadable viewing to folks back on 001, who are loving the Ensign-Capitán action and who are commenting all over the 'sphere with OMFGs and LOL;>s and ¡Muy calientes! Viewers delight in funding the starship's maladventures at such a reasonable download cost. Premium entertainment of this caliber is recession-proof. Obvs.

Online polls rage, as polls, and rages, tend to do. Some 45 percent of viewers think El Capitán will dump his Enseñita for the first hybrid fairy/gnome species he finds to seduce, while 86 percent of males aged 12–17 have voted Ensign Mermaid "Best Boobs on a Rogue Starship," a slap for sure to the 79 percent of females aged 18–34 who voted hard-bodied El Capitán way hotter than his Jell-O–bellied lover.

This episode is The One Where Enseñita Demands a Promotion. "To what?" El Capitán asks her as they lie sprawled on a long pool chair in a post-humpty-dance embrace, virtual sun beaming onto their glistening bodies. "You propose I promote you to, like, sergeant?" He sounds dubious.

She is not. She says, "I don't think we have sergeants on starships. I'd like to be . . . second in command. Affirmative. Number Two."

El Capitán wants to know, all commanding, "Number TWO! Dream big much? I mean, I could conceivably see you as Eighteen, or maybe Fifty-eight is more realistic, slacker. What makes you think you've earned that rank? Truly?"

"*I'll show you how I can earn that promotion,*" she murmurs, *straddling him.*

Fade to black, computer malfunction, CENSORED.

Very had thrown herself deep down back into the Internet black hole and, mmmmm, yes yes yes, ahhh, mmmmm, YES, such sweet relief.

El Virus had sent her a total of twenty-eight messages. She knew they were code for something. Very just had to figure out what.

As her fingers tapped the keyboard, she savored the rush—it was almost orgasmic. This laptop Jean-Wayne had hooked her up with was a virtual love machine. It talked back to her, flirted with her, played with her, adored her. It let her check out friends' photos and updates from around the world, it offered up visions of people doing naked tai chi, it approved when she IM'd everyone she'd ever known who could be found online at that very moment. It encouraged her to gamble her mythic fortune away in online poker. It practically applauded as she hunted the clues from El Virus.

That discarded computer clunker that Lavinia had loaned Very before this, what good was that? It had only let her type stupid papers. The typing part was helpful, obviously—Very had for once completed all her course work on time, and fairly cogently as well, without the online distraction. She hoped Dean Dean would be impressed. But still. The disconnected machine had helped her achieve no state of physical and mental satisfaction. It only got the job done.

Very rather liked this newly discovered flophouse approach to computing. As the boys *Dream*'d and Very surfed behind them, sharing in their green if not their screen, she liked the sense of community she felt with them, this den-sharing of an electronic vortex. Her drug of choice might have been different from the boys', but the goal was the same. Total assimilation Inside. No resident advisor interruptions, no studying, no money worries, no Real World nonsense.

He was being a tease, though, her El Virus. He'd left her a trail of messages, but sent her on a treasure hunt she had no idea how to decode. There was his posting on a Living Simple Listserv, providing a recipe for vegan maple cookies. A status update that linked to a new, alternative Wikipedia entry he'd written about Calvin Coolidge (who, according to the new entry, was *not* related to Calvin of *Calvin and Hobbes* fame, nor to Canadian singer Rita Coolidge; good to get that clarified). He'd uploaded images onto Very's different pages, picturing Amy Winehouse, photos of whom practically gave Very a hard-on of beehive-hair envy, and President Gerald Ford. He'd sent missives to her various accounts (Yahoo, Gmail, Mac, Hotmail, etc.—she had them all covered, even AOL, for quaintness' sake), but he only sent links. One link was to a message board of heated conversation by members of the Cooperative of Dairy Heartland Farmers, and another to a Walt Whitman poem called "When Lilacs Last in the Dooryard Bloom'd," an elegy for Abraham Lincoln in which Whitman used the hermit thrush as a symbol of the American voice. And so on. The messages' only purpose, as far as Very could deduce, was to inflict a smattering of information chaos upon her wounded soul.

Also, Very hadn't realized El Virus was *that* into American presidents. Personally, she found British prime ministers more fascinating and worthy of Wikipedia time.

He'd sent no monk photos.

She was intrigued, but disappointed.

No explanation of his disappearance.

Not one query of *And how are you?*

Not that their relationship had ever been genuinely chatty, but it would have been nice to know he'd been thinking about her in that benign kind of way, as bigger than just a text message or .jpg. Further, he'd disappeared for a whole month. He'd gone from communicating with her electronically several times a day to not at all. He owed her an explanation. Didn't he?

Still. The electronic hunt.

Total turn-on.

A nuclear explosion walloped across the green *Dreams* screen. Very looked up from her laptop daze to see that the boys' game had resulted in a decimated Pacific atoll, mercifully unpopulated, except by the schools of fried fish. Now she was hungry.

"Annihilation!" the voices in the chairs ahead of her cried out.

"Doritos!" she called out from behind them.

Break time. The games, and her laptop, were turned to Standby as a green trunk on a side wall was opened by Ghana. Inside, a treasure trove of munchies awaited consumption: Doritos and Twinkies and the mandatory Red Bulls. Perfection. These boys really knew how to party. That green trunk might as well have had a 7-Eleven logo emblazoned on it. The secret gaming room could only be improved with a green Slurpee machine.

And if she could ask her new benefactors to decode the messages from El Virus.

But El Virus was Very's secret man. He was not to be shared even with a secret society.

Very settled for some extreme caffeination and real-boy flirt time in the meantime. That green-splashed Ghana looked mighty tasty.

CHAPTER 15

Time Is Not on My Side:
Two Weeks Left to Figure Out a Plan

Very needed more.

More El Virus.

More ether (net).

She would find and rescue her monsignor.

Now that she was back in, no way was she going back out.

She even resented sleeping time. Any time that kept her off-line.

Her hunger to commune with El Virus burned deeper than ever.

And her hunger for the return of her own laptop burned even deeper than that.

Going online in *Dreams* world was awesome. But it was a fantasy that couldn't be sustained. Even Very knew that.

Summer break was right around the corner. The *Dreams* boys

would disperse, and their secret library nook would be locked up until the fall.

Perhaps it was a delayed reaction, but Very was finally, fully pissed at Bryan. She didn't know what she'd been thinking, not going completely ballistic on him when he said he'd taken away her machine temporarily. She'd let herself believe he was doing it because he cared about her that much. She'd let herself believe, because she wanted to believe.

The laptop had been Very's last material bond to her mother. The prior year, on Very's eighteenth birthday, Aunt Esther had handed Very a check for two thousand dollars. The money had been held in an account awaiting Very's passage into legal adulthood. It was money from a savings account that Cat had opened in Very's name when Very was a child. Cat had always been broke, but somehow, over the years, unbeknownst to Very, her mother had managed to tuck away twenty or fifty or seventy-five dollars at a time that she'd earned in various waitressing gigs, intending the funds to provide for her daughter's college education.

The couple thousand dollars would not begin to cover Very's university costs. But it was her mother's last legacy to her. Aunt Esther had suggested Very use the funds to buy herself a new laptop that Very could use when she went away to college. They'd both agreed Cat would have been pleased with that plan.

The laptop had been her proudest possession as an incoming freshman at Columbia University. She'd used that laptop for her schoolwork, her socializing—for everything. She'd used it to program The Grid. But now The Grid had been dismantled, and the foursome of friends hardly hung out together at all anymore.

Very realized she didn't even know what Bryan's plans were for the summer. Had his hope for an internship at a tech company in Portland worked out? Or would he spend another summer sweeping up his mother's yoga studio? Would any of the sexual confidence she hoped she'd imparted to him do him any good with the ladies back home in Oregon?

No, wrong. She shouldn't be having sympathetic feelings for Bryan. He was hiding her beloved machine. He had dismantled her online project. He was a dick. In the worst sense.

But Very was determined not to beg him for the machine back. She couldn't let Bryan know her hunger burned that deep. *The Grid? Who cares. That old thing. Whatever.*

With Jean-Wayne's help, Very could get her fix on the outside just fine until her gadgets were returned to her soon, and then she could take her habits back inside—to the privacy of her own machine.

Summer break loomed, and Very realized now how she would fill it.

She was going to go on an epic adventure to find El Virus. She figured she'd start with a road trip to various presidential libraries across the nation; that's probably where his clues led. She'd begin at the Franklin Delano Roosevelt library in Hyde Park, New York, then go on to the Harry S. Truman library in Independence, Missouri, and all the way to the Richard Nixon library in Yorba Linda, California, if that's what it took. She'd even backtrack to the Calvin Coolidge library in Northampton, Massachusetts, if necessary, although that one seemed so footnote-able.

What Very needed to figure out was how to finance her

journey. She also needed to buy one of those gorgeous GPS giz-mos and learn how to drive, but she'd worry about that part later. For now, she had to focus on fund-raising.

Could she sell her laptop and live off her iPhone to get her online fix, once her stuff was returned to her at the end of the se-mester? No, that wouldn't work. She couldn't sell off the laptop; her mother had provided that for her. And Very's thumbs were too chubby for full-time iPhone tapping—she'd go crazy.

She could sell sexual favors to the *Dreams* team. . . .

No, too sleazy. And it would make the groping sessions she'd resumed with Ghana in the hallway outside the *Dreams* room less fulfilling.

What an absurd idea, to sell sexual favors. What had hap-pened to Very that she would even consider stooping that low to finance her expedition? Maybe Dreabbie was right, and Very did have a problem?

Silly.

No way.

Next idea.

She could sell her eggs to infertile couples. The *Columbia Spectator* was always running classifieds looking for donor eggs from healthy, Ivy League–smart young women.

That could work.

Okay. At least Very had a backup plan now. But selling her eggs might take too much time, with all the paperwork and test-ing and blood samples and surrendering her genetic code and whatever. The summer could be over before she got paid.

What to do?

Very decided to turn to the one person who always had a good answer for everything.

She found her best guru, Hector the Janitor, mopping the floors in the dining hall.

"You're looking for a smoke?" he asked her. Hector reached into his uniform pocket and pulled out a hand-rolled cigarette for Very.

"I'm looking for something more," she said. She held up her customary payment to Hector—one of Aunt Esther's sweaters that Hector's mother-in-law apparently adored. "I need guidance."

"Do you ever, señorita," Hector said.

CHAPTER 16

Tonight We're Gonna Party
Like It's Finally the End of Finals

Hector had it all figured out in no time.

To set out on her summer quest, Very was going to need an epic amount of money. The most surefire way to get that money would be her old reliable.

Throw an epic party.

THE ASTRONOMY CLUB PRESENTS!

Top-Secret Extra-Credit Lab
Midnight Stargazing Event of Awesome*

Saturday, midnight till sunup.
Campus Observatory.
Follow the meme clues for event entry password:

lefreak / le-awesome productions.
You know the dot-com trail—URL it, baby.

* Beer and dancing *may* be involved.
($20 cover)
Harder booze may also be available.**
**(Cash bar—please tip your legal-drinking-age bar staff generously. 🍸)

She'd only had two weeks to put the whole thing together, *and* study for and take finals, but she'd pulled it off. Where there was an El Virus–inspired will, there was a way.

Very was not a complete idiot. She could learn from her mistakes.

1. Don't throw party in any residential dorm facility where persnickety RAs prowl, looking for inmate infractions.
2. Get Ghana, age twenty-two, to take on keg ordering and delivery duties. A student leaving the country the afternoon after the party to return to his native African homestead for the summer would be less likely to be called as a material witness in any potential but highly unlikely university investigation into party.
3. Exploit Barnard girl with the Very-crush who is also the student manager of the Barnard Bartending Agency for hooch and event staff.
4. Don't send out invitations on freaking paper-printed newsletter.
5. Circulate event info electronically only: pop-up

ads on select college gaming networks; fake e-mail chain letters purporting to solicit funds for some poor kid's kidney stone surgery in Lithuania; Columbia and NYU dining hall complaint message boards; and Ye Olde IM Favorite lists.

6. Guarantee spectacular attendance by inciting partygoer FOMO—fear of missing out—through viral YouTube campaign, a clip montage of the greatest party movies in the history of the world (*Animal House, Can't Hardly Wait, Superbad, Showgirls, The Exorcist*, etc.).

7. Biggest hurdle: holding the party in the observatory at historical landmark Pupin Hall, the famed astronomy and physics building where the atom was first split by Enrico Fermi. Overcome security concerns by exploiting janitor Hector's connections to campus security staff. Offer payola to Hector and on-duty officers, a cut of proceeds for looking the other way during party.

8. Rally Jean-Wayne's engineering *Dream* team to cross-circuit the building's security cameras for the event so playback of the previous night's empty rooms will appear on the main security monitors during the party's night of awesome.

9. Assure paid-off security officers that no acts of terrorism will take place during the party in the hallowed location, leading to no international incidents that will be splashed across the front

pages of the *New York Post* and *Daily News* the following day.

10. Also promise that any toilet backups will be fixed and cleaned by dawn.

11. Wear the sluttiest dress available—in Very's case, a psychedelic tie-dyed T-shirt she'd made the summer she was eleven (it fit back then), appropriately ripped so it drooped off one shoulder like in *Flashdance*, cut low for maximum cleavage effect, and cinched at waist, with a handyman's belt loaded with tools in case anything broke during the party and needed to be fixed. Plumbing equipment stored separately. No good way to accessorize a toilet plunger, sadly.

Now that she was back into the techno-game, Very was fully game ON.

Her party was a smash, even with no atom-splitting taking place (at least that Very was aware of; she would be *pissed* if any of those physics nerds got into any such antics on her party watch—Hector would never trust her again). Final exams were ending, and with students planning to disperse for the summer, the party people—hundreds of them—were primed to get down.

Ace DJ-ing from Very's party playlist, "Tear the Roof Down, Suckas"—a mix of funk, reggae, metal, disco, and bubblegum-pop classics that she'd created on her secret laptop in the *Dreams'* green-room den of iniquity—had the crowd pumped and gyrating on the dance floor. Why hadn't she thought of this before? An observatory with a world-class telescope was the ideal place for accommodating a huge crowd. A disco ball had been hung over the dance space, and it totally complemented the planet/stars vibe and shimmered sparkles over a lot of really bad dance moves, making everyone look suddenly sexy. The drunkenness helped liven the effect, too, as did the thick, cement observatory walls, which would not spill noise pollution onto the street below.

Seriously. She could have a big-event-organizer career ahead of her if she just put her mind to it. Even Lavinia said so.

"Look at this madness you've created. Have you ever thought what you could accomplish if you channeled all this brainpower and energy into something worthwhile?" Lavinia asked Very.

The massive room had a domed ceiling; somewhere between the floor and the high ceiling, a ladder had been situated across two opposing beams to make for extra seating space, and on that ladder Very sat with Lavinia. The disco ball hung from the ladder, and Lavinia and Very kicked it side to side to each other as their legs dangled high over the pulsing dance floor.

"What would you consider to be worthwhile?" Very asked. Generally, she feared heights, but with Lavinia sitting by her side, she felt immune to vertigo. Besides, Very was too high on the party's success to worry about how high she was sitting. She was smart enough to be sober up there, too. Nothing would ruin her party like having to unclog a toilet that was spinning before her eyes, or one that she'd just puked into.

Lavinia hadn't been mad about the party, surprisingly, saying only that she couldn't police Very's every technology whim and she was too busy studying for finals to try. So if Very was going to throw a party, Lavinia said, she figured, *If you can't beat 'em, join* 'em. She wouldn't give Very her spare 'Pod back, or lobby Dreabbie and Bryan for the return of her laptop and iPhone, however. The e-laws for Very had been laid down, and Lavinia, for one, was sticking with that original plan. What Very chose to do outside those boundaries was her choice.

Lavinia said, "I'd consider your time spent to be worthwhile if you could assure me you'll tap your brain for the good, and promise me you won't wind up in a post-party future, waking up barely alive in some tawdry ditch, then Googling the closest McDonald's location to make a french fry run instead of using the iPhone to call for help from the police."

"My, you dream so big for me." Very reached over to hold Lavinia's hand so she could steady her gaze to look directly down onto the floor crowd. She felt comforted that Lavinia knew the fries would be her priority. It was nice to be so understood by at least one person in the universe. "Want to go down and dance?"

"No, thanks," Lavinia said.

"Don't be a wallflower. It's a night for blowing off end-of-semester steam. Anybody who interests you down on the dance floor?"

"I'm about to go away for the summer. I'd rather just hang with my friends tonight than shout over the music to get to know new people down there."

Very said, "Understood. I see you meeting a hot fellow camp counselor this summer, anyway, having some crazy adventures in the Arts & Crafts building. Kinky stuff involving making pot holders?"

"*You*," Lavinia said, "could maybe dream bigger for *me*. C'mon, let's get off this ladder. I'm getting dizzy up here."

Together they descended the ladder and veered over to climb the stairs to the giant telescope viewing perch, where the actual Astronomy Club was assembled, taking looks up into the great beyond.

"It's too hazy tonight to see any good stars," the club president told the girls. "So we focused the telescope on the Empire State Building."

Very and Lavinia stepped up to the viewing lens at the same time. "Jinx!" they both said as their cheeks touched. They shared the telescopic vision, looking directly into the offices on the top floors of the Empire State Building, which appeared so close and large it was like the building was directly in front of them instead of a few miles away downtown. They watched some late-night office workers go about their business—typing on computers, talking on the phone, cleaning out desks.

Very said, "The workers seem so live and close. It's like they're in a video game. Except they look more real."

"They *are* real," Lavinia said.

Very hadn't heard from El Virus again since those twenty-eight messages on her first night with the *Dreams* guys, but when she finally found him this coming summer, Very was going to tell him about this magic. About the party she'd thrown so she could finance finding him, and about how Lavinia's cheek was so soft and delicate, and how the Empire State Building was populated by 3-D action figures at night, and how if she could observe stars in the sky with anyone, she'd probably choose Lavinia first, but El Virus would place a close second.

From behind them, a girl tugged on Lavinia's arm. "Jennifer! I was hoping to find you here! The crew team's all here. We were looking for you."

Very and Lavinia turned around. An Amanda, crew-girl specimen, stood before them, her face flushed and eager.

Lavinia jumped down from the viewing perch like Very wasn't even there. "Great!"

And Lavinia was gone, dragged away by the Amanda, who didn't seem to even notice Very glaring at her.

Well, then. If that's how it was going to be, Very had some end-of-semester celebrating to do herself.

She'd actually done it. Not just the party, but a legitimate 2.8 GPA. Not the 3.0 she was required to have, but she felt sure Dean Dean would put in the good word for her to keep her scholarship funds intact; she'd tell him so at the meeting she was scheduled to have with him the following afternoon to discuss her academic status. She'd survived without her iPhone and laptop—with a little help on the side, courtesy of J.-W. and the Green Team, but the Powers That Be would never know that part. She wouldn't know until her meeting with Dean Dean whether Dreabbie had signed off on Very's returning to student housing next year, but who cared? Very would worry about that later. Problems? She had no problems.

She was high on this moment that she, personally, Very Le-Freak, had made happen. The party was a few hundred people deep, and would probably go down as Extremely Legendary in the archives of Columbia party history. And now Very had the money for a cross-country adventure to rescue her El Virus. She'd leave as soon as she was packed out of her dorm room, or once Lavinia, exasperated and wanting to check out already, had done it for her. Very didn't yet know how she'd start her expedition. She'd plan the journey along the way. Life was more exciting that way. And to think she had accomplished every detail of this party electronically. Why anyone would try to curtail Very from her e-habits was, simply, ridiculous logic. Clearly, her best self came forward through machinery. She was all-powerful in that format. Practically a Cylon! (But she was the really hot blond Cylon, not those other sad sacks.)

Very eyeballed Bryan on the dance floor; he was doing an awkward white-boy two-step with the girl Dreabbie had tried to fix him up with. And since she, Very LeFreak, was feeling so celebratory, she was not going to take on her slut personage and sabotage his attempts to hit on the girl. Though she could. She could. But Very decided she could be bigger than Bryan. If Bryan got lucky and got some, he'd finally give Very her fucking machine back already. The two of them could be finished, cleanly and neatly, and without the need to scan his browsing history to see where he'd taken her machine, because she was over it, didn't care, just wanted to have this episode excised and to move forward in her life, onward to her El Virus–hunt presidential libraries road trip. Her friendship with Bryan was over. She'd find a newer, better cuddle buddy: E.V. himself.

Very approached Bryan on the dance floor, coming up behind him and tickling his back. Bryan turned around. He looked like a frightened cat when he saw Very; his back arched and his electric hair frizzed high.

"Debbie decides when you get your stuff back, not me," Bryan said loudly, over the music.

Very would be bigger than this. She *would*. She swayed to the beat of the song, grinding herself up against Bryan's front. She leaned in to tell him a secret.

"Faux-mo the girl," she said, gesturing to Bryan's otherwise dance partner.

"Huh?" Bryan said.

"Pretend you're not into girls. Let her think you're just ex-perimenting with her. Then she'll be all over you. A sure thing."

That's what Very should have done with Bryan to begin with, she realized. Pretended she was only into girls. So then she never would have hurt him, and never would have had her laptop taken away by him in retaliation. She would never have lost a cuddle partner. And friend.

Very abandoned Bryan to head over to the bar area, where she could scan the room for new victims. She needed some love tonight. An easier entanglement than the Bryan type, no strings attached. Of the most obvious pickings, Very considered: Ghana, grooving under the disco ball, who'd been giving her some some-thin' on the q.t. lately, but had held back on giving her the whole shebang because of his long-distance girlfriend; a really hot basketball player dude she'd been admiring in the dining hall all year, whom she'd really like to slam-dunk; the Barnard bartend-ing girl, whom she kinda owed anyway, and . . .

Very's scan was being most annoyingly uncooperative. Her gaze kept pulling in the wrong direction, away from her intend-eds, and toward Lavinia, dancing with the Amanda in a corner of the room. They were, like, *dancing*-dancing, not just snapping their fingers and mouthing lyrics, but actual hip-and-booty shak-ing up close and personal, while a parade of crew girls circled them, cheering them on.

The dance hall sight was just . . . disgusting. Who was Lavinia to behave so wantonly?

Very's slut personage triumphed, ultimately, redirecting her laser scan away from the so totally lesbo crew and directly back onto Ghana. Target lock. Beep beep beep.

Very had better things to do than worry about Lavinia's antics, which would probably culminate with the girls' crew team having a slumber party and cooing over an assortment of stupid Hugh Grant movies, none of the girls drunk or bold enough for more than slight petting—with each other, with themselves, or with the boys' crew team, undoubtedly having a pornfest in the next room. Very had superior ways to cap off her night. Like giving herself a parting party gift of Ghana.

Very and Ghana could be each other's going-away present.

CHAPTER 17

The Girl's a Superfreak / She's Really Freakin' Out

Full speed ahead. Engage!

Very stormed down the hall of her dorm floor. She wanted her fucking laptop back right now.

No appeasement. No compromising. No waiting even one more minute, much less another day. She didn't care what Dean Dean would proclaim he'd determined about her online privileges and other matters in their meeting later in the afternoon. She wanted her machine *this very second*, or she was gonna go Terminator on someone's ass.

What had she been thinking, letting Bryan keep it all this time, and acting like she could live with this treachery?

It wasn't that Very needed that particular machine so much. She didn't. She could get her fix anywhere, anytime. Top-secret military commandos could kidnap Very and deposit her down into the most remote corner of Siberia, and she'd still find a way to tune back in. She'd find the closest Eskimos, or Siberianos, or whoever the native species were, and she'd be partying with them and tapping away on their cellies in no time. Just *try* to shut her down! NOT. POSSIBLE.

It was the principle of the matter.

Who the *fuck* had Bryan thought he was to have commandeered the intervention?

And *what* had Very been thinking to have acquiesced so easily? So quietly?

Her true self could be contained no longer.

Ghana had spilled all the details. She knew the whole story now.

By bro-code, what happened in *Dreams* stayed in *Dreams*, perhaps—but what got discussed in the bathroom during *Dreams* was fair game. Jean-Wayne had 'fessed up all to Ghana in there. And Ghana had revealed all to Very.

It was Bryan who was in cahoots with Dreabbie. It was Bryan who'd suggested the intervention to Dean Dean, who then set it in motion with Dreabbie. It was Bryan who'd not only shut down The Grid but also, after swiping her laptop from her room while she was meeting with Dean Dean, wiped the machine clean. Jean-Wayne and Lavinia knew about it but hadn't had the heart to tell Very yet.

Her hard drive had been erased. All her favorite mementos of El Virus would be gone—their IM transcript logs, their photo and story exchanges, their PowerPoint love-letter presentations. Bryan had perused every nook on her machine before going on his destructive rampage.

It had honestly never occurred to Very that Bryan could go to that extreme. She'd assumed him to be holding on to her laptop in a misguided but sincere and only a little bit cruel attempt to protect Very from herself. How could she have been so naïve as to think he was only safeguarding the machine and not perusing it? She'd never imagined he cared that much. If she had absconded with *his* machine, she'd have stored it away. Look through it? Nah! What could possibly be interesting there?

It was eight in the morning, but Very was still operating on darkness time. She'd yet to sleep since the blowout party. She'd fooled around with Ghana, yeah, which had been satisfactory until he'd burst into tears afterward, despondent over having been fully unfaithful, in the biblical way and not just in the stoned making-out way, to his girlfriend. It was like he wanted to hurt Very for having prodded him. He'd retaliated with the most hurtful tool at his disposal: information.

Ghana was getting dressed, eager to bolt her room. Very had tried to entice him back into bed. "Your girlfriend won't mind," Very said. "Since we've already gone this far . . . why not go there again?"

While pulling up his jeans, Ghana said, "I really should be going. It's bad enough I did this. But if she finds out with *whom*, then I'm really in trouble."

"Why?" Very asked. "I don't know her."

Almost casually, while buttoning up his shirt, Ghana said, "But most everyone here knows about *you*, and that's going to get back to her." He leaned in to Very, like he was teasing. "Everyone in your residence hall thinks you're pretty nutty. You know that, right? I mean, people *like* you, sure. You're a cool gal. No doubt. But that thing the Bryan guy says about you—it's sort of become the party line."

"What's he say?" Very asked, her heart sinking.

"That anyone can see you're robotically attached to your machinery and have no real personality without your props."

OMFG WTF WTF OMFG?!

"What else does he say about me?" Very whispered.

And so Ghana had spilled the details about what Jean-Wayne had told him Bryan had done to Very's laptop.

Very had jumped out of bed and rushed out of her dorm room before Ghana'd had a chance to put his shoes on. She was glad Lavinia had spent the night away with her crew friends, because if Lavinia were in their room now, Very would want to kill *her*, too. Very didn't want any distraction from her primary goal.

Target: Bryan.

Mission: Annihilation.

She had to settle the score with Bryan. Before he turned her in to Dean Dean for the Astronomy Club party, too. Before he could wreck her life any further.

"BRYAN!" She pounded on his door. "BRYAN!"

She didn't care how early in the morning it was or that most students living on Bryan's floor were probably still asleep. No answer from Bryan. A few calls of "Shut the fuck up!" came from nearby rooms, but no response from Bryan's room.

Very reached for the doorknob. Times like these demanded no respect for privacy. "I KNOW YOU'RE IN THERE, YOU FUCKING PIECE OF SHIT!"

Sure enough, the door was unlocked. She pushed it open. Jean-Wayne's bed was made up—he'd obviously not come home the previous night. Bryan's bed was unkempt, with clothes tossed on it. But no Bryan.

Ahhhh-chooo!

That sneeze.

Very pivoted to face the side wall of the dorm room. She opened the closet door. And there Bryan was, naked, with the girl whom Very had so generously suggested he faux-mo standing behind him, wearing a G-string and nothing else, her arms clasped over her chest to cover herself.

Very tapped the girl on the shoulder. "You. Leave. Now. For your own good."

The girl scurried from behind Bryan, grabbed her clothes from his bed, and bolted out of the room.

Bryan and Very inspected each other warily, like gunslingers at a showdown. Nude Cowboy and Nude Cowgirl. For Very, too, it seemed, was not dressed. She'd left Ghana so angrily and hastily, she hadn't, she realized now, bothered to put on clothes.

And Nude Cowboy had the audacity now to try covering his junk with his hand!

Very pulled a pillow from Jean-Wayne's bed and flung it at Bryan, who positioned the pillow to cover his private parts. Still standing in the closet, Bryan reached for his newsie jacket and tossed it to Very. "Cover yourself up at least!" he hissed.

She let the jacket drop to the floor. What did she care about nudity? That's how her mother had raised her—to be free and open.

And to express rage at men, as appropriate. If only she had a lighter handy . . .

"I HATE YOU!" Very yelled. "I heard what you did to my machine. How could you have done this to me?"

Bryan tried to hand Very a robe from the closet, but she shoved it away.

"It was for your own good," he said.

"Give it back to me. Now. Give me my machine."

"I can't. The machine had to be put down. One of those El Virus files of yours—when I tried to open it without the right password, it launched a virus on your hard drive. Obliterated the laptop. It's useless now."

This was not possible. Weren't there constitutional amendments that protected Very from this tyranny? The right to bear arms, and laptops, and have private exchanges with an unseen electronic *amour*?

No. Please, no. This can't be happening.

It wasn't possible that tears streamed down Very's face. Such humiliation. She could feel the wetness on her cheeks, but she couldn't give in so easily. She couldn't let Bryan see this effect he'd had on her. She wiped her face with her hand and tried to steady her expression back into a hateful gaze.

"Give it back to me," she repeated. "Even if the hard drive is destroyed, it's still my machine. And I want it back."

He said nothing. Just stood there.

"NOW!" Very shrieked.

"You're not listening," Bryan said, all of a sudden speaking very East Coast fast for a West Coast granola spawn. "It's destroyed. I'm sorry. I didn't mean for this whole thing to go this far. I'm so sorry, Very. So sorry. I didn't know what to do. That El Virus guy is quite the masterful programmer. There was no saving your machine after the virus launched without the proper passwords. Very"—Bryan did have the decency to appear despondently sheepish—"when I realized what I'd done, I panicked. I threw away your laptop."

"Like, in the *trash*?"

"Yes."

Not only was his action completely environmentally irresponsible, but what Bryan had done was also the most unspeakable, vile act imaginable.

And yet he'd just spoken it, as fact.

This *was* happening.

"NOOOOOOO!!!!!!!!!!!!!!!!" Very screamed.

His conciliatory tone gone, Bryan added: "One more thing. That El Virus stuff was totally gross. I saw it all. You must be crazy to get involved in that kind of sordid mess with a stranger. You. Are. Such. A. Freak."

Very didn't care that a crowd had gathered outside the room, spurred on by the noise from her argument with Bryan. She didn't care that she was standing opposite him, completely exposed, in every manner possible. She would make him pay.

Very lunged forward, her hands reaching for Bryan's neck.

Yes, she was going to have to kill him.

"*Aargh!*" she cried out.

Very LeFreak was indeed the freakiest of the freaks. Not the cool brand of fun freak. She was the worst case of freak, a complete and utter loser.

And now, she was a monster, too.

PART TWO

White Noise (The Real Kind)

CHAPTER 18

ESCAPE, Emergency Services for Computer-Addicted Persons Everywhere, was a former fat farm fallen on hard times. Originally built as a summer vacation lodge during the post–World War II period, it developed a reputation as a refuge for plump housewives seeking to discreetly shed pounds at discount rates during the off-season. The lodge became a full-fledged fat farm during the dot-com boom of the late 1990s, when the Vermont lake resort targeted a new clientele and transformed to cater year-round to a pampered elite of suddenly wealthy/suddenly porky millionaires. But a shyster accountant and global economic turmoil ultimately forced the family who'd owned the establishment to sell it off. The controlling interest was bought by a faceless conglomerate (IBM and Microsoft were both rumored; a consortium of dot-com fat farm graduates was the more likely candidate—skinny people could get so mean and vindictive). The new regime was looking to profit from the flip side of the new technology economy: technology addiction. The conglomerate hired Dr. Joyce Kuntz, a New Age shrink who'd dreamed of finding a cheap resort that could be converted into a technology dry-out clinic, to run the new endeavor. She preferred to be known professionally as "Dr. Joy," for obvious reasons.

Very had seen the ESCAPE infomercial once, when she was in high school, on the television in her dentist's office in New Haven. The TV had been set up to distract patients during root canal procedures.

"Hi, I'm Dr. Joy. I'd like to tell you and your technology-addicted loved ones about a program I've started, at a place where overstressed, overstimulated people can go for guidance and strength, to learn about the beauty in their hearts, away from the numbing addiction of their machines. Located along the scenic Lake Champlain shoreline in Vermont, ESCAPE is a resort clinic where you or your loved ones can withdraw from technology and travel to the inner depths of the soul. At ESCAPE, you'll receive premium physical and mental rehabilitation, in a relaxed natural setting. Call the number on your television screen now for more information."

Lavinia had promised the place would be like spa rehab.

Lavinia had been wrong.

Newly technology-less residents roamed the ESCAPE grounds like automatons, mindlessly performing stupid provincial chores foisted upon them as "voluntary," like churning butter and picking berries to make into jam. They gardened and trimmed bushes and trees on the property, under the guise of "nature time." Residents had to launder their own clothes and sheets, using old-fashioned wringers and washboards, and then hang the laundry on outdoor lines to dry. There wasn't even a manicurist on site to fix inmates'—er, residents'—hands after all that hard work.

In Very's opinion, the "spa rehab" was more like a technology-free indentured servitude zone, without Google and iTunes and satellite TV and a Wii—in other words, all the perks that were supposed to come along with basic existence. The ESCAPE brochure—with all the pretty Vermont pictures and 12 Steps jargon and quotes from "healed" technophiles—was just a subterfuge.

Very didn't know if she'd make it through the first week, much less a whole month. She'd rather have a dozen root canal procedures than suffer through twenty-eight days of ESCAPE rehab. At least with dental work, you got painkillers to help you sleep away the time.

The experience as a whole Very didn't so much object to. It's not like she had something better to do with her summer.

It was the sheer quiet that was going to be her downfall at ESCAPE.

There was nothing to do at this place except think. Ruminate hard on all her failures in life that had led her to this rock bottom of disconnected indignity.

They tried to make me go to rehab and I said . . .
"Yes, yes, yes?!"

Indeed, Very had been a complete pushover when it came down to the decision.

Although she'd originally sung to the tune of "No, no, no."

But Aunt Esther had taken command of the situation. "Oh yes, you will, young lady," the senior lady had proclaimed.

And that was that.

In all honesty, Very was so very tired. And relieved to have the decision made for her.

She needed something to do, anyway.

So she'd agreed to go to rehab.

Whatever.

Snooze.

Her presidential libraries idea would never have worked out. What had Very been thinking? She didn't even have a legal driver's license, only that fake Montana one that said she was twenty-three and her name was Ermengarde Schnitzel—eyes: green; hair: red; weight: 'scuse me, that's personal. Very wouldn't know what El Virus really looked like even if she found him. And she didn't know whether going on a road trip to presidential libraries was, in fact, what his clues had meant.

Very didn't, quite honestly, know anything anymore.

She'd tried to kill a man. She was pretty sure.

She wasn't exactly a reliable narrator.

She probably wouldn't have gone through with it. But the desire had been there.

The memory was hazy. She remembered lunging toward Bryan, reaching to grab his throat. She remembered screaming or shrieking or some hellacious form of Mariah Carey trilling coming from her mouth that possibly could have broken the sound barrier. She knew that Bryan had shoved back at her, trying to deflect her and silence her. But her feet had been bare, and she'd slipped on the floor, knocking her head against a bed frame as she tumbled down.

What happened in between she'd have to consider A Lost

Chapter in her life. She preferred those memories silenced anyway. Who was she to protest her subconscious?

When Very came to, she was laid flat on a hospital gurney. With her hands in restraints.

"WHAT THE FUCK!" she yelled. Her wrists ached from the shackles; they must have been fidgeting beneath the restraints for—who knew how long?

Her gurney was parked next to a hospital corridor wall. A nearby nurse strolled to Very's side, unconcerned. "We're waiting for your room to open up, sweetie. Bed upstairs should be ready in about an hour. I'll let your folks know you've come to."

Very had folks now?

No, she only had Aunt Esther and Lavinia, who rushed to her side from a waiting room.

"You gave us quite a scare," Aunt Esther said.

"WHAT THE FUCK!" Very repeated. She spread and wiggled her fingers from beneath the restraints, intending to gesture, *How could this be?*

"Language," Aunt Esther chided her, paying no mind to Very's hands. "You know I will not tolerate that."

Trying to sound calm, Very singsonged, saccharine-sweet, "Please may I know how the frock I came to be here?"

Lavinia filled in the blanks. "You and Bryan got into a scuffle." (And may Lavinia always be such a blessed old soul to drop words like "scuffle" into conversation completely without irony.) "You fell and got knocked out. When the ambulance came and the medics tried to take you for help, you . . . resisted. It wasn't pretty. They sedated you. Doctor says physically you're okay, but mentally . . . you're going to have to stay overnight for psychiatric evaluation." Lavinia leaned down and cupped her hand around Very's ear to whisper one last thing. "Also, you were naked when it happened, and no one's judging you about that; everyone who saw agrees you look fierce au naturel, but don't mention it to your aunt because I didn't tell her that part."

Thank God. Aunt Esther disapproved of low-rider jeans with thongs showing through ("Oy, despicable!"), so nakedness to her was almost as unholy as the f-word spewing from the mouths of young ladies.

Funnily enough (not really), much of Very's "psychiatric evaluation" took place without Very's having the benefit of being present. It happened in the hospital waiting room the next day, in a conference attended by the attending physicians and Dean Dean, Aunt Esther, Dreabbie, and Lavinia. They made the determination—er, recommendation—that Very go into rehab. Apparently, charges wouldn't be filed against Very (FOR WHAT?!?! Very wanted to know—Bryan had gotten safely on a plane home to Portland, according to Lavinia) if she agreed to voluntarily go into treatment.

"I said 'No, no, no.'" Very actually sang it aloud to them.

"Oh yes, you will, young lady," Aunt Esther said.

"But I can't afford rehab!" Very tried to protest. The group had just come from their meeting and presented the idea to Very in her hospital room. She couldn't afford college. Who the hell would pay the costs for a rehab facility? Aunt Esther didn't have that kind of money to spare; she lived off a modest pension. And if Aunt Esther was going to spring for that kind of expense for Very, well, then, Very privately felt she would rather have the money go toward building a supercomputer station in her attic room in New Haven that she could one day use to teleport herself into outer space, thankyouverymuch.

"May we have a few moments alone?" Lavinia said to the group. The doctor left Very's room along with Dean Dean, Aunt Esther, and Dreabbie (who'd been pissed to have missed her flight home for summer break in all the Very drama, yet seemed pleased to have been on call through the episode for the purposes of practical experience on her resident advisor résumé).

Alone with Lavinia, Very begged her, "You asked them to leave so you can tell me the better plan you've figured out for me, right? What is it?"

Lavinia tucked a strand of Very's wild hair behind her ear, then tenderly patted her on the head. "You do have the money," Lavinia said. "I counted the money in the envelope you left in our room from your Astronomy Club party. You have about exactly enough for a month's stay at a residential treatment center. I found one for you. It's near the summer camp where I'm working. I'll be nearby. You won't be alone. I promise."

"No way," Very said. Her hard-earned funds would most certainly not go toward a nonsense idea like . . .

"If you don't use the money for rehab," Lavinia said, "I'll tell the dean how you made the money."

"You wouldn't."

Lavinia smiled. "I would. And Bryan and Jean-Wayne back me up on this. So it's your choice. We can lie and say you have some cash stashed away from various odd jobs you've been taking on all year, along with some contributions your friends kicked in, and you'll have the possibility of at least coming back to Columbia next year. Or we can tell Dean Dean how you really earned that money, and you'll never come back to the university."

"You are evil incarnate," Very said, shocked and offended that she'd had no idea about this sexy side of Lavinia's personality.

"I'm worried about you," Lavinia said. "Seriously worried. This is not a game anymore. You really scared me."

And because she was a sucker for stupid ol' Lavinia's concerned but dear ol' face, Very jumped on board with the ESCAPE plan. And because Lavinia blackmailed her. And because Aunt Esther said she had to.

They tried to make me go to rehab and I said . . .
"Whatever. Who cares. So I'll go."

CHAPTER 19

Very needed to silence the quiet or she'd go mad.

If she could locate the secret stash of MP3 players on the premises, Very figured, she could last the four weeks in rehab. Simple tunage would ease her music-deprived soul and ease her transition into being so harshly, and completely, de-technologified.

ESCAPE was not kidding about forcing residents to escape from technology. ESCAPE could teach the TSA a few things about security procedures.

There was a metal detector that residents, and visitors, had to pass through at the entrance. A full-on body search was also part of the intake process for new residents, and it had caused Very to lose the first-generation iPod loaded with 2001's Hottest Hits that she'd desperately bought off a long-term patient at the hospital following her psychiatric "incident" and then had slipped between her sock and shoe before check-in at ESCAPE. New arrivals were only allowed to bring a duffel bag of clothes and cosmetic supplies, which had to be thoroughly inspected by staff before residents could check in to their rooms. And so Very had also lost the Game Boy she'd acquired from that same hospital patient in exchange for a fully consensual but nonsexual back and shoulder massage (no oil or taking-off-of-shirt involved). Somewhere on the ESCAPE grounds, Very knew, there was a whole ESCAPE supply room filled with items confiscated from the arrival inspections: music players, phones, Game Boys, computers, probably naughty toys, too.

This was probably why Dr. Joyce Kuntz, aka "Dr. Joy," was *also* also known as "Dr. Killjoy," re-nicknamed by the original class of ESCAPE inmates, who'd passed the name down through successive cycles of rehabbers.

Very didn't think asking for one bloody iPod, or just a battery-operated AM/FM radio, was that big a deal.

Dr. Killjoy apparently thought differently.

"Veronica, you're missing the point," she'd said when Very presented the idea to her during their initial orientation session together. "The goal here is to check out from external stimulation and material communication. It's not meant as a punishment. It's a means for you to cleanse, and check in to, your own soul."

Soul cleansing at ESCAPE would include mandatory attendance at group therapy with Dr. Joy, art therapy, talk therapy, and kitchen-duty "therapy," but, frankly, Very thought her hygiene habits weren't all that bad, so she didn't understand what she needed to be cleansed of.

"Cleanse my soul of what, exactly?" Very demanded. "The devil?" Trapping Dr. Joy into defending the supposedly secular curriculum could be an entertaining diversion.

Conceiving devil-themed playlists would be more entertaining, though. Off the top of her head and without benefit of a search engine, Very would include "Devils Haircut" by Beck, "I'm Your Boogie Man" by KC and the Sunshine Band, "Shout at the Devil" by Mötley Crüe, "Christmas with the Devil" by Spinal Tap, "Satan Is My Motor" by Cake, "Devil Inside" by INXS, and, most obviously, "Satan Rejected My Soul" by Morrissey, which Very considered her personal anthem, in a song-title kind of way.

Better yet, Very could pass her ESCAPE time developing a Satan-inspired video game. It could be something like *Grand Theft Auto . . . in HELL*, brimstone and hellfire in really fast cars, and a seedy underbelly lined with John 3:15 placard holders, and death and tyranny and awesome motor raceway sounds.

Very had to find that secret stash of confiscated equipment soon. Who was she fooling? An iPod alone wouldn't do her. She needed access to programming software, which would require computer hardware.

Dr. Joy said, "Of course I'm not talking about 'the devil.' This program is not intended to engage in that kind of polemic debate. The goal here at ESCAPE is to achieve a simple spiritual purification from within, without artificial stimulation."

" 'Simple,' " Very said. "That makes no sense. I'd *simply* like to be able to listen to my music. Getting through the day without that is like asking me not to breathe."

Very had to figure out the sound track for her video game before she could develop the actual game. She'd like to get started right away.

"No one's asking you not to breathe. If it's simple music you think you are missing, you could learn to play an acoustic instrument here! We have classes available for that! You could learn to play the banjo, the recorder, the lute! We have so many exciting options."

Very laughed. Dr. Joy did not. Sarcasm did not seem to be included in the doctor's therapeutic repertoire.

What Very found fascinating about Dr. Joy was that she seemed to genuinely want the pathetic offerings at ESCAPE to sound fun and enjoyable, yet the expression on her face as she offered them was often strangely grim. It was like Dr. Joy's voice inflection was filled with exclamation points, but her facial tics indicated a dreary and indifferent same-old period mark. Unnaturally tall, slim, and pasty-faced, Dr. Joy looked to Very like the beleaguered Mother Superior who was always chasing after that rapscallion Madeline girl in the children's books. BTW, Dr. Joy's attire could use an infusion of cool nun's habit. At present, her clothing appeared to operate strictly out of the Lands' End bargain basement.

Very said, "I don't want to *play* an instrument. That's so much work to learn how to read music and be patient until you can get through the suck part till you actually sound good on it. I only want to *listen* to music and dance around my room, flailing my arms around like a maniac while I wail along with, like, The Clash. I think that's a healthy outlet, don't you?"

" 'Outlet' implies electricity, hence—no, absolutely not. And there will be no need for wailing or clashing here, Veronica! I assure you of that. We've already gone over some of the physical activities offered here—"

Did this woman even hear her?

"I'm not interested in churning butter like in the brochure," Very interrupted, imagining herself decked out in a peasant's

164

costume and singing "Ol' Man River" along with the other indentured servants. The appealing costume aside, the mental picture appalled her. Also, her arms would get really sore from the
physical labor, and just when her carpal tunnel syndrome was
getting so much better. Fuhgeddaboutit.

"Are you vegan?"

"Yes," Very lied. She was as vegan as that Jimmy Dean
sausages guy on the TV commercials was, such a good salesman
that the mere sight of him made Very also crave the glories of
scrambled eggs slathered in butter, crispy bacon, bagels with
cream cheese, and coffee with half 'n' half.

Dr. Joy said, "Then you are excused from butter churning and
cheese making. What types of exercise do you enjoy?"

Very laughed. "I'm sorry, did you just say 'exercise' and
'enjoy' in the same sentence?"

"I did." Dr. Joy's stern face acknowledged no humor in the
statement.

"Okay, I'll play this game. I love Wii bowling, and *Tiger
Woods PGA Tour* SimGolf is cute, too, but figuring out the golf-
ing outfit to wear while playing it is cooler. I like the haberdasher/
plaid kind of look, like sort of *Caddyshack* meets a Wii version of
Gossip Girl—"

"Let's discuss realistic options." Dr. Joy's eyes didn't offer
even the possibility of a twinkle. *Caddyshack* meets *Wii Gossip
Girl*?!?!? Totally hilarious! And what an awesome fashion statement that would be. But, realistically, Dr. Joy continued, "Each
night an activity schedule showing the offerings for the following
day is posted in the dining hall, so you may schedule your time
accordingly. You'll have group therapy or individual counseling,
but also time for exercise and other purifying activities. We have

canoeing, tai chi, tetherball, meditation sessions, yoga—we've even just added hot yoga!"

"What's that?" Very said, imagining a roomful of *Playboy* Playmates doing naked yoga, which could potentially be highly entertaining.

"Yoga! In heated rooms! The sweat you generate in that style of yoga is an excellent way to relieve your body of toxins!" Dr. Joy's face indicated the prospect might be as fun to experience as getting a Pap smear.

"Sizzle me not," Very sighed.

Very's first order of business after escaping the ESCAPE headmistress would be to find out where the confiscated loot was and, at the very least, get some music back into her life. The Internet she could maybe live without for a few hours—er, days—no, a whole week, even. Head-banging and thrash-dancing and music-electrifying she absolutely, positively had to have.

Like, right now.

CHAPTER 20

The quickest way to discover where the cache of confiscated machines was stored would be to hit up any institution's designated group of all-knowing information sources: the smokers. Very might only have been nineteen years old, but she had seen enough movies and TV shows about the subject to know that no [Insert Name of Any Bad Vice Here]s Anonymous meeting would be complete without the toxic air of cigarette smoke suffocating all those otherwise good feelings and affirmations going on. And where the smokers could be found, important information could usually be tapped.

The main lodge at the center of the property, perched on a hill and offering a breathtaking view of Lake Champlain, was ESCAPE's equivalent to a campus student union. The dining hall was there, along with many various spaces for group activities, socializing, counseling sessions, and administrative offices. The cabins for residents were located a few hundred yards away.

The cabins were simple one-room shacks that mercifully included private bathrooms. Each cabin was furnished with a bed, desk, chair, and wind-up clock, and oil lamps for light. Empty carcasses of plaster hung around the room's walls where outlets had once been, traces of wiring hanging loose, as if to tease the newly wireless into submission. Beyond the rows of cabins were gardens and paths and trees, then a tennis court, then the pool, then . . . finally, after all that useless nature walking, Very found the holy grail: the smokers' lair.

Despite nicotine's international fame as the last refuge for addicts, Dr. Killjoy's first order of business upon taking the reins at ESCAPE had been to banish the smokers to the farthest outpost on the grounds: the caretaker's house. In fact, Dr. Joy had banished smoking entirely at ESCAPE, but through exhaustive legal maneuvering by a former renegade group of ESCAPEes who'd taken the cause up with the Vermont chapter of the American Civil Liberties Union, Dr. Joy had conceded a small part of the property to be designated a smoking zone, pending a court-case decision.

The decided-upon smoking zone, not coincidentally, also housed the institution's one true legacy, a caretaker who was the last surviving resident from the family who'd owned the original resort, and was himself a smoker. He had been born and raised on the property, and was known as "Jones," both because that was his last name and because his part of the property was where residents gravitated when they jonesed for something: a cigarette break; casual hanging-out time with other residents outside the auspices of Dr. Killjoy's purification aura; wicked good vegan chocolate chip cookies that Jones made fresh daily and sold at fair market price; fresh fruit from the berry patches behind Jones's house (free); and caffeine, which Dr. Killjoy had also forbidden in the dining hall, but, after the threat of more legal wrangling, had been forced to agree to allow—by means of nonelectrical French press coffeemakers in Jones's kitchen, so long as Jones was amenable, which he was, though again at fair market price.

The ground floor of Jones's house, which had a wraparound porch furnished with outdoor chaise and rocking chairs, was known to have an open-door policy for residents. Jones kept private quarters upstairs, but the downstairs area was left unlocked, and residents were free to go there to socialize, play card and board games, make coffee, nosh, smoke, etc. Very had found out about Jones the same way most residents did—not because the jonesing location was mentioned in the ESCAPE brochure, which it most certainly was not, but through word of mouth in the dining hall, along with the map to Jones's house crayoned by previous residents into the bottoms of the desk drawers in many cabins.

When Very found the house, she approached the only person she saw there, an old guy probably as ancient as someone's dad, like late forties or early fifties. He looked Yankee-hippie relic—long and scruffy hair and beard, but wearing new and neat jeans and flannel shirt, with man sandals on his feet. He smoked a gentleman's pipe as he rocked on a rocking chair that looked out onto a gorgeous lake view.

"Greetings," he said to Very. "Got a name, newbie?"

Very said, "Veronica. Friends call me 'Very.' "

"Nice," he said, nodding approvingly. He took a puff on his pipe, then let out a sweet-smelling exhale of smoke. "Have a seat. Tell me about yourself. I'm Jones."

"So you're the famous Jones. Nice to meet you! Are you the

lone smoker out here? I heard people hung out on this porch all the time."

"There's a few of them inside the house. They discovered a road atlas on my bookshelf while they were making coffee. Young ones like you, hipsters who never used anything besides Google Maps. They're hunkered down over the atlas inside, if you want to join in with the new discovery."

"I know what a real atlas looks like," Very said, defensive.

"Do you also know that paper road atlases can't be zoomed and scaled, have no live satellite imagery, and require that driving directions be figured out manually?"

"Of course I know that," Very said. (*Shut the fuck up!* That was how you used nonvirtual atlases? What a waste!) She took a seat next to Jones. "Do you have a cigarette I could possibly bum?"

"I do," he said. He took another toke on his pipe. He rocked contemplatively in his chair, making no effort to retrieve and hand over a cigarette, as if he had all the time in the world.

"So," Very said. "Cigarette now? Later? Or were you teasing me?"

He stopped rocking and turned to face her. "What got you here?"

"You mean, how I found your house, or how I ended up at ESCAPE?"

"Whatever you want to tell me."

The finding-his-house story wasn't that interesting, so Very went with the latter option. "I landed here after a bad acid trip inspired me to hack into the CIA's Mongolian surveillance operation."

Jones smiled. And waited.

170

Very tried again. "I freaked out and thought I was a living Pokémon. I went on a hunger strike at City Hall, demanding the mayor put me up on a giant electronic billboard in the middle of Times Square displaying me as, like, the master Pokémon deity who was going to take over the world."

Jones chuckled. And resumed his chair rocking. Still said nothing.

Very gave in. "I was a freshman at Columbia this past school year. Went a little overboard with, like, being online and whatever. But it really wasn't that big a deal. Sending me here was a bit of an extreme solution, in my opinion, to a very minor problem."

He spoke. "Is that so?"

"Totally." Jones still did not extend a cigarette. But since he seemed to be a cool guy, Very figured she could straight-up ask for what she *really* wanted. "Where's the stash of confiscated equipment? 'Cause if I could get some music, and the tiniest amount of programming time, I think my whole 'recovery' would go better, and just be more efficient. You know?"

"I don't know, actually. I've never much liked the Internet myself. Don't own a TV. Never played on a Nontendo."

"*Nin*tendo."

"Sure."

Very asked, "Are you one of those Luddite people who don't deal with technology at all?"

"Of course I deal with it. Can't live life in this day and age without it. I just don't let it rule my life."

"Technology doesn't rule *my* life!" Very proclaimed. "I can do without it just fine."

"Obviously."

More rocking, more pipe smoking. Still no cigarette or information.

Finally, Jones answered her real question. "There is no stash of confiscated equipment here. If you'd actually read the liability waiver you signed before checking in, you'd have noticed the clause which very clearly states that any prohibited equipment you're found with upon arrival is donated directly to charity, and not maintained on the premises to be returned when you leave, since the condition of entry to begin with was to not bring the equipment at all."

"Harsh," Very stated.

"It's not so harsh," Jones said. "It just takes a desire to change."

"What do you mean?"

"I mean, I've seen people come and go from this program. Watched as some people made it through and flourished afterward, and watched as other people completely fell off the wagon and vanished in the night to find the closest gaming casino, or Internet terminal, or cell phone store. I've watched as many return time and again after leaving prematurely, relapsing and getting into bigger and more dangerous trouble again on the outside, all because they've refused to seriously attempt the time-out to try taming their inner beasts while they're here. From what I've noticed—and mind you, I'm a caretaker and not a professional therapist, but I like to think I have a keen enough sense for how things work in the world—what separates the ones who flourish from those who fail is the simple desire to seek change in their lives. To try this path and give it their best, honest effort." He shrugged. "It's not so complicated, really."

"Oh," Very said. She could try to try living without an iPod for a while, she supposed. Think about it as an experiment, rather than a death sentence.

Jones reached into his shirt pocket and pulled out a pack of smokes. He leaned over toward her chair to extend a cigarette to her. "You wanted one of these, my new friend Very?"

Very looked at the cigarette pack. They were American Spirits, but probably still not as good as those hand-rolled cigs that Hector made. She didn't really smoke that much, anyway. Maybe she should not smoke even casually anymore. Make ESCAPE sort of a one-stop-shopping place for healthy living, at least in terms of giving up nicotine, and eating a vegetable or two, and she supposed she could try one of those yoga classes or something. Since her party money was going toward the nonparty manifesto anyway.

"Never mind on the cigarette," Very said. "But thanks. Where'd you say that atlas was?"

Jones returned the cigarette pack to his pocket and set his pipe down on a nearby table. He reached for a baseball cap there, placed it on his head, and tipped the cap down to cover his eyes for a nap. "You'll find the kids in the den inside. Tell 'em Jones said to play nice with the new girl."

He shooed her inside with his hand and stopped his chair rocking to settle into his quiet shut-eye time.

CHAPTER 21

Very was wary of making new friends or even going on her typical hunt for crush prospects at ESCAPE. She was starting to worry she might be a toxic personality. She didn't want to cause undue harm to unwitting rehabbers. They had enough going on without worrying about whether Very needed someone to take care of her, or if she might cause them to be unfaithful to their significant other, or if she might suddenly have the desire to kill them.

She was bad news. Very understood that much. She still didn't think she was such a problem as to have warranted being sent to ESCAPE, but she also knew enough to know she didn't want to be the person who created new problems for other people. For as long as she was stuck at ESCAPE, Very vowed, she would do her best not to form attachments, in either the friends or the friends-with-benefits category. She would be as celibate as . . .

a stick of celery—a pleasant enough filler, especially with peanut butter or cream cheese slathered inside, but not a dangerous tool of emotional fortification or caloric fornication, either.

Yet still, Very had one very important question she couldn't help but reach out and ask: "What the fuck am I supposed to do with my hands?"

Gesturing *jazz hands*, Very directed this question to the boy and girl sitting on a couch in Jones's den, who looked up at her from the atlas they were poring over. The boy wore green eyeliner, so Very already knew how he'd gotten to ESCAPE. The girl Very immediately recognized from an unfortunate high school prom night after-party video that a mean prom king had recorded on his phone, then posted on YouTube, where it had gone viral. The drunk prom queen from the clip was known to the world as "Big Gulp."

The boy said, "You're new?"

Very nodded.

The girl said, "That's the toughest part the first few days. Trying to figure out what to do with your hands if you're not texting or holding a joystick or typing. Right?"

"Exactly!" Very said.

"Do you smoke?" the boy asked. "That's the first line of defense."

"No," Very said, feeling like it wasn't a lie. She didn't. Anymore.

"Needlepoint?" the girl asked.

"Ew," Very said.

"Try it!" the boy and girl said, in unison.

The boy's name was Erick; the girl was Kate. Erick had lost it after a *Dreams* game at Harvard. He jumped into the Charles River, thinking he could go after underwater prey there. Problem was, he didn't know how to swim in actual water. Pretty blond Kate from Atlanta . . . Well, everyone knew Kate's story. There was even a Yahoo! group created by 7-Eleven employees who wanted to marry her. She obviously never joined that group. She had to drop out of her freshman year at the University of Georgia because she was too famous. No sorority house would have her, not even the really slutty ones.

They were nice, this Erick and Kate, and helpful, too. They located a spare needlepoint kit for Very to help her get started. For their art therapy projects, Erick was working on a needlepoint cat that somehow looked more like a dolphin, and Kate was working on a hydrangea bloom that somehow had evolved into a picture of a cell phone that was also a gun.

"Freedom of expression," Kate said.

Erick said, "Needlepoint is a really awesome and safe way to keep your hands occupied, but go deep down, like, in the sea of your soul to see what's really in there."

"Cool," Very said.

Over coffee, vegan cookies, and stitching, Erick and Kate filled Very in on how to survive her ESCAPE tenure.

"The first week is the hardest," Erick said. "Figuring out how to stay occupied. Trying to figure out how to breathe when there's no wireless energy source you can practically feel pulsing through your body."

These kids really got it!

"Yes!" Very said, excited for the first time in a long time. Jean-Wayne had been the only one of her outside friends to really understand this—the hunger that felt like it burned through and pillaged your body, the infinite lust to connect, to game, to be online all the time.

Kate agreed. "Yeah, when I first got here, just learning what to, like, think about, if you're not hitting Refresh on your friends' pages every two minutes, or IM-ing, or texting, or video chatting, was way hard."

"Or meme-ing!" Very said.

"Or listening to music!" Kate said.

"*Dreaming!*" Erick sighed.

Kate said, "You know what's been the weird part about making friends here? Getting to know people in the first-person present instead of through their third-person updates. It's a bit disconcerting at first. But then you get used to it."

Erick said, "Yeah. After a while, you get used to not checking e-mail, or browsing your friend lists, or needing to be in an online game round-the-clock. It seems to just happen. It gets to be pretty mellow to hang out in the real world, and do needlepoint, and play tennis and stuff. I'm not saying it's better like this. It's just . . . different. But okay. Like, totally survivable."

"Really?" Very said.

"Really!" Erick and Kate answered.

But they warned her: Beware the ones who weren't serious. You could tell the ones who were going to fall off the wagon. They tried to flag down passing boats from the dock to ask to borrow sailors' cell phones. They stood at the road to wait for SUVs to go by, hoping to get a glimpse of a GPS system or the backseat video screens playing *Wall-E* for the kiddies on a long road trip. They gnawed at the empty electrical outlets in their cabins, pining to be re-electrified. They stood on the roofs of their cabins, framing their hands as if they were holding a phone to try to find a good connection out in the boonies, then gestured wildly like they were having an actual conversation, when their hands were actually empty and they were alone up there.

Those were the ones who'd fall and wouldn't make it through the program. Watch out for them.

This one guy, he'd been to ESCAPE three times already. He escaped, but kept getting sent back by his rich, angry parents, who didn't know what else to do with the guy. He was the most fun guy in the world, until the hunger bit him so hard that he turned crazy, and he broke into the church charity store in town in the middle of the night to loot the confiscated equipment supply that ESCAPE donated every week after its new recruits checked in. Stealing from the Congregationalists! What kind of desperate jerk took it that far?

Erick pointed to the collection of framed needlepoint pieces on the wall, which looked like it could be a picture-book window into the minds of past ESCAPEes. "Check out the clown one," Kate told Very. "It was made by him."

It was hard not to find the clown-face needlepoint. It was the most disturbing image on the wall, scarier than Kate's phone/gun-in-progress. The clown face had searing black eyes with pointed red eyebrows, a Star of David for a nose, big purple lips opened to reveal one blue tooth, and bright red cheek rouge like a transvestite. The clown also wore a turban, but like the kindly Auntie Mame kind, not the Indian kind, which was particularly upsetting. The clown looked like the meanest mofo from Mental Clowntopia since, like, ever.

Very shivered. "Yikes!" she said.

On the less serial-killer-potential side of the ESCAPE gossip, Erick and Kate updated Very on ESCAPE's most winning long-running soap opera: the war between Dr. Killjoy and Jones. He thought she was a New Age quack; she wished the old-school Yankee crank would just move off the property already. They tried to avoid each other, but if you were lucky enough to glimpse Jones walking down to the main lodge, be sure to follow, and listen outside Dr. Joy's door to the ensuing conversation. The drama was better than any reality TV show, and the dialogue was totally real.

"Outstanding!" Very said. Sign her up to tune the fuck in.

CHAPTER 22

Today's Talk Time was brought to Very by the letter K and the number 7.

Her therapist's name was Keisha, and Keisha met with residents in studio number 7 in the main lodge.

Very wasn't too keen on having to go to regular talk therapy. But if she was going to try to try . . . she'd *try*. Although she really didn't see how a stranger who had no emotional investment or personal connection to her could actually give a care about what Very had to say.

It helped that Keisha appeared totally casual. Very couldn't imagine truly confiding in someone who dressed in Birkenstocks and chinos and sweater sets, like Dr. Joy. But Keisha wore faded, vintage jeans, and she was barefoot with sparkly blue-painted toenails, and she wore a shirt that Very recognized from Threadless.com, a baby blue tee that said, "Let's ESC together," but the "ESC" was a picture of a computer Escape key. Her dreadlocked hair was tied back with a piece of twine.

"Is the shirt meant to be ironic?" Very asked as she sat down with Keisha for their first session together.

"What do you think it's meant to be?" Keisha asked. She wasn't really old like the rest of the staff at ESCAPE—she looked at least young enough to have come of age after e-mail was created.

"How old are you?" Very asked, sitting down on a sofa opposite Keisha, who'd settled cozily into a cross-legged position on a comfy chair.

"Does it matter?" Keisha asked.

Very thought about it. *Did* it matter? She shrugged. "Guess not."

"I'm thirty-two," Keisha said. She pointed toward her diplomas posted on the wall behind her desk. "Undergraduate degree in history from Mount Holyoke, master's degree in clinical psych from the University of Vermont. Will this package work for you?" She didn't say that last sentence in a mean way. She had a relaxed, kind manner that Very appreciated.

"Do you have candy?" Very asked.

Keisha reached over to open a drawer from the coffee table that was placed between them. "M&M's do ya?"

"Plain or peanut?" Very said.

Keisha pulled out a crystal candy dish, so fancy it had a top to it. She placed the candy dish on the table, lifted the top off, and said, "Almond."

"Almond," Very said, impressed. "You're one classy broad."

"I try," Keisha said.

Very dipped in for a handful, which went right into her mouth. Crunched, chewed, swallowed: delicious.

Therapy maybe wasn't so bad.

"So what would you like to talk about, Veronica?"

"Friends call me 'Very.' "

"So we're friends?"

"Yeah. I think so. Are we?"

Keisha took a handful of M&M's for herself. "I hope so, Very."

"I don't know what I'm supposed to talk about," Very said.

"Talk about whatever's on your mind. How you got here. Which color M&M's you like best. How you're managing this first week here at ESCAPE. Your family. Your friends."

"I'd like to know the name of that nail polish color you're wearing on your toes."

"It's called 'Am I Blue.' "

"That's a good one. I hate it when they call the colors something that has nothing to do with an actual color. Like, a really whore-red color gets called 'Night on the Town.' And stuff like that."

"A whore-red color? Describe it."

Very said, "You don't need to do that with me."

"Do what?"

"Use what I say to lead me into something you think I'm supposed to be talking about."

"Like what?"

"If you want to know if I'm a whore, it's okay to ask me straight out. I don't mind."

"Well, that's maybe not the word choice I'd go with, but tell me, Very . . . what do *you* think you are?"

"I'm a bit whore-y," Very allowed, laughing.

"How so?"

"I like to fool around. Get together. Hook up. You know."

"Do you have unprotected sex?"

"Fuck no!" Very said, offended.

"Good. So when you 'fool around,' tell me about that. Have you been in a long-term relationship, or are you more casual?"

"Casual. Haven't been lucky in the long-term department."

"How so? Are there relationships that you've had so far in your life that you might have wished to be more than casual?"

Very couldn't believe she was going to say what she was going to say—she'd never even talked with Lavinia about this stuff, not seriously, at least. "Well, even though I am the first person to make out at a party, I've only been with, you know, *really* been with, six people." Very counted on her hand. "Or wait, seven, if we're being technical."

"What's the distinction?"

Very spoke down low. "Penetration with a guy totally counts. But when it's with a girl, it's more . . . vague."

"Why?"

"There's six people I've been with. Well, more like six and a half. Okay, seven. Five guys I've slept with. And two girls. But the first girl, she was just practicing, although it went as far as it could go."

"Which is how far?"

Very started to feel exasperated. She was about to tell Keisha something important that she'd never shared, but Keisha was leading her to the wrong story. Very didn't answer Keisha, but took another handful of M&M's instead.

Keisha said, "If you don't feel comfortable talking about it, that's okay. Our time together is to explore what you feel comfortable discussing."

Very had always been a girl who put out too soon. Why should therapy be any different? Very let out, "I'm totally comfortable talking about my sexuality. It's that you're asking about the wrong girl. It's the second girl who doesn't quite count that really got to me. That first girl, she was nothing, just experimentation. She was someone I met at a party when I was in high school. We went upstairs to watch a movie in someone's bedroom. But there was one of those Skinemax movies on TV when we turned it on—"

"Skinemax?"

"Late-night soft-core movies on the Cinemax channel."

"Oh. Thank you for clarifying. Please continue."

"That first girl and me, we were just imitating what was happening on the TV. We were drunk, the usual. I don't even remember her name. Strictly experimentation."

"So who was the second girl, who doesn't quite count as your seventh person, if I'm following you?"

"That's right. The second girl was Kristy. She would only go so far with me, so that's why I don't count her all the way."

Dammit, Very could feel the potential for tears forming in her eyes. She had been so determined not to even talk about anything meaningful with this stranger, yet here she was, ten minutes into their session, giving it all away.

"How did you know Kristy?" Keisha asked.

"She played on the field hockey team at my high school in New Haven. She was really blond and beautiful, but in that no-makeup, casual, athletic kind of way. She looked like she should be on the cover of, like, rich people's equestrian magazines."

"Was Kristy in your classes?"

"Oh, no. She wasn't that smart. At least academically. She was really into sports. She did okay at school, but she didn't put in much effort. I was in all Honors classes, got mostly A's back then; the work was so easy in high school. I met Kristy because I was assigned as her peer tutor."

"So what happened between you and Kristy?"

"Well, she used to come over to my house to study. I live at my aunt's house because my mom died. New Haven's kind of a nothing place, but I have a really nice attic room there, so I didn't mind it that much. And my aunt is old and doesn't like to climb stairs, so I had a lot of privacy. Kristy had a big family and her house was always in chaos. So we always studied at my aunt's place, in my room."

"How did your mother die, may I ask?"

"Drug overdose," Very said. She could only get through Kristy today; she couldn't fathom opening up that other bottle of disaster.

"I'm sorry to hear that. Your father?" Keisha asked, jotting away on a notepad.

"Never knew him."

"How do you feel about that?"

"Robbed," Very said.

Keisha placed her notepad on her lap. Very couldn't read the words, but she could see that whatever Keisha was writing about Very had already taken up a whole page. "This is a lot we're stepping into, Very. Do you need a break?"

"I'm okay." Very wasn't lying. She hadn't realized how much she needed just to talk. Like, *talk*-talk, to a live person, not online-OMG-talk. "Let's finish what we started."

"Okay. Tell me more about Kristy."

"I was totally into her. Maybe even thought I loved her. But when we were together, you know, she'd only go so far. Kissing, and cuddling, and sometimes my hand was allowed to wander, but she was so embarrassed by it after. She barely acknowledged me at school. Then one time after school when my aunt was gone, Kristy and I were alone for real for the first time. And she let me go farther."

"Do you want to tell me how so?"

"My hand in her panties."

"Did she do that to you also?"

"Never progressed that far. It took so much whispered sweet-talking just for her to let me touch her there. I don't know how teenage boys put up with all that yes/no, stop/start stuff from teenage girls, let me tell you. Drove me crazy! But then finally one day, like I said, we were truly alone for the first time ever, and she was really into it, and she let me take it farther than just kissing. She let me slip my hand there. Inside."

"I notice you talk very openly about sex."

"Doesn't everybody?"

"Frankly, no. Especially at your age. Was your mother very open with you about it?"

"Totally. She walked around naked at home whenever she could; she hated clothes. She had boyfriends over all the time. She took me to the doctor to talk about birth control as soon as she knew I was sexually active."

"How old were you then?"

"Sixteen," Very lied.

Jot jot jot, wrote Keisha. She looked up from her notepad again.

186

"So. Kristy. What happened when she let you become that intimate with her?"

Very paused.

Jot jot jot.

"Could you stop writing while I tell you this?" she asked Keisha.

"Of course." Keisha set the notepad over on her desk and returned to her comfy chair. "Does the notebook bother you?"

"No. But if I'm going to tell someone about this, I'd like to know they're really paying attention to me. If I see you writing, in my mind, you're also IM-ing your friends, or returning e-mails to coworkers, or . . ."

". . . technological multitasking? Five screens open at once?"

"Yes, something like that," Very said.

Keisha said, "The notepad's gone. You have my full attention. I'd like to hear what you have to say."

Very hesitated one more time, then let it out. "Kristy let me put my fingers in there. And she seemed like she was really into it. But then she came so fast, I was almost frightened. It was amazing, too, though, to give so much pleasure to someone I cared about so much. Beautiful, even. She smiled at me for a second and then kissed me; it was like this one perfect moment of happiness. But then, just as fast, she turned on me. She shoved me away and started crying, then hitting me, saying she wanted to go home. She completely freaked out."

"Why do you think that was?"

"Her family was really religious. The conservative Catholic kind or something, not the chilled-out types. I guess she wasn't ready to accept that she wasn't straight."

"So what happened after?"

"Kristy left. And never talked to me again."

"That must have felt bad."

"It did. It felt *awful*." Very felt the sadness and rejection revisiting her body, squeezing the breath from her lungs and making her heart want to collapse as a spray of tears rushed down her face. But the tears felt okay: safe. And when she got her breath back, Very found it was deeper, and better. It seemed weird that letting out something so sad could actually make her feel kind of glad, but she couldn't deny the sense of relief flooding through her.

Keisha passed a tissue to Very.

"Thanks," Very said. She sniffled into it.

"Do you think there's anything you would have done differently then, knowing what you know now?" Keisha asked.

"Yeah. Don't fall for a girl who won't admit she likes girls. Pretty simple, if you ask me."

"Do you prefer girls?" Keisha asked.

"I prefer a pulse," Very said. "I know it's lame to say this, but I'm probably one of those It's the Person, Not the Gender people on the sexual orientation spectrum. I'm pretty equal opportunity. Well . . . maybe I trust women less than men."

"Why do you think that is? Because of Kristy?"

Very paused a moment, to give the question fair consideration. "I don't know, really. I didn't realize I even felt that way until I just said it. I mean, I feel like I am a feminist, and I was raised by women, and Go, Girl Power! and all that. But yeah . . . I think I do trust women less than men. Partly because of Kristy. But also, with men, I just don't expect anything of them, anyway. So they can't let me down."

"Sounds to me like you're saying you don't trust men *or*

women, then? Do you think the feeling of being let down and not able to trust ties in to your feelings about the loss of your mother?"

Very's head was officially ready to explode, and not with a need to connect to a machine, but from connecting to too much personal feeling.

"Keisha, may I be honest with you?"

"I sure hope so."

"I really just want a nap all of a sudden."

Keisha stood up. "You're not the first to sit on that couch and tell me that before our session is over. It's good to listen to what your mind and your body are telling you. So go back to your room and rest. We'll pick up where we left off next time. Deal?"

"The M&M's will be here?"

"They will. Perhaps, contrary to Dr. Joy's notes to me, you might not really be a vegan if you'll eat milk chocolate candies?"

"I was trying to get out of butter churning."

"Good move." Keisha smiled and patted Very's shoulder. "And great work here today."

CHAPTER 23

You could take the song out of her ears by taking away her headset, but the song remained the same: always in her heart.

The best way for Very to make it through kitchen duty was to make a song game out of it.

Kitchen duty was a mandated ESCAPE chore. With no automated food-processing machines or dishwashers allowed, Dr. Joy cleverly managed to cut ESCAPE's labor costs by forcing the residents—who were *paying* to be there—to help with food preparation and cleanup. Dr. Joy should be featured on the cover of *Forbes* magazine rather than *Psychology Today,* Very figured. "Shrink Shrinks Costs by Squeezing Joy from the Hands That Feed Her," the headline would read. The inside pictorial spread would show ESCAPE residents in kitchen-duty servitude— preparing vats of glutinous oatmeal for breakfast, cutting cucumbers to put into elegant-looking lunch sandwiches, peeling and chopping vegetables for dinner—and post-meal cleanup glamour poses featuring residents washing plates with Joy brand dishwashing liquid (whose manufacturer would gladly compensate for the product placement, as would that of Glad, for displaying its plastic wrap and storage containers) and cheerfully mopping floors with the maniacal gleam of Mr. Clean on their faces.

Very survived kitchen duty by thinking of the experience as an experiment in socialism. Everyone did his or her part to contribute to the collective whole, and if she signed up for duty alongside Kate and Erick, her comrades-but-not-friends (for their own safety), the time passed more quickly.

What was timeless to the experience, Very would discover, was disco music.

Kitchen duty was as segregated as eating in the dining hall. It wasn't a scene like the high school cafeteria with the popular people in one corner and the rejects in the other; the social breakdown was more like a case of Olds versus Youngs.

The Olds at ESCAPE were the forty-plus crew, who were not as technologically adept as their younger comrades but perhaps had more to lose because of their addictions, having had more time on earth investing in material accumulation. They were people at kitchen duty like Bob from Phoenix, a fifty-five-year-old architect, who had lost his once-thriving business to online gambling. Or Irma from Atlanta, a mother of eight, grandmother to eighteen, and great-grandmother to four, who had her house foreclosed on when she went into credit card debt from online shopping. (Luckily, one grandchild in there was solvent and could afford rehab.) Minnesota Suzanne had lost tens of thousands of dollars—and her powerful status as president of her local Leisure World Tenants Association—when too many too-trusting residents at her retirement community entrusted her with their online stock-trading choices.

The Youngs were people like Very and Kate and Erick, and like Enrique from Miami, a twentysomething music promoter who, when so many people showed up for the electronica club night he conceived, thought it meant people *wanted* to be electronically Tasered during their music reverie. Or people like young mom Raelene from Alabama, thirty-one, whose live Internet sexcapades during her kids' school hours went awry when her oblivious husband came home early with a sick child in tow, and the ensuing fight was streamcast for all the pervy online world to watch. So deeply Inside, Raelene hadn't thought to power off the webcam.

The Olds versus Youngs tended to segregate themselves, whether consciously or not, in the dining hall and at other group activities, and even, Very discovered to her horror, in kitchen duty. The Olds were some bossy bitches.

It was the second night of kitchen duty toward the end of her first week at ESCAPE, and Very was assigned to dinner preparation.

Bob took charge first, announcing, "I'll fold the napkins tonight." Which meant Raelene would be stuck setting the napkins out at each table, while Enrique had to set the cutlery out.

Irma seconded with, "I'll measure the flour." Which meant Very would be stuck kneading the bread dough.

Suzanne topped it off with, "I'll make sure the refrigerator is stocked with the necessary ingredients." Which meant Kate and Erick would be peeling and chopping the carrots and potatoes.

The Olds then "supervised," in the form of sitting at a corner kitchen table playing gin rummy after their meager tasks were completed, while the Youngs had no choice but to pick up the slack. Raelene and Enrique took on setting up the tables in the dining hall, while Very, Erick, and Kate set out to their food-preparation tasks in the kitchen.

Erick arranged carrot sticks on a platter to resemble fishies.

Kate spewed invective at the Potato Men she sculpted with the potato peeler. "You! Potato Man! Can't-be-trusted, lying, no-good, mean jerk! How I hate you! I bid you be chopped into french fries and devoured by gluttons!"

Regrettably, Very had to admit that there was something to Dr. Joy's assertion that kitchen duty had therapeutic value. For Very, it came as she was kneading bread dough while singing aloud to the KC and the Sunshine Band song in her heart, if not on her iPod, at that moment: "I'm your boogie man . . ."

To her surprise, from the corner of the room, a man's voice—Bob's!—answered with: "That's what I am."

Very had thought it a fluke, but then Suzanne and Irma chimed in with: "I'm here to do . . ."

And then the voices united to include Kate's and Erick's: "Whatever I can."

The Youngs and Olds all looked up from their respective tasks, wondering if what they thought had just happened had indeed happened.

To test it, Very tried a new song—her signature song, as it were. Again she sang aloud: "Young and old are doing it, I'm told."

The Youngs and Olds collectively answered with: "Le freak, c'est chic."

So it was true, then. Disco music *was* the great equalizer.

And even if the Youngs and Olds bridged only this one gap, the irrefutable evidence was now clear: At this moment in time, Very was in the exact place where she belonged, with the people, whether friends or not, whom she was meant to share it with, and vice versa.

This rehab was straight-up for real.

CHAPTER 24

Resistance is futile. You will be assimilated.

Erick and Kate had been right.

Very was getting used to ESCAPE. She wouldn't describe herself as fully assimilated, but her resistance had worn down, and she was, after a week in, fully acclimated.

The withdrawal pains had subsided. Very no longer sprang out of bed in the middle of the night to search for messages from El Virus. She wasn't mentally calculating all the unread e-mails she was unable to answer, nor was she visualizing emoticon responses to substitute for human interaction. When she walked, she saw white clouds and blue sky and green trees, and not artificial yellow smiley faces and jumbled-together black punctuation marks. *:/phew.* Without the constant stimulation of video games, Very felt her blood pressure going down, as if her body was acknowledging gratitude for not rushing a constant adrenaline surge through it. Certainly, Very's mind felt clearer, and her balance much improved from not regularly swerving and jumping to match the fast and furious goings-on of an on-screen virtual world.

The hardest bite of all? Her body had acclimated to not being on constant alert for a buzz against her flesh that indicated new messages vibrating through her iPhone.

Oh, her iPhone.

She could give up all the other crap, but that one, it was so exquisitely beautiful, such a perfect little piece of technology, so smooth and compact and powerful and . . . well, she missed that one a hell of a lot, but she didn't *need* it. She was doing fine without it; she wasn't going into withdrawal-pain shock spasms or anything anymore. iPhone. Whatever. Totally casual. She'd get back to it whenever. Not a big deal.

The bummer part was just as she was getting used to ES-CAPE, the place changed. Erick and Kate were graduating. They'd made it through their twenty-eight days and were headed back into the world, to their real lives. Once back on the outside, Kate planned to start a support group for teen girls who were the victims of cruel Internet games. Erick planned to learn how to swim, for real. Very would have to find new people to needlepoint with. Or maybe not. The Christmas-stocking elves Very had been working on in their company had turned out complete disasters and looked positively satanic. The needlepoint elves frightened Very, and not in a beguiling goth-metal way, but in an ickily creeped-out way. Maybe Very would have to find a new form of art therapy once she lost the companionship of Erick and Kate.

"Are you scared to leave?" Very asked them.

Per tradition, the almost graduates were being thrown a

campfire get-together on their last night before legitimately escaping from ESCAPE. A small group of fellow ESCAPE convicts (Youngs) sat around the fire at the designated fire pit behind Jones's house, celebrating Erick's and Kate's imminent reintegration into the world. The group drank herbal tea and munched on trail mix. Someone strummed an acoustic guitar, but no one was singing. The sounds of fire sparks and cicadas were enough backup.

Very's last campfire had pretty much put the death seal on her relationship with Bryan. She was like her mother with fires. Dangerous.

Kate said, "I'm scared to go back out there. Absolutely."

Erick said, "Mostly I'm scared to talk to people again in a real setting. You know, in an environment that's not artificially maintained for nonartificial living. I don't know what I'm supposed to talk about if I'm not all the time talking about my addiction problem."

Addiction. That was the basic component of the ESCAPE program Very just could not get on board with. That one simple word. It implied so much desperation and lack of control. Addiction meant alcoholics, and people who abused narcotics, and bulimics who couldn't keep their Twinkie habits in check. The a-word didn't really apply to the people at ESCAPE. It was a word Dr. Joy bandied about to sound smart, Very assumed. It wasn't possible to be *addicted* to technology, because even Dr. Joy acknowledged that when ESCAPEes went back out into the real world, they could never escape technology. An alcoholic needed to stay sober to survive, but a "technology addict" couldn't maintain a job or a relationship or any kind of life in the modern age without reconnecting in some way, shape, or fashion. Dr. Joy said it was all about "finding the inner tools" so that "balance in the outer realm" could be achieved. Very suspected it was more about getting over the hump of one problem in life before moving on to the next one.

Very could recognize she had a problem. Sure. No problem to acknowledge the problem. She was too attached to technology and had let that problem get an eensy bit out of control. But was she an *addict*? Too heavy a label, IVHO (In Very's Humble Opinion).

"I'm really going to miss you guys," Very acknowledged to comrades Erick and Kate. Needlepointing with them had been the highlight of her days at ESCAPE so far. It kept her hands occupied, and she could talk with kids her age who understood and had been through similar experiences. It was like college, without all the thinking. Kind of awesome, and with better cookies and fair-trade coffee. "How did your reintegration go?" Very asked.

Just before leaving, residents who'd been cleared by Dr. Joy were allowed a night out on the nearby town, to begin the process of integrating back into the Real World.

"Scary," Erick said. "Everybody in town looked . . . green. It was like a swamp of human algae. I wanted to be sick."

Kate said, "We walked by a 7-Eleven and I almost freaked out when someone came out of the store holding a Big Gulp."

"But you didn't freak out?" Very said hopefully. "You were okay?"

"I managed," Kate said.

"You'll be fine on the outside," Very said, not sure of that, but wanting to reassure.

"You'll be fine on the *inside*," Erick reminded Very.

"We're really going to miss you, too, Very," Kate said.

Kate smiled sexily at Very, then over to Erick.

Erick smiled sexily at Kate.

Erick's and Kate's sexy gazes both circled back to Very.

"Final celebration?" Kate asked.

Erick gulped. Like he knew what maybe was about to be proposed. All that sexual-tension-by-needlepoint, about to approach its crescendo, in flagrant disregard of ESCAPE's "no fraternization" policy, which no one followed anyway, judging by the condom stash that could be found buried under the mattresses at most cabins.

Very's body tensed anew.

Danger. Danger.

There would be no three-way, no thought of a three-way, no dalliance whatsoever. The poison girl would not strike these young lambs.

Very leapt to her feet. "Good luck out there in the world, guys!" she said. She had to get out of this scene before she caused more trouble. No matter how attractive her fellow coeds were— and they were hella attractive—Very's celibate loins would not be tempted. She'd made that promise to herself, and she intended to stick to it. "See you in the morning for a final goodbye."

"I guess you and I will have to frame our pieces to hang on Jones's wall without Very's help," Kate sighed to Erick.

"Disappointing," Erick said.

Back in her cabin, alone, Very sat on her bed and fondled the One Week medal she'd received that morning at breakfast. Dr. Joy—and pretty much everyone else—said the first week was the hardest. If you could make it through the first week, the rest would be smooth sailing, relatively speaking (and Sunfish only, please, no thoughts of powerboats).

Very indeed felt a small sense of accomplishment. She hadn't achieved anything in a long time, not since getting into Columbia, and once there she'd gotten involved in so much online hustling that she'd stopped trying to do well at academics. Her only accomplishment her whole time at Columbia, Very realized, was that she hadn't alienated Lavinia so badly that Lavinia had abandoned her. That, and her wicked parties. And, Very had cocreated The Grid. That had been a rather cool thing she'd pulled off, even if it didn't count as an accomplishment. (Did it?)

Why hadn't Lavinia abandoned her? Very would abandon Very, if she could.

She was a complete fuck-up. Very would admit that about herself without hesitation.

Very looked over to the 12 Steps chart that a previous resident had needlepointed and left framed on the wall of her cabin. Obviously Very wasn't an *addict*, but she figured it wouldn't hurt to give the steps a thorough read and take stock of whether any of them legitimately applied to her. The primo party girl had nothing better to do, since she'd opted out of the campfire night.

Step 1—We admitted we were powerless over our addiction—that our lives had become unmanageable.

So okay. Step 1 applied to her. Before coming to ESCAPE, her life had become unmanageable. She couldn't survive the pressures of school; she'd alienated her friends; she was in love with an on-line rogue who probably didn't even exist! She'd brought on an information overload that had finally crushed her. She'd done it to herself. And it hadn't crushed her because she wasn't strong enough to take it. It had crushed her because it was just too.fucking.much. Sensory malfunction. *Beep beep beep*. Systems crash.

Step 2—Came to believe that a Power greater than ourselves could restore us to sanity.

Very wanted to be restored to sanity. The problem was, she couldn't be sure she'd been sane to begin with. She loved her mom, but Cat had been iffy on the sanity scale. And Very didn't have the luxury of knowing about the paternal half of her DNA. Was Very genetically predisposed toward crazy and didn't even know it? And if that was the case, maybe Step 2 had some merit, and she indeed needed to call upon a higher Power to steer her through. Very didn't know for shit how to do it herself.

Step 3—Made a decision to turn our will and our lives over to the care of God as we understood God.

Very had never been introduced to God, so she didn't feel comfortable turning her will and life over to Him. But if she could think of Step 3 as an algorithm, perhaps it could work.

If God is Captain Jean-Luc Picard of the starship Enterprise, *then Very could turn her will and life over to Him.*

No, that imagery made her too hot. Nix that one.

If God is the luscious-voiced Ella Fitzgerald, then . . .

That one could work. Very could willingly give herself over to the Great One, her favorite singer ever. God could be Ella—hella yella yeah.

Praise be and give Very back her iPod already.

Step 4—Made a searching and fearless moral inventory of ourselves.

Well, duh. Had Very been doing anything else at ESCAPE? Not really.

The "fearless" part sounded kind of egotistical, but the "moral inventory," yes, that part was crucial, and helpful, and Ella would probably agree that Very could use a lot more of that activity.

Step 5—Admitted to God, to ourselves and to another human being the exact nature of our wrongs.

Are you there, Ella? It's me, Very LeFreak. I hurt other people because of my problem. But maybe I hurt myself most of all. Shabba dabba deeba doo?

Step 6—Were entirely ready to have God remove all these defects of character.

Ella, if I'm being honest, it pisses me off that the word "defect" has been introduced here. I like machines, but I'm not an alien. My parts

are all in order. I just need a little tuning up. I resent the word "defect"
being thrown into the equation, on behalf of myself, and all other
might-be addicts of any race, sex, orientation, religion, etc.

Step 7—Humbly asked God
to remove our shortcomings.

Ella, here's the truth. I do need help. I am lazy, and irresponsible, and
selfish, and I curse too much, and I'd subsist on Red Bulls, Doritos,
and chocolate chip cookies if I could. I prefer the virtual world because
the real one is hard, and cruel, and scary, and I don't know if I have
what it takes to make it on my own.
  I'd like to do better.

Step 8—Made a list of all persons
we had harmed, and became willing
to make amends to them all.

This was an easy one. Very loved lists. She'd put Bryan at the
top of the list, then Lavinia, and maybe Aunt Esther because
Very had been such a handful of a niece for an old lady to be
stuck taking on. Also, there was that girl in kindergarten who
lent Very her Barbies because Very's mom wouldn't let her have
Barbies; that poor, generous girl who'd gotten those Barbies returned with their hair cut off and feet amputated deserved an
epic apology. Very had given Dreabbie and Dean Dean some
grief, too. Add them to the list. Plus, that boyfriend in high
school whom Very swore she hadn't cheated on but she totally
had, and . . .

Cat. Her mother. Cat should probably jump ahead of Bryan to number one on the list.

Very had been the reason her mother had gone into the downward spiral that ended her life. But her mother was gone; it was too late now for Very to make amends to her.

This hurt worst of all.

> Step 9—Made direct amends to such
> people wherever possible, except when
> to do so would injure them or others.

She was cut off from technology right now, but when she was released, Very decided, she could do this. Make amends to those she still could make amends to. Send some *sorry* e-mails to the people who mattered.

Or tell them herself.

Maybe.

> Step 10—Continued to take personal
> inventory, and when we were wrong,
> promptly admitted it.

Very would think about that one later.

> Step 11—Sought through prayer and
> meditation to improve our conscious
> contact with God as we understood God,
> praying only for knowledge of
> God's will for us and the power
> to carry that out.

*Ella, when you know what I'm supposed to do, please send me a sign.
I know you can't do it through my iPod . . . yet . . . but I'll be waiting to hear from you. And hear you.*

Step 12—Having had a spiritual
awakening as the result of these steps,
we tried to carry this message to other
addicts, and to practice these
principles in all our affairs.

Very didn't know what kind of messenger she'd turn out to be once back on the outside, but—*Hallelujah, Miss Ella!*—perhaps she had indeed experienced a spiritual awakening.

"Addict," Very said aloud. She spoke only to herself, alone in her room.

Miraculously, she didn't melt away and die from the utterance.

Instead, Very fell asleep, exhausted. And relieved.

CHAPTER 25

To usher in Very's second week at ESCAPE, Keisha suggested they discuss what had ushered Very into ESCAPE to begin with.

"Microwaved Chewy Chips Ahoy! cookies," Very told Keisha. "They brought about the Fall of Very."

"Tell me more about that," Keisha said.

"I'll need some M&M's," Very said.

"Today I have chocolate peanut butter cups." Keisha held out a box from a proper candy store. She opened it up to reveal rows of peanut butter cups.

Very took one and popped it into her mouth. "You own me now," she told Keisha. "You're not playing fair."

"So tell me what's on your mind."

"Well, I think I figured something out. I was friendly-ish with two people my age here, Kate and Erick—maybe you met them?—who just left. And I was so determined not to become truly intimate with them. I don't mean in the sexy way—though believe me, it occurred to me. I mean, in the really good friends way. We talked and all, and had a lot in common, but I really tried to hold back from becoming friends with them. To the point that, as they were leaving, Kate slipped me a piece of paper with her and Erick's e-mail addresses, and I tossed it in the trash as soon as she couldn't see."

"Why?"

"To protect them from me! The whole reason I landed here to begin with is because of fraternization."

"What kind of fraternization?"

"Well, you know how I told you about my friends from the dorm at Columbia? How my friend Bryan and I had created The Grid together for other students to use as a private networking forum?"

"Yes. You originally said you felt like Bryan's destroying your laptop was the catalyst to your ending up at ESCAPE. Do you still feel that way?"

"Yes, but it's bigger than just that one incident. The Grid we'd created together—it was a pretty powerful feeling, to be honest. To be in control of that universe. And to share that with him. But I let it break apart when I slept with Bryan."

"You slept with Bryan? How did that come about?"

"It was Spring Break. Most everyone had gone away—you know, all the rich kids with parents who can afford to send them on fancy vacations. And I was sort of bored, and lonely. . . ." Very couldn't bring herself to discuss the El Virus longing that had factored into what happened that day. She didn't know why, but El Virus was the one part of herself she didn't want to share with Keisha, who was already privy to so much of Very's personal life. "There was always this tension between me and Bryan. I knew he liked me as more than just a friend, and I really wanted to like him that way, too. He was so puppy-dog cute. Like, you just wanted to take him in and play with him and cuddle him. But what happened between us—in all honesty, he might have just caught me at a really horny moment. Sorry to be so crude. Especially when I just referenced him as being like a puppy. But that's how it was. There wasn't this big buildup of sexual tension between us, at least on my part. It was just like he walked into my room when Lavinia was gone, at the exact moment I was wanting to be with someone. And I let him in, and everything fell apart after."

"How so?"

"Because he wanted to be in a relationship, and I didn't."

"Why didn't you?"

"I just had no feelings for him that way."

"What way?"

"The way, you know, I'd felt with Kristy. That buzz of excitement and wonder and wow and feeling completely alive. Even if it was hopeless."

"Is that how you view love? As hopeless?"

"Not as hopeless, generally. But for me, specifically—probably."

"My hope for you is that as you evolve in life, your opinion on the subject—and faith in yourself—will improve. But back to Bryan. How did the incident of his destroying your laptop play into your winding up here?"

"It wasn't that, I don't think. I mean, yeah, that incident ultimately caused me to lose it, but I'm trying to think harder about what came before. It feels like sleeping with him to begin with was what triggered a lot of messed-up shit in me."

"Explain."

"Sleeping with Bryan wasn't just fooling around. It meant more. It was, like, real intimacy—opening a box that should have been left closed. That Pandora thing, you know? Bryan was a friend. He cared about me. We shared this online creation. And I treated him terribly afterward."

"Are you saying you think you deserved his ultimate reaction—convincing your resident advisor to take away your laptop, then destroying it?"

"Deserved, no. But I was ready for a fall. Almost like I willed it to happen. In high school, you know, I had mostly been a star student. But when I got to Columbia, the pressure got so big. *Everyone* there had been the smartest kid in their high school. It was like I had to create The Grid just to stand out. And it wasn't just academic pressure. The pressure of simply surviving on my own was tremendous. I mean, I'd gone from losing my mom to landing on the doorstep of an aunt who was practically a stranger to me, but her home had been nice, and safe—but it was just a bubble, maybe. Suddenly, at Columbia, truly on my own for the first time, it felt like I was flung into a life that was much harder and more demanding than I'd expected, with no one, really, to help me, and on top of that, at a school that's in a city that's really exciting but also that's really, really hard. The pace was too much and I couldn't survive financially and . . ."

Keisha handed Very the candy box again. "Whoa, sister. Take a breather."

Very nibbled on the chocolate, but set it down quickly. She pondered a moment more and said, "It's like I never had a landing pad. I just flew from thing to thing, always by the seat of my pants, but never stopped to take stock, or deal."

"How did Bryan fit into that?"

"I guess I used him like a landing pad. A safe and convenient one. But the wrong one. And I don't want to do that anymore. Land in the wrong places, and hurt good people in doing so."

"I think that's half the battle," Keisha said. "Acknowledging the problem, dissecting it, and then trying to make a conscious choice to take better actions in the future."

"Should I throw a party to celebrate the realization?" Very asked. "Because that's what my old self would have done."

"You tell me," Keisha said. "I thought you were resolved not to make friends here. Who will you invite?"

There was only one person Very would want to invite, she realized.

Wasn't Lavinia just up the road? So where the hell had she been, anyway?

CHAPTER 26

Yoga made Very fart and burp too much, and she was too ADD
for meditation, but the laundry thing had some possibilities, at
least as random contemplative, spirit-cleansing time went. It got
her clothes clean, too. Bonus.

At Columbia, Very had typically taken her laundry to a
nearby wash 'n' fold place to be done for her—an expensive
habit, but the Laundromat took credit cards, so it seemed cheap,
almost as free as that first week of school when Lavinia did Very's
laundry. (By the end of the week, Lavinia had copped to Very's
texting and video game habits, and consequently made the connection that the wrist problems Very purported to have that
would hinder her coin-operating, washing-and-folding abilities,
in fact, would not whatsoever.) But at ESCAPE, not only was
Very required to do her own laundry, but she was required to use
an old-fashioned washboard and wringing contraption that took

211

forever, and made her arms sore and tired. And yet it was strangely satisfying work.

To Keisha, Very had confessed, "Bryan said I was robotically attached to my machinery and had no personality beyond my electronic props."

Keisha responded, "Ouch. Do you think that's true about yourself?"

"I want to think that's not true about myself."

Perhaps laundry-by-hand was a step toward debunking that myth.

Very liked the simplicity of the experience. Clothes and linens were dirty. She swished and wrung and rinsed them. She hung them to dry on a line out in the sun behind her cabin. And hey now, the stuff not only turned out clean but smelled extra nice and fresh, and felt crisp and lovely against her skin, and she'd made that happen herself. Quite possibly when Very was sprung from ESCAPE and had to get a real job, she might become a laundry person. She'd listen to her 'Pod while washing clothes all the day long, never getting into trouble. She'd sing to herself to pass the time, and make people really happy with the results of her labor and her off-key but endearing song stylings, and she'd possibly win the Nobel Peace Prize because of her community service work that made her neighborhood, and its citizens and their stuff, so much cleaner, and brighter, and musically well-versed. Or, she could become a nail salon lady, also an important community asset, because doing so much laundry was chipping away at her nails, and her cuticles were a mess, and really, it didn't seem right that ESCAPE did not offer beauty services in exchange for all the indentured servitude it required of its residents.

It was time to lodge a complaint with Dr. Killjoy about this problem. Or better yet, perhaps Very could circulate a petition on the subject, so that when she presented her case to Dr. Killjoy, it would seem more . . . fair, and reasonable, and not entirely self-ish, because it was a grassroots campaign.

Another strange thing about laundry. The grass. Since the Vermont summer was so pleasant and mild, Very was able, joy-fully, to roam the grounds barefoot. On the other hand (or foot), this roaming had created calluses on her feet, but the feel of her feet sinking into plush green grass was so fucking sweet. Very loved standing outside in the fresh air with her feet bare, her toes dancing through the grass as she stood at the laundry line, hang-ing sheets. She couldn't believe such a simple chore could bring her so much sheer pleasure.

Others, apparently, could not, either.

"I don't believe it," a voice called to Very from behind her as she stood at the laundry line, hanging sheets.

Very's toes curled in recognition of that voice. It belonged to . . . Very turned around . . . "Lavinia!" she cried out. She was so happy to see her friend's familiar face, she didn't care that the last time she'd seen it had been in the psych ward.

Very threw her arms up to welcome Lavinia into a hug, drop-ping her pillowcases to the ground as she did so, but no matter, she'd wash them again; more fun for Very later. Lavinia stepped into Very's hug. "You smell good, like eucalyptus detergent," Lavinia said, sniffing Very's hair. Lavinia let go of Very to ap-praise her. "But seriously, I've been watching you for a couple minutes, and you look like a flame-haired Snow White out here, chirping as you hang laundry. I half expected some birds to land on your shoulder and sing along with you."

"That would be so awesome if that happened," Very said, shaking her head in envy at the idea. (But she'd rather be the voluptuous St. Pauli girl instead of Snow White—she wanted at least the promise of some beer and/or fornication after the chirping-along-with-nature costume fantasy.) She grabbed Lavinia's hand and led her to a nearby bench to sit down. "What are you doing here?"

"I promised you I'd come visit. So here I am. My camp's not too far away down the lake. Sorry for the lack of warning. This other counselor at camp asked me to switch days off with her at the last minute, so I ended up having today off, and I obviously can't call you first to schedule a visit, so I figured I'd just show up and take a chance that it was a good visiting time. Is it?"

"It is!" Very said. "I had group therapy already this morning, did my penance at Dr. Joy's daily lecture, so I'm free until I have to report for kitchen duty in a couple hours."

"You? Do kitchen duty?" Lavinia said, disbelieving.

"I'll have you know I am this facility's most ace user of a Brillo pad on roasting pans, missy."

"I'm impressed," Lavinia said.

Very liked that. Impressing Lavinia. It seemed like a worthy goal, beyond the simple technological sobriety Very was now striving to maintain. "I'm eleven days clean," Very said, in case Lavinia wasn't impressed enough already.

"Congrats!" Lavinia said. "I'm proud of you. I really am. Sorry I couldn't visit you during the first week. They told me new people were considered to be too vulnerable then. But they said that if you made it past the first week, then I could come visit."

As happy as Very was to see Lavinia, she couldn't deny that seeing her former roommate also brought back hard feelings:

humiliation at her Jay friends' "intervention," and anger, and a sense of displacement that they could apparently carry on so casually with their own lives while Very was left muddling through the muddy, grassy swamp-mess she'd enmeshed herself in.

But the joy—and relief—that Lavinia had come to see her more than outweighed any sheepishness Very might have felt at their reunion. "How's Camp Hoochie going?" Very asked Lavinia. "Since I obviously can't read the blog updates you've undoubtedly been compulsively posting." Lavinia, an avowed non-blogger, shuddered. She loathed blogs—or "brags," as she called them.

Lavinia was a camp counselor at Camp Hoochinoo, an all-girls camp a few miles down the lake from ESCAPE. It was known as "Camp Hoochie" because of the wealthy, sophisticated tweens who visited the camp each summer, eight-to-eleven-year-olds going on thirty-year-olds, whose favorite game was role-playing *Sex and the City* episodes and quizzing one another on "Are you a Carrie, a Miranda, a Samantha, or a Charlotte?" (Very thought of Lavinia as a Charlotte, and herself as a Samantha-who-wanted-to-be-a-Miranda. Carrie was just . . . blech. Who'd want to be that shallow bitch?)

"Camp's fine," Lavinia said. "Although most of the girls in my bunk this year are Carries. Yuck. The Carries are the worst. You'd think it would be the Charlottes who'd be the most annoying—too high-maintenance—but at least the Charlottes tend to be sweet. The Carries are just brutal. If I see one more mean girl at camp trading candy for designer shoes, I'm going to lose it."

"I'm trying to be more Miranda, less Samantha," said Very.

"Just be Very," Lavinia said. "Please."

"You'll still love me even without my gadgets?"

"Even more so. For putting in the time and work to get yourself together."

"Thanks," Very mumbled. This impressing Lavinia thing was . . . almost as satisfying as doing laundry. "Wanna take a look around and see the mortuary—I mean, grounds—here?"

"I do," Lavinia said, standing up.

Per familiar pattern, they locked pinkie fingers and began a leisurely stroll. As they wandered past the buildings and the other residents, Very explained the social order. "There are two sets of social hierarchies here that I've been able to identify. The first applies to the old people versus the young. That stuff mainly only plays out in the dining hall, though. The second applies to all spectrums of ages. I call it the 'Acolytes versus the Resistance Movement.' "

"Acolytes? How so? I thought this place was nondenominational."

"Acolytes like groupies," Very clarified. "The people who've fallen hook, line, and sinker for Dr. Joy's 12 Steps / New Age blah blah blah. They're the ones who talk at group therapy while the others just shrug and feign listening or try to nap."

"Don't tell me," Lavinia started. "You're in the—"

"Napping category," Very finished. "Affirmative. So the Acolytes worship Dr. Joy and want to do things for her all the time, like trim the hedges so Dr. Joy won't have to pay for professional gardeners and shit. She's got them convinced that it's part of their spiritual purification and that they're learning valuable skills."

"Aren't they?"

"If they live in New Jersey or something, maybe."

"I'm from New Jersey. Trimming hedges might be a useful skill at my parents' house, actually."

"Whatever, Jersey girl. The point is, you might want to garden, but you probably have enough sense of your own identity that you wouldn't fall under the Cult of Dr. Joy. See, look at them."

Very directed their walk toward the gardens, where a parade of Acolytes stood at attention for Dr. Joy. The Acolytes wore gardening gloves and rubber boots and had determined smiles and glazed eyes. Dr. Joy pointed to a pile of shovels. She directed them: "Today we're going to dig areas for placing these tomato plants in the ground. These tomatoes will sprout roots to your souls. You must dig, and irrigate, and tend to these souls."

"I had salad for lunch," Lavinia remarked. "It was good. So who are the people in the Resistance Movement?"

Very steered them toward Jones's house. "They're the ones who smoke, and obsessively needlepoint, and bitch about being here, but they're not so much against the whole thing that they escape or drop out of the program. They're progressing."

"Are you in that camp?" Lavinia asked.

"I'm sort of in the middle. Indifferent. Trying to put in my time and make it through, but not really socialize too much with either camp, really."

Lavinia laughed heartily. "Yeah, right."

"Really!" Very said.

Lavinia fondled a strand of Very's flame-red hair and tucked it behind Very's ear. "Sure, sweetie," she said.

Lavinia's lack of faith in Very was unsettling. "So how many counselors at your *all-girls* camp have you been—ahem—'socializing' with?" Very countered.

Lavinia said, "FYI, there are men at Camp Hoochie, too. Lifeguards and administrative staff. It's not entirely sapphic there. Sorry to disappoint you."

"Any special sapphic someone in the Arts and Crafts building you've got your eye on?" Very asked. "Perhaps a nice sophomore from Oberlin College, a folk singer double-majoring in Women's Studies and Bioethics?"

"Ha-ha," Lavinia said. "But if you really want to know, yes, there is someone special I might have my eye on. A lifeguard. Just finished junior year at UMass. Sports Management major, on the football team. Fills out a Speedo nicely. And smart, too."

Very covered her ears with her hands. "La la la," she said. "Can't hear you. Don't want to know."

Lavinia wasn't supposed to have a romantic life unless Very could be there to oversee every aspect of it. The first person who took Lavinia's innocence and hurt her . . . Very would kill him. Or her. Whomever.

They'd passed the smokers and the sewing circles on the porch at Jones's house and circled back to the pool, nestled under several large trees. Because the pool wasn't heated in the summertime, few people used it, preferring the natural pleasures of lake swimming, available not too far away. Because of its lack of popularity, the pool was poorly tended. Parts of the cement around it were cracked, the handrail on the ladder was broken, and the water had leaves and dead bugs floating on top.

Lavinia grabbed a cleaning net propped against a pool chair and swatted it through the water. "Shame this nice pool doesn't look like it gets used much," she said. "The girls in my bunk would go crazy for a pool. The Charlottes, especially. They hate swimming in the lake. Those girls are *so* prissy."

Lavinia wasn't really a priss. Perhaps she wasn't such a Charlotte after all. What would that make her? Just . . . a Jennifer?

Very sat down on the pool ledge and dangled her feet in the water as Lavinia cleaned it. "So what's happening? You know, out in the world?"

"Politics and war and stuff?"

"No. I mean, everyone from school. How's everyone doing?"

"Bryan's fine, if that's what you mean. Got that internship in Portland; it's going well. Haven't heard from Jean-Wayne. Haven't heard much from anyone, really. I hardly ever go online to check messages. Since I have my phone with me for anyone who really needs to reach me, I don't bother using the computer terminals at camp much."

"How do you live like that?" Very asked. She genuinely wanted to know. How was it possible to have online access, whenever, and not care about that privilege?

"Are you kidding? It's a *relief* to be offline. I'm enjoying this quiet summer by the lake, away from the world and information overload, just swimming and canoeing and, yeah, making the occasional pot holder with the Mirandas, who are more industrious than the other ones, let me tell you."

"What do you want to be?" Very asked Lavinia.

"What do you mean?"

"I mean, like, after you've finished school. Have you decided on a career?"

"Funny you should ask that," Lavinia said, circling the pool and tending to it like an experienced nature expert. "It's what's been on my mind. One of the reasons I went back to camp was to give myself one last year of fun and no pressure, but I also wanted to try to figure out what I want to do during this downtime. I've been going to this camp since I was eight. Now that I've graduated to camp counselor, I wanted one last summer there before I have to start doing internships and getting on a real career path. I think I've decided I'd like to be a doctor."

"That's what *I* want you to be!" Very exclaimed, excited.

"So I can take care of *you*?" Lavinia asked.

"No," Very said, deflated and insulted. "Because I think you'd make a great doctor. I think you'd enjoy helping people. Don't worry about me. I can take care of myself."

"Can you?"

"Watch me." Very jumped into the water, fully clothed. She let herself fall to the bottom, flailing her arms wildly, as if she couldn't swim.

From above the water, she could see Lavinia looking down at her, shocked, and concerned, and not sure whether Very needed to be rescued, but taking off her clothes to dive in just in case. Wow, even from beneath the water, Very could see Lavinia's muscle definition now that she was down to her skivvies, and the girl was in some tight-ass shape. All that exercise Lavinia did really paid off. Too bad Lavinia was always covering up the results of her hard work under nondescript jeans and T-shirts. Maybe Lavinia was more a Miranda than Very realized. Hopefully this Speedo lifeguard whom Lavinia was sweet on wouldn't turn her into a Samantha.

Very waited until just before Lavinia hit the panic button. Then Very pressed her feet hard against the pool's cement bottom and pushed herself to the surface, flinging her arms out as she sprang from the water. She swam to the ledge where Lavinia was poised to dive. "I wouldn't jump in if I couldn't swim," Very told Lavinia.

Lavinia sat down on the ledge and extended her hand to help Very up and out of the pool. "Okay. Good. I wasn't sure."

Very sat down next to Lavinia. "I can handle it," Very muttered. "The pressure." She wrung the bottom of her shirt onto Lavinia's leg so Lavinia could share the cold shock of wet.

Lavinia took Very's hand, pressing her thumb along the inside of Very's palm. "I want to believe you," Lavinia said.

"Believe me," Very said. She turned her face to look into Lavinia's eyes. "Please. Believe in me."

CHAPTER 27

"You're wearing *that?*" Aunt Esther said as Very greeted her in the main lodge for their scheduled visit, repeating the classic refrain from Great-Aunt Esther's Greatest Hits.

"You're Wearing *That?*" could have been Aunt Esther's Native American tribal name when Very was in high school. (Very would have chosen "Tender Morsel" for her own tribal name, only no one had bothered to ask.) Very had never understood how someone so nearly blind as Aunt E. could be so consistently critical of every outfit Very wore. Very knew that if her great-aunt had her way, the seemingly nice old Jewish lady would have sent Very off to public high school every day wearing a Catholic school uniform—the nonsexy, not the Britney, kind, long skirt with shirt-buttoned-to-the-neck—and a Muslim burka covering her head and face. As it was, Aunt Esther could barely contain her contempt for cutoff jeans, jeans ripped at the knee, any shirt that exposed shoulders or cleavage, halter tops, T-shirts with suggestive words printed on them, miniskirts, flip-flops, and so on. In fact, Aunt Esther didn't contain her contempt at all. She simply pursed her lips, raised an eyebrow, and said, "You're wearing *that*?"

"Yes, I'm wearing *this*," Very said, tugging at the ends of the sweater she wore over her jeans. It was the sweater Aunt Esther had made Very for her nineteenth birthday.

"I didn't know you liked my sweaters," Aunt Esther said. "I've never seen you wear one before." Her lips pursed, as if she was about to express displeasure; then, as if she realized the automatic reaction was inappropriate to the circumstances, her mouth changed course and turned into a hesitant smile.

"I freaking *love* your sweaters," Very said.

"Language," Aunt Esther scolded.

"I said *freaking*, not *fu*— Oh, never mind. Yes, I love your sweaters. Thank you."

"Who knew?" Aunt Esther said. She shrugged, but was clearly pleased. "You look well, young lady. Better. Did you change your hair?"

"No," Very said. "I just bothered to brush it today."

Aunt Esther grimaced, but pleasantly. "Who knew?" she repeated. "Such a lovely face. Nice to finally see it."

Very knew her aunt wouldn't want to walk all the way to Jones's house, where the cool kids hung out, so Very led her into the crafts room in the main lodge for their visiting time. "Would you like some tea?" Very asked Aunt Esther.

"Excuse me?" Aunt Esther said.

Thinking the old lady was going deaf, Very started to repeat herself, loudly. "I SAID, WOULD YOU LIKE—"

"I heard you the first time," Aunt Esther snapped. "I'm just not used to you extending such courtesy."

223

"I'm not a completely feral beast," Very said. "I know how to offer a person tea."

"Who knew?" Aunt Esther said again. "Yes, I'd love some tea. I prefer English Breakfast, with two sugars. Thank you."

"I'll be right back," Very said. She darted off to the nearby kitchen to prepare Aunt Esther a tea. She dreaded the next two hours. What could the two of them possibly have to say to one another for that long a period? Very hardly knew anything about her aunt and what was going on in her life, which was probably Aunt Esther's fault, for refusing to learn to use e-mail. How else could Very be expected to maintain a relationship with this woman whom she appreciated, but who was essentially a stranger to her?

Ugh, *tick-tock, tick-tock,* please let the next two hours go by quickly.

"How did you get here?" Very asked Aunt Esther when she returned to the crafts room with her aunt's tea. Her aunt no longer drove more than short distances; the only places she drove now were all within a five-mile radius of her house— primarily to the grocery store, and to her card games with the New Haven Benevolence Society ladies.

"I took the train from New Haven to Burlington. A friend of mine used that Global Spider thing . . ."

"The World Wide Web," Very said.

". . . the interconnectivity thingamajig, right. She used that to find a car service to take me from the train station in Burlington to here. The driver will be waiting for me at the main gate promptly at four, so we must be careful not to let our time run over. I have a train to catch back to New Haven, and a friend picking me up at the train station there to take me home tonight. I don't drive in the dark."

It had taken rather a huge effort for this octogenarian to make the pilgrimage to see her, Very realized. "Thank you for coming all this way to see me," Very said. She sat down opposite Aunt Esther at a worktable. Aunt Esther's eyes widened. She started to say something, but Very spoke first. "*Please* don't say 'Who knew?' again. I'm perfectly capable of expressing thanks."

"You're welcome," Aunt Esther pronounced. "I'm glad to see you looking so . . . calm. For you, that is."

Very took a medal from her jeans pocket to show her aunt. "My Two Weeks medal. It's pretty, isn't it?"

Aunt Esther said, "We should sew that to your sweater!"

Now that Aunt Esther mentioned sewing, Very realized how they could spend their time together. "There's a box of clothes in the corner over there, left behind by former residents. Dr. Joy stores them in the crafts room so that people can make art therapy projects out of them. Most people choose needlepoint—it's all the rage here. But I'm sick of needlepoint. Want to make some projects out of the old clothes? Pick some fabrics to put together new sweaters?"

"Really?" Aunt Esther said, clearly touched. "You'd want to make sweaters with me?"

"Love to!" Very said. *Tick-tock, tick-tock.*

Very lugged the box of old clothes to their worktable, and together she and her aunt sifted through old flannel shirts, jeans, sweaters, and T-shirts to identify the garments that could be turned into the best sweater pieces.

"We could bedazzle, too, you know," Aunt Esther said.

"Huh?" Very said.

"Add pretty pieces to spice up old things." Aunt Esther held up a pair of old Levi's. "See where the pants are ripped at the knee? We can fix that."

"The jeans are supposed to look like that."

"Nonsense," Aunt Esther said. She reached for a pink and turquoise raincoat from the reject box. "We can cut out pieces of this jacket into the shape of a flower and sew the flower over the knee. And maybe add some parts of the jacket lining—look at that gorgeous pattern on the raincoat's lining—to embellish the back pockets, and add lining pieces to the leg bottoms to hem them?" Aunt Esther held up the pair of jeans. "Yes, I think these will fit you. A bit too long, so the hemming will work perfectly."

"Awesome!" Very said.

As they cut and sewed and buttoned and trimmed, Very figured now was as good a time as any to ask her aunt a little question: "Do you know who my father is?"

Aunt Esther didn't look up from her sewing, but she answered matter-of-factly, as if she'd been waiting for this question at just this bedazzling moment. "I have some records of your mother's that were given to me after she passed. His name is on your birth certificate and some other documents. And she had a few letters she'd saved from him, from when you were a baby. I don't remember his name. But I've got that box of her things in a safe place for you in the basement at home."

"Can I look through the box?"

"Of course you can look through the box! I'm not hiding anything from you."

"How come you never mentioned the box before, then?"

"You never asked before. You always preferred to go straight

226

to the attic. And you're always so distracted by your machines. I figured when you were ready, and able, you'd ask. And now you have, and I think you are, and the box will be yours. When you come home."

"Is that what I'm doing next?" Very asked. "Going back to your home?"

There was no chance for Aunt Esther to answer over the loud arguing that now was coming from the next room.

"YOU ARE IMPOSSIBLE!" yelled Dr. Joy.

"YOU ARE COMPLETELY INFLEXIBLE!" yelled Jones.

Dr. Joy and Jones must have assumed that the crafts room next door to where they were arguing was empty; it usually was, since the Resistance Movement people preferred to do their needlepointing near to where they could do their smoking, at Jones's house, and the Acolytes didn't dare try new crafts projects without Dr. Joy present to tell them how their creative minds were supposed to work.

Very leaned in to Aunt Esther, excited. "Jones and Dr. Killjoy are going at it! The best entertainment to be found here!"

Aunt Esther dropped her sewing materials on the table and turned her ear sideways to give the argument in the next room her full attention.

"I JUST WANT TO TAKE THE GROUP OUT FOR SOME FLY-FISHING! YOU OF ALL PEOPLE SHOULD REC-OGNIZE HOW GOOD THAT ACTIVITY WOULD BE FOR THEIR, WHADYACALLIT, 'SOUL CLEANSING'!"

"FISHING IS FINE, JONES! IT'S THE MOTORBOAT I OBJECT TO! THE RATTLING SOUNDS WILL THREATEN THEIR RECOVERIES! I DON'T WANT TO LEAD THEM INTO TEMPTATION!"

"A MOTORBOAT IS NOT GOING TO LEAD THEM INTO TEMPTATION, JOY!"

"*YOU* ARE THE ONE WHO IS IMPOSSIBLE, JONES!"

Then, the sound of a door slam and footsteps. A book being thrown against a wall. Then, another door slam, and the sound of more footsteps following the first ones.

Aunt Esther nodded and said to Very, "You're right. Quality entertainment." Very was pleased to have so pleased Aunt Esther, who hadn't found a "story" she liked on the television since *Passions* had been canceled. Aunt Esther picked her sewing materials back up and resumed her work. "And yes, your home in New Haven is there for you, should you choose to come after your time here in Vermont."

It was funny to hear Aunt Esther use the words "*your* home." Very had never thought of it as more than the place where circumstances had forced her to take refuge. She'd never considered that she had a real home.

Aunt Esther added, "I've got a letter for you in my pocketbook. I wanted to see how you were doing before I gave it to you. It's from Columbia. I can tell you what it says if you want."

"You read my mail?" Very asked. She should have known better than to think she could start trusting her aunt.

"Of course I didn't open your mail. I had a phone conversation with the dean, who told me he'd send an official confirmation by mail. I understand the boys from something called the Green Team are also receiving this letter."

"May I see the letter?" Very asked, trying to sound casual.

Aunt Esther took the letter from her pocketbook and handed it to Very, who opened it and skimmed it quickly for the target phrases. The highlights: "regret to inform you . . . ," "concerns have been raised regarding improper use of university facilities," "academic suspension pending a disciplinary committee hearing," and "Yours sincerely, Robert Dean."

Very placed the letter down on the table.

"Are you mad?" she asked Aunt Esther.

"Livid!" Aunt Esther said. She didn't look up to meet Very's eyes, but her sewing hands shook more furiously than usual, and Very could see that her breathing was faster. "I'm a retired old lady bound for an assisted-living home soon enough. My resources are limited. I've tried and I've tried with you. Hoped for you. Prayed for you, even. But this, too, now? You'll lose the New Haven Benevolence Society scholarship funds. I can't in good faith advocate that money going to you any longer." Her eyes finally looked up to meet Very's. The eyes weren't so much mad now as sad. "I don't know what I'm supposed to do with you. I'm at wits' end."

"I don't know what I'm supposed to do with me, either," Very said. She paused. Then added: "I'm sorry, Aunt Esther."

CHAPTER 28

Keisha would know what Very should do with Very.

Their first session together, in which Very had given up some of her most intimate secrets within minutes of meeting her therapist, had left Very feeling like she'd put out too quickly on a first date. But somehow that first date had turned into a relationship that looked like it might be a keeper—at least for the duration of Very's ESCAPE time. Talking to Keisha had become the most meaningful aspect of her stay, besides doing laundry.

"The irony," Very explained to Keisha on Day Eighteen, "is that the university has called a disciplinary committee hearing for me *for the wrong offense*. I totally did worse things than hang out with the *Dreams* guys in a secret room below the East Asian Library"—Very rolled her eyes—"while 'utilizing unauthorized university bandwidth.' What. Ever."

"What worse things?"

"Like, that party I told you about, the night before my melt-down."

"Why was that worse?"

"It was held in the observatory. It's, like, in a famous build-ing, where nuclear physics or something was invented."

"That probably would be considered a more severe crime, yes."

"And all the alcohol for profit. With underage kids in atten-dance."

"Yep. Pretty bad."

"If those buttfuckers only knew . . . ," Very said.

Keisha didn't respond.

"What?" Very asked.

Keisha said, "I don't know if you realize you do this, but you tend to revert to vulgar language when you're confused about an issue."

"Am I confused about this issue?"

"Are you?"

"Keisha! Please. Don't answer a question with a question. Tell me what you mean."

What Very liked especially about Keisha was that when called upon to call it straight, Keisha would do exactly that. And so she did. Keisha said, "I think that, if you looked deep down, you might have ethical concerns about this adjudication matter, and you use vulgar jokes to deflect that. I don't mean to suggest this to you, but from what you've been telling me, I wonder if perhaps you *want* to tell the dean about the irony of the discipli-nary action, to come clean about everything?"

"You mean, now that I'm clean of being online all the time and will acknowledge that I'm addicted to my iPhone and all, I want to wipe the whole slate clean?"

"Something like that. You tell me."

If she was being honest with herself, Very would admit that the idea of wiping the whole slate clean had appeal. "I do have a filthy mind that could probably use extermination," Very said.

" 'Extermination,' " Keisha responded. "That's a harsh word. Do you think you're perhaps being rather hard on yourself?"

"I'm not being hard *enough* on myself, Keisha. My mind thinks of the most disgusting and crude things. You'd be shocked if you realized how depraved I am." Very wanted to be a Miranda, but forget it; she was a Samantha, just without the Botox. There probably wasn't really hope for her. "Once a hoochie, always a hoochie, I guess."

"And how exactly do you consider yourself to be a hoochie?"

"Well, when you start having sex when you're not even thirteen yet, for one thing . . ."

Keisha looked down at her notepad and shuffled back several pages. "Shall I note that you originally told me you were sixteen when you first became sexually active?"

"Lied."

"Care to tell me why?" This was another thing Very liked about Keisha. Very could flat-out admit she'd lied about something important, yet not feel like Keisha was judging her because of it. Keisha seemed to want Very to figure out the reasons instead of punishing her for the reasons. That was cool of her.

"It's just . . . sort of embarrassing, is all. That's way too young to be starting up with all that stuff. If I had a daughter, I would never let that happen to her."

"So do you think your mother should have prevented it from happening to you?"

"Well, she's dead, and I'm the reason, so she can't really defend herself from that accusation."

"That's quite a statement. And I didn't intend to make an accusation. But since you've opened up what sound like some heavy issues, do you want to tell me the story of what happened when you became sexually active so young? Or how you think you may have contributed to your mother's death?"

Very fidgeted on her chair. "The two things are sort of connected." If the beast was to be unleashed, it needed to be coaxed out as gently as possible. "Can we listen to music?" Very asked. Music, and not the usual chocolate recourse, was what she needed to get through this particular discussion.

"Of course."

This was why Very trusted Keisha most of all. She knew when to be flexible. When it mattered.

Keisha got up from her chair and retrieved an iPod attached to speakers from inside her desk. "It's battery-operated," Keisha said. "So technically we're not breaking any rules here. But can we keep this between us?" Confidence begat confidence. If Keisha could trust Very not to tell the other residents about the iPod-playing, Very could trust Keisha to know how she came to be such a terrible person. "What would you like to listen to?"

"Background-music type of thing, preferably. Nothing I have to think about too much."

"Mozart?"

"Too fancy for a sordid story."

"Miles Davis?"

"Perf."

Keisha spun *Sketches of Spain* onto the player, and despite the album being one of Miles's not-obscure, mainstream offerings, Very decided not to hold that against him, or Keisha. The sweet trumpet sound instantly soothed Very.

"Talk to me," Keisha said. She settled back into her comfy chair, sitting cross-legged, without the notepad in her lap, and looking at Very with an intent listening face.

"This song reminds me of the last place my mom and I lived," Very said. "Goa. It's a state in India, on the western side, on the Arabian Sea. It had been colonized by the Portuguese, back in those conquering times, and lots of the buildings there, especially the churches, have this Spanish look and style. And the Portuguese-Indian food there! Ohmygod, so good."

"How did you and your mother end up in Goa, of all places?"

"The usual way. A guy my mom met. He was visiting back home in the U.S. when we were living in Seattle, I think. He owned a little hotel on the beach in a northern town in Goa. He invited us to come visit him. Of course, to my mom, that meant we should move there. So we went to his hotel, and we lived there for a while. Cat worked there, as like a maid or cook or receptionist—whatever needed to be done."

"Where did you go to school?"

"This guy who owned the hotel, he had a younger brother who'd just graduated from college in the U.S. and wanted to see the world a bit before he returned home to start a job and, like, his adult life, I guess. His name was Carter. He was our teacher. It was a very segregated place. The white kids there, mostly kids of expats from Europe and the U.S., didn't go to school with the native kids. There weren't too many of us expat kids in that small beach town, so we were sort of informally taught by Carter."

"Did you go to an actual school?"

Very laughed. "Hah, no, that's funny! There were only, like, ten of us, ranging in age from twelve to about seventeen, and we were a wild bunch. We'd all been moved around a lot, all over the world, and the beach in Goa was so amazingly beautiful. Really, a tropical paradise. We never would have survived being in a real school. So Carter taught us on the beach in the mornings, before it got too hot, or in someone's house, during the monsoon season. It was pretty informal."

"Did you enjoy it?"

"It was great. Until it wasn't."

"What happened?"

Very closed her eyes, to extract the memory. She could see the whitewashed sand and azure sea, the palm trees, the gorgeous old Catholic churches and Hindu temples. She could taste the bebinca—coconut pudding—in her mouth. She could see the flame-red hair of her beautiful mother, who was on the hotel veranda in the distance. She could see her "classmates," all of them darkened to a crisp by the sun, sitting on surfboards and waiting impatiently for Carter to end the lesson so they could hit the waves. Often, they didn't wait for Carter to finish at all.

"I was the youngest of the group," Very said. "The other kids were teenagers, already experimenting with drugs and sex. Most of the parents were wanderers, sort of hippie throwbacks, or die-hard beach slaves, and the way they raised their kids was pretty loose and free. There weren't many rules set down for us. And because I was with those other kids so much, of course I wanted to do whatever they were doing. Also, I looked much older than I was. I got my period when I was eleven, and was totally filled out by the time I was twelve. It was almost embarrassing, the way tourist men at the hotel would look at me. When I was twelve, I looked more like I was twenty-five."

"So was it another student, or one of the tourists, with whom you became involved?"

"No," Very said. "It was Carter."

Keisha nodded. "I see." It was hard to tell on her dark skin, but Very almost suspected Keisha's face was flushing with anger. "How did that happen?"

"It was during monsoon season. Earlier in the week, I had gone to Carter's room to find out where class was going to be that day. The hotel was almost empty. Cat usually went into town in the mornings to buy produce for the kitchen, and Carter's brother, who owned the place, was in Mumbai on business. There weren't any guests staying at the hotel because of the rain. When I got to Carter's room, he said class was canceled for the week. One of the kids had been hospitalized with a serious influenza, and the parents had decided to suspend class-time until the danger of it spreading had passed. But . . . don't laugh . . . I was sort of a geek. I actually liked school, and I didn't want to miss out. So Carter said we could do lessons together. Alone, in his room."

"Did your mother know about this?"

"She did. But her relationship with Carter's brother was falling apart. I don't think she gave it a second thought, me and Carter. She was probably more concerned with other things. Carter was a nice guy. And really, really shy with women. I think he's the last person she would have suspected would have preyed on her daughter."

"Was that what he did? Preyed on you?"

Very could feel the tears and pain and hurt rising, threatening to spread through every cell in her body, but she was determined to see the story through. She'd made it this far. Might as well go all the way. "This is the really confusing part. I'm *not* sure he preyed on me. I knew better than to do what I did. I was twelve, but I was pretty sophisticated, at least in the sense of having had to be pretty self-sufficient most of my life. I was older than my years, and looked it, too, so it was like people validated that to me all the time. But I was so lonely. I was by myself a lot in Goa. Cat was usually working. The other kids thought I was too young to really party with them. But Carter paid me so much attention. We had all these great geeky talks about literature and history and stuff, which we could never do when the other students were around, because they just wanted to hit the waves. They didn't care at all about learning.

"So then, on the last day of the quarantined week, Carter and I were reading a book together, I think it was one of those moody Brontë ones, with all the moors? And the rain was coming down so hard, it was like *bang bang bang* on the roof, but sort of romantic, too, you know? Because it was all gray and mysterious outside, and the wind was howling, and we could hear the waves crashing hard. It was kind of dreamy, maybe. Like, it was us alone in that room, and it felt melancholy and sweet at the same time, and we knew it was the last day we'd be alone together like that. And he leaned over to kiss me, and I let him, and things just happened very quickly from there. I can't say I even consciously made the choice, *yes, I want this to happen.* It was just, boom, done. It hurt, yes—but maybe my heart hurt more."

Now the tears streamed down Very's face, but they were not

bang bang bang tears. They were quiet, and easy, and necessary, and just fine.

Keisha said, "Do you think it was wrong, what happened?"

Suddenly, furiously, Very spat out, "I think it was wrong, what *he* did!"

"Whoa!" Keisha said. "That was quite a reaction. Tell me why it was wrong, what he did."

"Because I was a kid, and he knew that! And he was the adult, and he should have been the responsible one! I *always* had to be the responsible one. It was tiring."

"You're right, Very. It *was* his responsibility. He *should* have acted with restraint. There's a legal phrase for what happened between the two of you. Do you know what it is?"

"Idiocy?" Very said.

"This isn't a joke, Very. It's called statutory rape. Regardless of whether you were willing, or thought you were willing, the fact of the matter is, you were too young to make that distinction. And as the adult, and as your *teacher,* for goodness' sake, it was his responsibility to protect you."

"So you don't think I'm a slut?" Very asked.

" 'Slut' is a self-defining term. I think you should stop thinking of *yourself* as a slut because of one unfortunate incident a long time ago that could have caused the partner in question to be prosecuted if you'd been back home. I think you should stop internalizing that 'slut' label and then behaving accordingly. You were a child then, and you were taken advantage of by an adult who undoubtedly knew better. You are a woman now—capable of choosing for herself who she wants to be and how she wants to act."

"Oh," Very said. She'd never considered the label that way,

or that she could make a conscious choice to think of herself in a better manner, and try then to meet that expectation. The power belonged to her. *Who knew?* as Aunt Esther might have said.

Keisha said, "We still haven't gotten to the other part, about your mother's death. Do you still want to go there, or wait for another time?"

"Well, the two parts are one and the same."

"How so?"

"Because Cat found me with Carter. She had been looking for me, so she went to Carter's room, where she knew we were studying. She walked in on him and me, in his bed, right after. A sheet was over us. But it was obvious what had just happened."

Somehow, having made the decision to at least try to spin negative thoughts into positive ones, Very was finding that what she had admitted to Keisha felt less horrible than she'd anticipated. Very had always thought she could never tell another person about what happened, that the shame was too great, but actually it wasn't. It was just a fact of her life that needed to be aired. The past didn't deserve to be locked up in the attic of her mind. It deserved to fly out the window along with all the other ghosts, to be free, and in turn to free Very from living with it.

"Are you okay?" Keisha asked.

"What? You mean now, or then?"

"This is a tremendous amount you're working through today. Do you want to tell me the rest of the story, or do you need a breather?"

"May I e-mail you the rest of the story?" Very joked.

Keisha smiled. "No, you may not. Miles Davis is the most you're getting out of me."

Very felt a small laugh escape from her throat. "You're making me laugh when I'm spilling my guts to you?" But the smile Very felt returning to her lips was a welcome one.

Keisha didn't respond. She, and Miles Davis and his lulling trumpet-playing, waited for Very to come forth with the next move.

Very considered bolting the room; certainly the instinct was there. But her legs felt glued to her chair. Or maybe it was her heart that was keeping her there, not letting her go until she finished what she'd started.

Finally, Very said, "Cat freaked out when she saw us. But not in the crazy, screaming kind of way. She very calmly—like, too calmly—told me to get up and go upstairs to our room. Which I did. And then I heard shouting between her and Carter, but with all the rain, I couldn't make out what they were saying. Or maybe I didn't want to. In any case, Carter was gone by that night. No note, no goodbye, just gone. It was the next day that my mom really freaked out. When I woke up in the morning, our bags were packed, and she said, 'We're moving,' and just like that, we were on a bus to another beach town a couple hours away. Completely uprooted."

"Did you and your mother talk about what had happened between you and Carter?"

"Not really. She wouldn't look at me the whole bus ride. She had a scarf on her head, and her face was pressed against the window, but I could tell she was crying. When we got settled in the next town, she took me to see a British nurse to make sure I wasn't pregnant. The nurse told me Cat had asked her to tell me to please wait and talk to my mother first before I considered having sex again. And that was it."

240

"Did you feel changed after this experience?"

"It was Cat who changed. Not me. I was just this dumb kid who'd made a mistake. Even *I* knew that. I just wanted to go back to being a kid. But I also knew Cat wasn't going to help me figure out why I'd let it happen. It's like, I was very aware that as this traveling family, we were a ship with no captain."

"How did your mother change?"

"She sort of shut down. She got really quiet, and serious, and wasn't her usual flirty self with men. She'd gotten another hotel job, and she wanted to work all the time, any extra job she could find. Before, when she wasn't working, we'd go exploring together, looking at old churches, and biking through nearby villages when there were festivals and stuff. But after, she just wanted to work, all the time work."

"Why do you think she did that?"

"She said it was because she needed to earn enough money so we could go back home. To the U.S. She said I needed to go to a proper school, and have a proper home, and she said she was getting too old to wander the world. For the first time that I ever saw, she seemed like she wanted to be settled. She said once we got back home, she would figure out a new plan. Find a place where we'd stay for a long while. But it felt like she was working so much to avoid me."

Keisha said, "It sounds like, in her own way, your mother was trying to do the right thing by you. Learn from the mistake, and try to make a better life for you afterward."

"I know that was the reason. But it didn't feel that way at the time. The saddest part is, she achieved her hope for me to have a proper home, and go to a proper school, in the worst possible way. I got those things at my aunt's house in New Haven. But I got those because the U.S. State Department sent me there. After my mother died."

"How did she die?"

"She loved a good fire, my mom. Late one night, when I was asleep, I guess she saw a group of people partying on the beach, with a fire and dancing and food and all that. She went down to join them. It was a group of backpackers traveling across Asia. Those kids passed a *lot* of drugs around. Cat wasn't a drug user; I don't want you to get the wrong idea. I mean, I definitely saw her smoke a joint now and then, and she was open about the fact that she experimented a lot when she was young, before she had me. But she wasn't irresponsible that way. She just knew a good party, like me. So she joined in that night on the beach, and one tainted tab of X was all it took. Five other people died from that batch, backpackers at that same party. But Cat was the only one of the bunch who had, you know, a life outside of backpacking."

"She had a child. She was responsible for you."

"And then she wasn't."

CHAPTER 29

Suddenly Very wanted her machines back, but not for the old reasons. She didn't want to update or comment on a needless blog, or dot-com shop for things she didn't want or need, or participate in an online romance that was as meaningless as it was fake. She wanted to reconnect with her old life. She wanted to hear the songs her mother had taught her to love. She wanted to look at pictures of Goa, and use the Global Spider to revisit the other places she'd lived with Cat. She wanted to connect to a possible future. She wanted to find a service in New Haven that drove elderly people around where they wanted to go. She wanted to see her biological father's name, and put her Google skills to work to see what she could find out about him.

Very wanted a laptop she could use to make a list, but not the simple paper kind of list. She wanted a Very-style list, with too many (parenthetical) asides,[1] photos added, graphic images blended into the text, and a sound track to complement the list,

1. And footnotes.

too, most obviously. It didn't seem unreasonable to want to use machines again for this purpose. Even Keisha, who'd set Very on the task of making the list, acknowledged that the list could be made better through technology. But Keisha said that although the No Techno sentence was admittedly harsh, it seemed to be serving its purpose for Very, allowing her to take the time-out she needed to unload the nonelectronic baggage that was cluttering the hard drive of her soul. (Keisha acknowledged borrowing Dr. Killjoy's lame-ass terminology with that last metaphor and apologized for it, thereby endearing herself to Very for eternity, and allowing Very to see that Keisha was right on this point, even if she was quoting Dr. Killjoy.)

In therapy, Very had made the connection that perhaps her overdependence on technology had been her way of not dealing with other, deeper pains. It wasn't about the technology so much as it was about something to do, to stay busy all the time, and to not connect to what was really in her heart. Keisha said that Very, when she left ESCAPE, would have all the time in the world to reconnect and learn how to live with technology again, hopefully with better boundaries. But since Very was here and starting to make such personal progress anyway, why not really use her remaining time to process what she was feeling, in order to make the best steps moving forward once she was released?

It wasn't like Very didn't have some major shit to figure out once she was sprung into the world. She was more or less kicked out of Columbia, at least until she could defend her case at the disciplinary committee hearing that would be scheduled upon her release from rehab. But what case was there to defend? What could she say? *Um, guilty as charged, on this count, and so many more. Like, sorry, and can I just pick back up with my schooling like this never happened, even though I'm pretty vague about whether I'd want to go back to Columbia at all?* Lavinia was the only reason worth being there.

More scarily, Columbia was only the beginning of the list of life issues Very needed to sort out. She still had to make her amends to people once she went back out. She had a mountain of credit card debt she had to pay off. She had to figure out where she would live.

Problems? Oh, *hell yes*, Very had problems waiting for her on the outside.

Now was the make-or-break time for rehab patients, according to Keisha. Once they figured out how and why they got to this position in life, then they had to decide: Who am I going to be now? Would they resume old habits, or pick up the pieces, grow from the experience, and move on, stronger and better?

Very had no.fucking.clue how she was going to sort out the problems awaiting her on the outside. One thing Very did know was that she didn't want to be guilty anymore of falling into relationships for the wrong reasons. In that spirit, Keisha had suggested that since Very liked lists, she should make a list of her past relationships, to take inventory and see what there was to learn from them.

Very chose to make her list on Day Twenty, during group therapy time with Dr. Joy, who didn't mind Very sitting in a corner of the room with pen and paper in hand, as that's how Very typically spent group therapy time. Most of the people in group were both Olds and Acolytes, and their technical skills didn't extend beyond using the Internet (which a baby could figure out).

Very preferred to sit in a corner and doodle during group time with them, which Dr. Joy actually allowed, saying everyone had the choice about how they wanted to participate, and if Very wasn't breaking any rules otherwise, and if that's how her artistic expression called to her within nontechnological bounds, it was fine for Very to write and draw in a paper composition book while the oldsters bemoaned their unforgiving/unreasonable spouses/employers and discussed with one another why it was embarrassing to their kids that they still used AOL to go online. Snoozers.

5 Guys and 1½ Girls
(with some others in between):
A List, by Very LeFreak

1. *Carter. The first. Hello, Very LeFreak.*
I, Veronica, forgive you. Goodbye.

2. *Hideo. He was my second first. We competed at*
high school. We both wanted to be valedictorian.
He won; I pulled a major senior slump and didn't
break the top ten, but I did come in ranked
eighteenth overall, which wasn't too shabby now
that I think back on it, so yay for me. Not so yay
for me was that by graduation, Hideo wasn't
talking to me anymore.
    Hideo and I were in a lot of the same Honors/

AP classes, and we were also together in Computer Science Club (I was the president) and the Japanese Art Appreciation Club (he was the founder), both extracurricular activities that were basically résumé padders for college applications. We were competitors, but also friends. I loved that his name looked like "Hideous" but was pronounced "Hee-day-oh." He was Japanese and a really nice and handsome boy, nothing hideous about him. His mom made great teriyaki. Hideo and I finally got together in our junior year (it was the sake tucked away in his parents' liquor cabinet—and his folks were away for the weekend). By that time I was pretty acclimated to living in a regular house in New Haven, and going to a regular school, and I'd gotten to the point where I didn't cry through the night alone up in the attic, grieving for my mom; and I also had stopped expecting that I was going to be completely uprooted at a moment's notice, so I guess I was, like, relaxed enough to finally form attachments. I was Hideo's first. I guess he was sort of my first, too? Like, my better first? He was so sweet, and happy, and nervous, and awkward when we finally did it. It was really nice. Nothing AH-MAY-ZING, but good. Comfortable. The problem was, he wanted us to be a proper boyfriend-girlfriend couple. And I liked it better when no one knew we were doing it.

3. Skinemax girl. After he and I started doing it, Hideo became jealous. Every guy who looked at me, he'd be like, "Do you like him?" I guess, in retrospect, he was mad at me for not giving him back what he was giving me. He was always doing sweet things for me and making me little presents and I didn't really do that back for him and now I wish I had because he was a good guy and deserved a kinder girl and I hope he's found someone like that now. Because I wouldn't commit to being "outed" as his girlfriend (just as Kristy later wouldn't with me), he started assuming I was cheating on him with other guys. He accused me of it enough that finally I did cheat on him, only not with a guy, but with the girl at that party. I was drunk, and she was drunk, but that's just an excuse. The truth is, I probably used the alcohol to let loose that side of me that I'd always known was there, but hadn't done anything about yet. But since I can't even remember her name, she probably counts

as the half girl. The whole girl, even if physically
we didn't go as far as me and the half girl,
would be:

4. Kristy. It hurts just to write her name. Still.
I think I really did love her. Straight-up, sober
love. I had all these fantasies that I would go to
Columbia (which was my first and only choice—
I thought I couldn't wait to move back to NYC and
live on my own—hah, what did I know then?!?!),
and Kristy would go to a college somewhere not
too far away. She'd come into Manhattan on
weekends, and we would be a real couple there,
free and happy and out—at least, to each other.
I'd have waited into eternity for her to tell her
family even if that meant her being mine only
privately; though now, I have to say I would never
accept that. After Kristy freaked out on me and
stopped seeing or talking to me, I, too, freaked
out. Got together with several different guys (guys
seemed safe—they couldn't devastate me like a
girl could). Nothing all the way. But several
Everything But situations. I became a real party
girl—I'd do anything to get attention and not
think about the hurt.

5. Brendan. He was the boy I used to get back at
Kristy. He was her cousin, a bronze California
surfer god who went to Yale. I'd met him when he
was using her family's car and came to pick Kristy
up at my house one time when she and I were
studying together. (Our study sessions really were
Kristy and me kissing and talking and holding
each other for hours up in my room, and I swear,
those "study times" with her felt like the happiest
moments of my life to that point, truly AH-MAY-
ZING; no schoolbook ever got opened.) Soon after
Kristy dumped me, I found Brendan online and
posted a comment on his page. He invited me to a
college party, and we hooked up. We went out a
couple more times, and I posted pictures of us
together on his page—nothing really dirty, but it
was obvious we'd gotten together—because I knew
Kristy would see the sexy pix. She worshipped
Brendan like a brother. I know it was mean and
manipulative of me to do that, but I have no
regrets on that one. All is fair in love and war—
isn't that the saying? Also, every girl should get to
be with a beautiful surfer god at least once in her
life, I think. Especially if doing so will hurt the
girl she really loves. Although Brendan was rather
vapid and vain and way too into working out, but

holy shit, he was so nice to look at, and touch.
Really, no regrets. Not really, really. OK, so maybe
it was sort of sleazy of me. But satisfying, in the
moment.

6. Bryan. Oh, regrets. Big-time regrets. I regret
hurting him. I really, really regret losing a good
friend. But . . . after what he did to me, and
said about me . . . fuck him. He got his payback
on me. The score is settled. Even if I *might*
try to make amends to him when I get out. But
it's entirely possible that I am not that big a
person and won't. I don't know. File him under:
"Dilemma Dude, to Be Figured Out, and Possibly
Amended, Later." (I might also swing out a
"sorry" e-mail to Hideo while I'm at it. We'll see.)

7. Ghana. I think I was having some sort of
manic peak when I went after him. That night of
the Astronomy Club party, I was as high as I'd
ever been on what my technological prowess could
accomplish. I needed to burn off some of that
energy. I wish I hadn't done it with someone who
had a girlfriend, though. Note to future self: Don't
do that fucked-up shit that hurts people. Be
honorable in your relationships.

Hmmm . . . that seems like a good goal. Strive to be honorable. It's not all about sex. The heart matters, too. Mine does, at least. Or should.
<u>WANTS TO.</u>

Well, lookee here, Very thought as she finished writing her list and flipped to a fresh page in her composition book. The beginning part of the book was filled with her handwritten thoughts and feelings and lists, but this new, empty page presented possibility. Space was available on the page, and in her heart. Not that Very was planning to go on a romantic hunt, especially not at ESCAPE now that she had barely a week left, but the possibility loomed. She was a free woman. She could act accordingly. When the time was right. And, more important, when and if the right person came along.

Maybe she could be not such a disaster, in the future?

CHAPTER 30

"There's disaster," Jones muttered to Very out on his porch as she sat next to him in the early evening of her Day Twenty-two. Jones was smoking a pipe while she sorted through a container of old buttons for the right ones to sew onto the cardigan she was bedazzling and planning to give to Aunt Esther upon her escape from ESCAPE.

"No," Very explained, "that's the genius of the sweaters. They *seem* like disasters, but they're really quite fashion-forward. You have to look beyond the mismatched pieces and—"

"I wasn't talking about your sweaters," Jones interrupted. He gestured with his pipe to a young male walking toward the house. "I'm talking about the gentleman there. Repeat offender. Went AWOL last time—disappeared into the night and broke into the church charity store in town. He arrived this morning for his fourth rehab stint here. Fun kid, but a complete disaster."

Very thought it strange that Jones would gossip about a resident; she'd never heard him do so before. She said, "I thought the rule was no more coming back to ESCAPE after three failed attempts."

Jones said, "You're right. The rule is supposed to be three strikes and you're out. Unless the parents are so rich and desperate to palm their kid off that they'll offer to finance constructing a dedicated space for smoking and caffeine if Dr. Joy will take their son back one more time." So that explained Jones's out-of-character gossiping. Jones's cookie-and-caffeine income, and the pals-dom of regular visits from residents, could be threatened by the proposed new space. But being genial Jones, he still extended his hand to shake the hand of the stranger, who'd now reached them on the porch. "Greetings, Vikram. Welcome back. How you holding up?"

He was a tall, dark, handsome stranger, this Vikram. He had skin the color of a yummy soy latte; a 'fro-like shock of thick, curly black hair standing straight up, seemingly without the aid of mousse or other hair products; Bollywood-film-star-worthy hazel eyes; and a jaw and chin graced with black stubble. He was the tiniest bit chubby, in a way that made Very instantly want to pinch the small fold of his stomach. His height and girth made him look rather like a black bear, but the really tender, cuddly kind that wouldn't massacre people camped out in the woods in the middle of the night. He wore jeans and a T-shirt with a bird picture stenciled on it, and he was barefoot, like Very.

Vikram said, "Holding up okay, Jones. If being sent back to rehab by court order after a little hacking incident"—Vikram here cough-hacked over the words "hacking incident"—"is considered to be 'holding up okay.' "

"What'd you hack into this time?" Jones asked. "Not the feds again, I hope."

"No, not the feds. Even my parents couldn't have saved me from jail if it had been that again. Nah, this time it was a big toy company. It just pisses me off the way some dolls are built to send fucked-up body-image issues to young girls. I have a younger sister, man, and she is so messed up in the head about her body because of those stupid dolls. I decided to send a little protest message to the manufacturer. Changed the images for some of the key products on the company's Web site, to something closer to explicitly porno."

The wonderfully contradictory thing about his tirade against sexualized dolls was that as Vikram proclaimed it, he was staring at Very's boobs with unabashed admiration. Honestly, she couldn't help but like him.

Jones said, "Your clown needlepoint from last time is framed now. It's inside the house if you want to see it—use that marker from your previous stay to help ease you back in this round."

Very suddenly remembered Kate and Erick's needlepointing story about the repeat ESCAPEe, and them pointing out the clown face he'd left behind. "You're the guy who made the needlepoint clown face?"

Vikram smiled. Hot hot hot. Very's knees wanting to buckle buckle buckle. Vikram looked to Jones. "You *framed* my needlepoint and put it up on the wall? I'm touched. Truly touched. Thanks, man."

Jones turned to Very. "Very, it's your turn to lead the newbie. Why don't you show Vikram his spot on the wall? I want to finish my pipe out here. Vikram, cost of coffee has gone up twenty cents. Cash only."

Vikram saluted Jones. "Aye!"

Very and Vikram went inside the house and approached the wall of framed needlepoint pieces, which looked like a collection of art therapy projects gone psych ward, with pictures of cell phones turned into guns, elves beaming demented laser rays from their eyes, and "Home, Sweet Home" turned to "Help, Somebody, Help!"

"This is the most mental wall I've ever seen," Vikram said.

"I know, right?" Very said. She extended her hand now to shake Vikram's. "I'm Very. It's short for Veronica."

A huge smile erupted across Vikram's face now. "Of course it is. Was your online handle, perhaps, 'Very LeFreak'?" He looked to her boobs for confirmation.

She returned the stare to his chest, to that bird on his T-shirt. "Is that . . . ?" she said.

"The hermit thrush," Vikram affirmed. "Yes. The state bird of Vermont."

She imagined a turban covering his 'fro of black hair.

VIKRAM WAS EL VIRUS!

"Twenty-eight messages!" Very exclaimed.

"Twenty-eight days!" Vikram said.

"Calvin Coolidge! WHAT THE FUCK?!"

"Also from Vermont."

"Gerald Ford? What did he have to do with it?"

"Married to Betty Ford. Famous rehab place in California. Get it?"

"Oh!" Very sighed. Then she shoved Vikram. Hard. "You asshole! I almost went on a mission to presidential libraries looking for you."

"Really?" he said, flattered.

Very plopped down into a chair and buried her face in her hands. "This is bad," she muttered. "Bad."

He plopped down next to her. "Why?" he asked.

The girl who couldn't shut up in Keisha's office now felt reduced to a blubbering mess. ". . . was doing so well . . . didn't even think about you . . . Why now, El Virus, why *now*?"

He leaned over to whisper into her ear. "It's fate. Us, meeting here of all places. Finally. It's meant to be."

Very stood back up, intending to leave, but her feet remained planted on the floor. She couldn't decide whether to stay or go. This was too confusing.

El Virus—rather, *Vikram*—inspected her more thoroughly this time, going from her chest down to her feet, then up to the crown of her head. "Sometimes I could see strands of your red hair around your shoulders. Especially in the Elizabethan-costume pictures. Well done, by the way. Funny, though. You don't look at all how I imagined."

"What's *that* supposed to mean?" Very huffed.

"You look better," Vikram said.

She took her turn to appraise him. Truthfully, he looked better than she'd imagined. Starship captains had nothing on this chunkiest of himbo specimens.

The problem was, she'd stopped imagining El Virus at all. And she'd gotten rather used to not thinking about him, or obsessing about him, or letting him be the fantasy through which she spiraled out of control.

"Are you Indian?" she asked him. She'd always wondered about this.

"Half Indian, half Jewmerican." *Haji Jew-boy*. Of course. "Don't worry. I'm just a nice boy from Scarsdale, underneath my mad confidence and sexy swagger. Loves me a good brisket along with a good game of cricket." Vikram performed what appeared to be, confusingly, an Irish jig around Very.

This was too much, having El Virus here now. Very had less than a week left to go. She hadn't caused any trouble, made any waves, formed any attachments. She was clean. She wanted to stay that way.

But this boy! He was so luscious to look at. And a good dancer! Maybe Very could get a little bit dirty with this one. Maybe? Pretty please?

Although, seriously. Everyone knew the outcome of online romances that turned into Real World meetings. Either they were complete disasters and the two people in question turned out to have no chemistry together whatsoever, or one of the two people turned out to be a serial killer. These would be BAD outcomes. Alternatively, there was historical precedent for the couple in question finding the fairy-tale ending, two virtual people turning out to be real, live soul mates, and together walking off into the sunset (real or virtual, no matter at this point), The End. This would be considered GOOD. There was no in-between for this type of situation. Who ever heard of "Oh, we had this passionate, intimate online affair, and then when we finally met, we were sort of lukewarm on each other, and we fooled around a little but fizzled out quickly." HO-HUM. That never happened.

Very inspected Vikram now. She sang out the song that had immediately cued to her brain: "Psycho killer, *qu'est-ce que c'est?*"

Vikram responded in the same song: "Please don't 'Run run run run run run run away.'"

That's exactly what Very should do.

Run run run run run run run away.

She darted out the front door, away from Jones's house, and back to the privacy of her own cabin.

This was a disaster. She thought she could deal.

She couldn't.

CHAPTER 31

El Virus was watching her. Since his arrival, Very had felt his demon eyes upon her, everywhere and all the time: in the dining hall, during morning calisthenics, while she hung linens to dry outside. Forty-eight hours since his arrival at ESCAPE; two excruciatingly long days and nights of prying eyes, curious looks, psychic inquisition.

She'd been doing her best to ignore him, to pretend her final week at ESCAPE hadn't brought her this disaster that had landed in her lap like a tiger and not like a kitten. But Very had never been a person who could survive the silent treatment. Or, the plain curiosity. Plus, tigers were as cute as kittens, just more . . . dangerous to deal with.

The only way to put out this V-match fire was to contain it.

Late at night as Day Twenty-four wound down, Very resolved to fight the El Virus / Vikram combustion head-on. Technically, lights-out (or "lamps-off") was supposed to happen at 11 p.m. for residents, who were of course welcome to cleanse their souls in the privacy and darkness of their own cabins, in whatever non-technological manner they saw fit, no judgments. But people still managed to wander outside the confines of their cabins, with only moonlight and starshine to guide their steps.

Very appeared at the back window of El Virus's cabin just before midnight. She knocked on the partly open window. "Come out, come out, wherever you are," she whispered.

Through the window, Very saw a light that was most certainly not an oil lamp brighten under some bedcovers. Then Vikram appeared at the window, wearing women's pajama shorts (Hello Kitty! He shopped at Target online, too!) that made Very want to lunge for him through the window. "I thought you were giving me the cold shoulder," he whispered to Very.

She'd like to warm him up but good. She couldn't help herself. But she'd stay strong. Get to know him first.

"I'm thawing," Very said.

"Finally!" Vikram said. He threw a shirt on and climbed out the window. "C'mon!" He grabbed her hand and started to sprint.

"I can't see!" Very protested.

Vikram reached under the elastic band of his shorts and handed her an iPhone.

Behold, sweet Jesus!

He said, "There's a flashlight app on there. I invented it. $1.99 download, includes police lights, disco lights, strobe lights, the works. Made a shitload of money on that app. We can escape now and just go get married if you want. I've got enough banked away to support us for a while."

"Just let me hold your iPhone like this for a while," Very

murmured. How beautiful and smooth the machine felt against her skin. She tapped it on, found the flashlight application, and let Vikram lead the way. "Where are we going?" she asked.

"Shhh," he said. "There's a secret path. Leads to a cozy spot just above the ESCAPE grounds."

"You mean, the other end of Jones's watchful eye."

"Exactly."

They tiptoed through the forest and let the moonlight and iPhone light lead them to a spot at the shoreline just past the ESCAPE grounds' perimeter, separated by a thick stand of trees that hid the escape route. Vikram found the cove like a pro. He led them to a rocky patch of beach, where they sat down on the ground as the lake lapped nearby.

They paused for barely a minute to catch their breaths and admire the moonlit lake, and then Very started the for-real conversation. "If we're going to get married, I should probably know something about you first. So, you. Tell me about."

Vikram said, "I'm a Leo, with Capricorn rising, I believe. Age: twenty. Height: six-two. I like long walks to private lakeshore spots, I prefer not to wear shoes, I secretly want to be a ballroom dancer or covert electronic assassin, and I really dig beautiful redheads. I'm a great cook. Could we please have the sex now?"

Very laughed. "Where'd you get the iPhone, husband?" She tapped it back on to inspect it thoroughly, checking out the games he had loaded, making sure his music selection wasn't sucky, and avoiding looking at his photo collection—what if other online girls had played with him as she had? Very didn't want to know. She handed the gadget back to Vikram, surprised that she didn't mind letting it go so easily. She'd made it this far. No use cheating now.

Vikram said, "I left the iPhone buried under a clothesline last time I was here."

"You knew you'd be back?"

"Just playing it safe."

"How'd you slip the phone past security, anyway?" Very asked.

Vikram shrugged. "Bribe. Cash."

How simple! Cash. Very hadn't even thought of it. She was almost glad she hadn't. The time away from it had maybe helped her head to clear somewhat.

Vikram said, "So how have you been surviving ESCAPE? Here in the cozy-quaint wilds of Vermont? What offense got you slapped into this wasteland?"

Very said, "I went overboard with being online and whatever. Then my friend Bryan destroyed my laptop. And I sort of tried to kill him over that."

Vikram sounded impressed. "*That* is passion. Did Bryan live?"

"Oh please, I barely had him in a strangle before I fell. The bruise on my ass was probably bigger than any bruise on his neck. Wuss."

"So I don't need to fear that I'm marrying a homicidal maniac?"

"You're in the clear. For now. Are *you* a homicidal maniac?"

Vikram said, "Only on certain days of the month." Sweet, sweet woo-words.

"I like those shorts you're wearing. Target online?"

"Maybe. Not sure. I stole 'em from an ex-girlfriend back in my college days. Before she, and the universities, kicked me out."

"She had good taste," Very said.

"Only in boyfriends," Vikram said.

Very and Vikram sat together silently then, for a measure of time that didn't seem to matter. That they could sit together comfortably, without talking, *or* computing, seemed a hopeful sign to Very. The lakeside spot was almost romantic, with only bright, twinkling stars, a half-moon, and a fully loaded iPhone flashlight to help them find their way to one another.

When she spoke again, she asked, in all sincerity, "What else should I know about you?"

Vikram answered in kind, telling her about himself, this time without pretense. Like her, he'd been raised all over, in India, and Paris, and London, and Washington, DC, until finally his parents had landed in the refined suburbia of Scarsdale, New York. They sent him to prep school, where he did well enough to get into Dartmouth, where he didn't do so well, and he subsequently transferred to a smaller college in Connecticut. Like Very, he could excel at academics when he wanted to, but he, too, burned out quickly, distracted by nonacademic pursuits—machine pursuits. Also, all the hacking and whatever, it had caused some problems with administrative types, wink-wink. Very understood. Wink-wink.

She gave him her abbreviated report. The unknown dad, loss of mother, move to New Haven, on to Columbia—a broad sweep of the general facts, with none of the specific hurts and joys and real feelings.

Dawn approached over the horizon behind the trees. They needed to leave hastily in order to return to their cabins before light broke and the staff at ESCAPE awoke and could possibly report the Double V infraction.

Very dropped Vikram back off at his open window. He leaned in for a good-night kiss, but she turned her cheek. The feel of his stubble-fringed mouth upon her skin was exquisite. But no. She wasn't ready yet. But his breath on her neck. Sigh. She wanted so badly to be bitten.

"I think I love you," he said, half-teasing, half-sincere, before he vaulted into his window. From the other side, inside his room, he added, "Even if you don't fornicate before marriage."

Very laughed, and hurried back to the comfort of her own cabin.

Alone in her bed, aware of the condom stash beneath the mattress, she regretted that she'd given in to her stupid resolve not to give in again until she was truly ready. She wished for a Vikram to snuggle up to. Or maybe it was merely a warm body she craved. She couldn't be sure.

This was love? Very wondered.

CHAPTER 32

Very assumed it would be hard to reconcile the El Virus person who'd starred so prominently in her fantasy life with the Vikram creature who'd appeared live and in person at ESCAPE. In fact, it wasn't difficult at all.

Vikram was exactly like El Virus, only a fully dimensional, awesomely cute version. And as dimensions went, his proportions fit nicely against hers. The expiration date on their ESCAPE time together loomed near, but as of Day Twenty-six, they were holding steady on holding out. No kissing, or fondling, or any of the other usual rest stops on the road to fornication occurred between them. Instead, they settled into a relaxed, dreamy state of cuddling, in her room, without his iPhone, between chores and therapy sessions.

Very considered it a sign of her improved mental state that she even distinguished between the online and Real World versions of El Virus / Vikram. And she actually preferred the live version. The online version had been fun and naughty, like the real version, but the real version had bonus add-on features, like being able to breathe on her neck, and let her nuzzle her head against his, with no adrenaline surge rising in Very demanding *more more more*. It was almost like their cuddling time together was a pleasant, stoned haze. Except it was real. And as if to prove that, Very could occasionally feel Vikram's boner pressed against her, but he was considerate enough to leave for the privacy of his own room when that happened, and not press the moment, or her, too far. Cuddling was a nicer way of getting to know a person, Very thought, rather than learning about him online, or jumping straight to Real Time sexual mischief. When Very went back out into the world, she might try to start a whole new crusade, International Cuddling Day or something.

She'd prefer not to move even that fast with Vikram, but the rehab schedule necessitated the accelerated leap to cuddling. With only a few days left before Very graduated from the program, they had no choice but to fast-forward to some form of intimacy. There was no time to grow the relationship; better to just jump in and act as if they'd known each other significantly longer than a few days—when, sorta, they had.

Very didn't bother mentioning El Virus / Vikram to Keisha *at all*, and, sure, holding on to secrets had been a path to darkness in her past. But this time, Very was confident she could handle it. Truthfully, it was still too embarrassing to admit this one detail of her past online life. Not embarrassing in the Deep, Dark Secrets way, but embarrassing in the Sheer Stupidity way, which was a harder distinction for Very to reconcile than the simple El Virus / Vikram fantasy versus the real person.

Anyway, it wasn't like Keisha knew *everything*. It wasn't like Keisha could really help Very with this situation.

(It was more like the situation would probably make Keisha answer Very with more questions. Questions, questions, questions, just when Very was starting to figure out answers, answers, answers, and, just . . . No, thank you. Situation under control. No need to drag it to death in therapy.)

Vikram would probably turn out to be no more than a nice little footnote to Very's ESCAPE experience, and who ever bothered to read the footnotes? Surely Keisha didn't.

"Guess what?" Very said to Vikram during their postdinner cuddle on her Day Twenty-six.

"What, my little cherub?" he said.

"Keisha authorized me to go out for reintegration tonight."

Reintegration was a time-honored ritual, and now it was Very's turn. With Keisha's authorization, she'd be permitted to go into town with a staff member for a night's entertainment at a music or spoken-word performance, so long as it was acoustic. The idea behind Reintegration Night was for residents to be exposed again to the outside electronic world, but, according to Dr. Killjoy, they'd be reintegrating in a safe, relaxing, and non-threatening manner (which was why hip-hop spoken word or tribute performances to the music of Laurie Anderson were, alas, not permitted). The night out was residents' celebratory first step toward the reintegration that would happen once they left ESCAPE and returned to their regularly scheduled, fully powered ON lives.

At Very's announcement, Vikram pulled out of their cuddle and jumped to his feet. He stood over her, looking angry and scary—a side of him she hadn't seen yet, online or real. "Who's leading reintegration tonight?" Vikram demanded.

"Jones," Very answered, confused by Vikram's sudden hostility. "He's taking the few of us who are graduating out tonight to some music event. I think it's some acoustic banjo? It will probably be shit. But it will be fun to go out, finally." Vikram stared at her with utmost venom. "What? Why are you looking at me that way? What did I do?"

Vikram said, "I just don't think it's fair, the way Dr. Joy does this. Separates the haves from the have-nots."

"I hardly think it's an issue of fairness. It's a reward system. For people who've made it through. For instance, Raelene the sexcapade mom? She isn't allowed to go even though she's almost at her twenty-eighth day. Not after the rooftop spectacle with Enrique the club promoter after his graduation last week. Wow, were they loud—"

"Fuck you!" Vikram interrupted. "I could make it through this program perfectly fine, if I chose to."

This time, Vikram chose to storm away, leaving her cabin with such a heavy door slam that her bed shook.

"Psycho killer," Very mumbled.

Poor Vikram. She should be irritated at him for storming away like a stupid girl, but she was more sad for him. She was almost all the way through the program, and she indeed felt a righteous sense of accomplishment. She'd made it through, and, except for fondling Vikram's forbidden iPhone a couple times, she'd made it through fairly, without falling off the wagon, and she was feeling brighter and lighter as a result.

Very hoped for Vikram to one day also share in this sense of accomplishment for himself. It was a sweet feeling, despite knowing that the life awaiting her back out in the world looked to be nasty for a while, until she could straighten out her many problems. But at least now she genuinely wanted to straighten out those problems. And she felt like she might possibly be capable of doing so.

At the same time, Very understood now why Kate and Erick had left ESCAPE with so much trepidation. As exciting as the prospect of leaving ESCAPE was, it was equally terrifying. Reintegrating into the electronic world would be the least of Very's hurdles; tackling the Real World, and her place within it, head-on loomed largest.

CHAPTER 33

Going into town for Reintegration Night, and seeing real lights, and people with phones, and television screens through store-front windows, was not the shock to the system Very had imagined. It felt more like returning to everyday life after a long vacation—a bit abrupt, then business as usual.

Jones had chosen a bluegrass band at a local coffee bar for the group's night out. It was the perfect safe haven, Very thought. The place was designed like someone's oversized basement, with comfortable chairs and sofas, but no alcohol to make people too fun or too mean, just heavy doses of caffeine to make them jumpy and happy within a mellow setting. As expected, the band a little bit sucked, but Very loved hearing the pure sound, anyway. Life was good. Music made it so.

Sharing the experience with Very were about-to-be graduates from the Olds school: Bob from Arizona, architect and misfit online gambler; and Suzanne from Minnesota, scourge of her retirement community's online investment assets. Suzanne sighed over her java brew. "So sad not to share this night with our Irma."

Bob said, "Who would have thought an eighty-year-old, retired Ma Bell great-grandmother would sacrifice all her progress to run off with a newly checked-in thirty-year-old Blackberry dealer?"

Very said, "Ah, cross-generational, cross-platform love. Warms my heart. Icks my soul."

The three clinked mugs, exclaiming, "Cheers!"

Very felt no sentimental loss that she'd probably never see these people again. What they'd shared—the addiction, the disco music during kitchen duty—had been adequate bonding for a lifetime. She wished them well, with no hopes for a future connection. She suspected they felt the same, and liked them all the more for their indifference.

She wished Vikram could be so indifferent, but no such luck. He apparently could not let the good moment on the outside happen without him. He, too, had to participate in Reintegration Night. He walked into the coffee bar just as the group clinked glasses and then brazenly seated himself between Very and Jones.

Jones shook his head. "This isn't good, Vikram," Jones said. "You know that, right?"

Vikram waved his hand nonchalantly. "It's not a big deal."

"It's a big deal," Jones said. "Dr. Joy won't be happy. How'd you get here, anyway?"

Vikram extracted a hundred-dollar bill from his pocket. "This way. Could I, perhaps, interest you in one of these, Jones?

As a very humble thank-you for not telling Dr. Joy about my un-fortunate case of premature reintegration tonight?"

Jones pushed Vikram's hand away. "I can't be bought," Jones said.

Since he was here anyway, and facing some major hostile stares from the Olds, whose faces indicated that reintegration was earned and not bought, Very took Vikram's hand and led him away from the group's table, toward the dance floor. She said, "Are you here because you missed me too much, or because you couldn't stand the thought of me having a night out without you?"

"A little of both," Vikram said.

At least they could share one last dance together, before Very graduated, and before Vikram got kicked out of ESCAPE again.

There was no chance for a dance. The song ended just as Very and Vikram wrapped arms over each other's shoulders. As the band cleared the stage for a break between sets, people in the audience shuffled, getting up to head to the bathroom, or to re-turn to the coffee bar for refills. Standing on the dance floor as the crowd dispersed, Very had a clear line of vision to the far end of the room. Shocked at the sight her eyes discovered, Very let her arms fall from Vikram's shoulders to her sides. Her mouth was agape.

Two girls sat at a remote table, lost in each other's eyes, hold-ing hands across their table.

One of the girls was Lavinia.

Who the hell was that other girl?

As if feeling Very's laser beam of a stare, Lavinia looked up and away from the monster who was affectionately stroking her hand. Lavinia noticed Very, and her face brightened. She raised her hand to amiably wave *Hi* in Very's direction.

Very felt no compatriot amiability. She suddenly felt nervous and weird and alive, and not at all because of the night's caffeine infusion.

WHAT. THE. FUCK. was Lavinia doing *here?* And with a *girl?*

"Don't follow me," Very demanded of Vikram. She didn't need him to distract her while she sorted out this disgusting situation.

Very walked over to Lavinia and Monster's table. "Hi," she said, trying to sound casual, but really wanting to shoot daggers into Monster's soul. (Also, Monster was very butch-looking, and Very had always assumed if Lavinia went in that direction, she'd go more femme. Like, preppy crew girl, or hedonist has-been hoochie. Or something.) "What are you doing here?"

Lavinia smiled at Very. "Hi!" she said, not sounding guilty at all. Lavinia said to Monster, "Annie, this is Very, my roommate from college I was telling you about. Very, this is Annie. Annie is another counselor at camp. It's our night off, so we came into town to hang out, have some fun. What are you doing here? Are you allowed to be, you know . . . out?"

Very said, "It's a reintegration event. For people who are almost finished with the program. We get to go into town for some live entertainment." She turned to Annie-Monster. She accused: "Are *you* the lifeguard?"

Monster said, "I'm working as a lifeguard this summer, yes. Why?"

"Do you go to UMass?"

"Yes?" Monster said, puzzled.

Very turned to Lavinia. "I thought you said he was on the football team!"

Lavinia, responding to Very's tone, answered with similar antagonism, "*She* does the scheduling for the UMass football team."

Monster said, "What's going on here? What's the matter?"

"NOTHING!" Very and Lavinia both said. Then they both amended, "Jinx!"

This was too much. Infuriating. Outrageous. NOT. HAPPENING.

Very said, with no sincerity whatsoever, "Well, have a great time tonight, you two. Don't want to interrupt your time together. Catch up with you later, Lavinia." Very turned away to return to her group, hoping the girls noticed the full-on fuck-off effect of her dramatic exit.

"Lavinia?" Very heard Annie ask Lavinia. "Who's she talking about, Jennifer?"

UGH.

Could Monster be more ignorant?

HATE HATE HATE MONSTER MONSTER MONSTER.

Someone at the coffee bar had turned on a stereo during the band break, and the speakers overhead let out the sweet soul sound of Mr. Otis Redding.

> *I've been loving you a little too long*
> *and I can't stop now.*

As good a make-out song as any.

Very's target-lock stare-glare relocated Vikram, now sitting in the opposite corner of the room, separate from the ESCAPE group. She headed back to him and seated herself on his lap. With the subtlety of a giraffe, she caressed his stubble cheek and breathed hot onto his neck. He didn't bother to question her intentions. He knew when opportunity knocked; he closed his eyes and opened the door to his mouth wide to meet Very's.

Very wrapped her arms around his neck and ground her pelvis into his lap, loving the attention it immediately extended to her. Their mouths met in a forceful kiss, tongues meeting, hands exploring, minds totally not caring that they were in full spectacle at a crowded coffeehouse.

Very felt a tap on her shoulder. She opened one eye from the sloppy kiss with Vikram to see Lavinia standing over them. "Can I talk to you?" Lavinia said. Very shut her eye again and stayed inside the Vikram kiss—harder, more insistent. *Tap-tap* on Very's shoulder, one more time. "Outside," Lavinia commanded. "Now."

Very whispered into Vikram's ear, "I need to go outside and deal with this for a minute. I promise you I'll make the wait worth your while."

Vikram smiled lazily, seeming to appreciate the conflicting messages Very was sending him, perhaps misconstruing her behavior as foreplay, or as some potential three-way action coming his way.

Although it wasn't like Very gave him a chance to question her behavior. She immediately jumped off Vikram's lap to follow Lavinia outside, to a dark, empty alleyway behind the coffeehouse.

"What was that?" Lavinia asked her.

"What was what?" Very said.

"You. Being so hostile to me. Then turning around to make out with some guy. Just to prove how hot you are, I'm sure. *We know*, Very. You don't need to pull that act."

"Are you jealous?" Very asked.

"As if," Lavinia said.

"How come you never told me you were gay?" Very accused.

"Because you always assumed it to be so!" Lavinia said, her voice rising.

"How long have you known?" Very asked.

"I've always known," Lavinia said. "I just didn't fully accept that about myself, or feel ready to get out there, till recently."

"You're on a date, aren't you?"

"People our age don't date, Very. It's casual. It's hanging out. It's— Wait a minute, why am I defending myself to you? Why do you care? Why can't you just be happy for me, especially since you were caught up in a gross display of affection with some dude in there?"

"He's nothing!" Very exclaimed.

Very didn't understand this angry energy erupting so violently from her heart. Because really, Lavinia had a point. Why *did* Very care so much about Lavinia being out on a not-really date?

"If he's nothing," Lavinia said, once again matching Very's belligerent tone, "why were you doing *something* like that in there with him?"

"I don't think you should date that Annie," Very deflected.

"I don't think you should make out with some guy just to prove how hot you are. This isn't about me."

"It *is* about you!" Very said, and suddenly she lurched forward, pressing Lavinia against the brick alley wall. She didn't know what the hell she was doing, but her lips had to touch

Lavinia's. She leaned in to meet Lavinia, and their mouths joined for a kiss that was angry, and surprised, and gorgeous, until Lavinia shoved Very off.

"What the *hell* are you doing?" Lavinia said. "I can taste him on you."

Very didn't care. It was like an out-of-body experience, this need for her lips to touch Lavinia's. She couldn't be held accountable. She leaned in again, this time more tenderly, her lips softly touching Lavinia's, as her hands reached around to trace into the outline of Lavinia's back. And this time, Lavinia dropped her guard, and not only let the kiss happen, but encouraged it, let it go deeper, and longer, reaching her hand around Very's neck to pull Very closer to her.

Very had been privy to more than her share of romantic kisses, but this kiss, now, with Lavinia, this kiss she knew to be different from all those past nothings. This kiss felt like the only one that had ever mattered.

But, then, Lavinia turned her head to stop the kiss. She softly pushed Very's body away, keeping it from pressing into hers. Still, Very kept Lavinia trapped in place, extending her arms on either side of Lavinia's shoulders to the wall behind her.

"What?" Very whispered.

"I can't do this," Lavinia said.

"Are you scared because I'm a girl and now it's real?" Very ventured.

"No. I'm scared to care about someone so determined to hurt herself." Lavinia wriggled herself out from under Very's arms and ran away, back inside the coffeehouse.

But I'm changing, Very thought. *Or trying to. Lavinia didn't even give me a chance to explain.*

Not that Very really could have explained, had Lavinia given her the chance. Very didn't understand what had just happened. She had no idea what had taken over her. She'd only known that she had to kiss Lavinia, and right away, before that Monster got any closer to Lavinia. And without a doubt, Very knew that the kiss she'd shared with Lavinia was the most meaningful one she'd ever experienced. Ever ever ever. It was for sure the best kiss in the whole history of Reintegration Night, and possibly the best Most Unexpected Kiss in the history of the entire world. Never, ever had there been a more beautiful girl to share it with than Lavinia.

But Very also knew she couldn't put herself through it all again: the hope, followed by the rejection.

Fuckfuckfuckfuck, Very realized, as tears welled in her eyes. This was not fantasy. *This* was love.

CHAPTER 34

Very had to come clean to Keisha. Not about Lavinia—that situation was too much to even start dealing with on her next-to-last day before leaving ESCAPE, and obviously that whole thing was doomed and headed only toward epic disaster if Very tried to pursue it further. She had to tell Keisha about El Virus / Vikram.

Since he was a footnote, Very gave Keisha only the generalized, one-sided Wikipedia account, about their online meeting and subsequent message exchange, and about finding one another here at ESCAPE, now. Very didn't bother with any of the details that would have required CliffsNotes analysis. Keisha didn't need to know about the boob pictures, or the erotic-vampire story exchanges, or, most especially, about the pathetic neediness that had fueled Very LeFreak's online relationship with El Virus.

"Why do you think you neglected to mention this before our last session together?" Keisha asked Very. Vikram had never been Keisha's patient, so their discussion was free of that conflict.

"*You* tell *me*, please. I'm tired."

"You're not tired. If anything, I think you're more invigorated than ever."

"I'm not. I'm lazy. Incapable. I'll probably self-destruct immediately when I return to the outside."

"Do you really have so little faith in yourself?" Keisha asked. When Very didn't respond, Keisha kindly didn't answer her own question with another question again. Instead, she told Very, "*I* have faith in you. That you've come clean about this experience, even at this late stage, shows me you really do want to learn and grow and move on."

"But what if I don't?" Very asked. "Vikram's pretty damn cute. I'd maybe just rather, you know, wait for him to break out of here again and just be with him and, like, live off his application-development profits. He's got a *lot* of money socked away! Being with him could make the whole transition so much easier."

"Really? Have you asked yourself whether Vikram really wants to change and do better, as you seem to be asking of yourself?"

"Rich people don't have to do better," Very pronounced. "It all gets taken care of for them."

"I doubt that," Keisha said. "Vikram's been here four times now. Have his problems gone away because his parents can afford to keep sending him here, or have they gotten worse, because he seems to use money to buy temporary solutions that only

281

sabotage his long-term prospects? Just because a person can pay rent or his student loans or not worry about the next paycheck doesn't make him immune to problems."

"It should," Very said. Then she added, "I might just leave today instead of wait for tomorrow. I'm done here."

"Where will you go? I thought your aunt was arriving tomorrow to attend your graduation and to take you back to New Haven with her."

"I'll make sure someone calls her to tell her not to come. If I'm all empowered and shit, I think I ought to leave right away. Before Vikram tempts me any more. I'm in the danger zone, Keisha. I totally want to be really naughty with Vikram. *Really* naughty."

"How naughty?"

"*Depraved* naughty. Sex and machines and tuning out the world and just being together with our stuff and our orgasms, probably. I want to run away with him. But if I leave now, ahead of schedule, I'll save us both from that temptation. I'll hitchhike my way out and not look back."

"Safety concerns of hitchhiking aside for the moment, you don't think you can survive the Vikram temptation even one more day?"

Very shrugged. "No."

"You're sure?"

"No."

"Then stay for me," Keisha proposed.

"What do you mean?"

"I mean, you've worked so hard and come so far. It will be my honor to watch you graduate tomorrow. Please do not deprive me and your aunt of that. I feel confident this temptation you think you feel is just anxiety about leaving."

The anxiety, Very knew, had nothing to do with leaving, and everything to do with Lavinia. But that unexpected situation had to be hopeless. It had been a crazy moment, that was all. Even if Very did entertain the notion that she possibly had deeper feelings for Lavinia than she'd realized, the reality was that no way would someone as together as Lavinia ever want a girl as fucked-up as Very. Right?

Keisha added, "And even if you think you want to run away with Vikram, at least for pragmatism's sake, wait another day. If you ever hope to be readmitted to Columbia, you'll need to show that you officially graduated from this program. Ride out the anxiety if only to get that graduation certificate."

"Okay." Very sighed. "I'll stay another day." *Even though every basic instinct in me right now wants to prove how fucked-up I am. Where the hell is that box? I want to force it wide open.* "But I'm going to lock myself in my room as soon as I leave your office, and no goodbye campfire parties tonight, or final crafts projects on Jones's porch tomorrow morning. I'm staying away from temptation. At least until tomorrow."

"Good girl," Keisha said.

Very returned to her cabin. She was going to shutter herself inside so she could stay true to her vow to Keisha. If she could make it through the next twenty-four hours without succumbing to what she knew she wanted to do—bolt—maybe she'd be all right after all. Pandora's box would stay shut this time. *Should* stay shut.

Alone on her bed, bouncing on it in great agitation, Very decided to pack her belongings. That activity hardly took up any time. Next, she opened up the frame of the 12 Steps needlepoint that hung over the desk in her cabin. She took a Sharpie pen from the desk drawer and inserted the word "fuck" into the needlepoint at amusing places.

Step 2–Came to believe that a fucking Power greater than fucking ourselves could restore us to sanity.

Step 10–Continued to take personal inventory, and when we were wrong, promptly admitted it. Sorry, mothuhfuckah. I was wrong, yo.

Stay busy, stay busy. Stay out of trouble, for only one more day.

She could do it.

Very skipped dinner, wanting to steer clear of any temptation she might find in the dining hall, in the form of Vikram. She bolted her cabin door before going to bed, as a final defense against him. She willed herself to sleep at eight that evening.

But Vikram just had to pry that box open.

At eight-thirty, the smell of freshly baked cookies coming from her half-open cabin window awoke her. Very looked out the window. Dammit! Vikram stood outside, holding out a plate of cookies to her.

"Go away!" Very said. "Please?"

"You missed dinner. I thought you might be hungry," he said.

That just proved it. Vikram was a provider. A goodfella.

She opened her window all the way to let him in. So what about that stupid box? For cookies, she'd sell out her own soul.

Vikram stepped inside the window and passed her the plate of cookies. "They're the vegan cookies. Sorry. But they're still pretty tasty. My last batch at ESCAPE, I guess."

"What do you mean?" Very asked, biting into a dark-chocolate munch of delicious.

"I'm kicked out. For good. Jones reported me for leaving the grounds on Reintegration Night. And for fraternizing. Interestingly, he didn't report that I'd fraternized with *you*. Just that I had engaged in behavior that showed I wasn't serious about the program. Again."

"So what will you do now?" Very asked.

"My parents are arriving tomorrow morning. But I can't deal with that scene one more time. All the crying and screaming and blah blah blah. I'm hitching a ride out tonight."

"How?"

"There's a boat coming to pick me up at our secret-cove spot." Vikram took the iPhone from underneath the elastic band of his shorts and waved it in the air. "I arranged it this afternoon. Just came here to tell you goodbye. We'll find each other again, on the outside, later. Right? We have to. We're kind of the same person. You're like the female version of me. Don't you think?"

"I guess," Very said. She didn't think she liked the idea of a male version of her. She didn't think she wanted to be the female version of anyone but herself.

Very felt bad for Vikram. He looked so defeated. Should she go down on him, to make him feel better? And make herself feel . . . more like herself?

Vikram sat down on her bed and made himself comfortable. He patted the empty space next to him, inviting her in for a cuddle.

Danger. Danger.

Fuck it.

Very lay down on the bed and skipped over the cuddle, grinding her body directly into his as her mouth found his for some serious hard-core tongue-and-mouth action.

They had to consummate this already, before it was too late. As a final goodbye. Very would do anything not to let her mind indulge the fantasy she really wanted.

But what Very really wanted refused to be held at bay. Very couldn't get the picture of Lavinia out of her head as her mouth kissed Vikram. His kiss felt haunted, and wrong. It was giving her a headache.

Very removed her hand from the equatorial point on his body that it had reached and pushed Vikram away from her. "I can't do this," she said. "I'm sorry."

"Fuck!" Vikram said, breathing heavily. "You're torturing me with this hot-cold act. What the hell do you want?" He beat his head into the pillow on her bed.

"I don't know!" Very said.

Vikram jumped out of bed, shaking with anger. "Well, figure it the fuck out!" He tried to storm out of her door, but it was bolted shut, and that was just awkward, so he retreated back out the window, and was gone.

Go back to sleep, Very, she told herself. *That never happened. You're almost there.*

Vikram returned, however, soon enough. Calmed down, and at her window once again. Through it, he whispered, "Hey. You. So I've given it some thought. Since it seems the only way to get you is to marry you, why don't we just elope? You, me, leave together, tonight? The boat's coming in twenty minutes. Are you in? Adventure awaits. All you have to do is say yes."

Welcome back, Pandora! It's official now!

The world outside, it really was too much. What Very truly wanted she'd never have. Very needed someone to provide the path for her. Do the work for her. Vikram was nutty, but fun, and he'd get the job done. At least in the short term. She'd worry about the long term later. The sex would probably be all right. The adventure would be awesome and perhaps terrifying, but she'd worry about that later, too.

"Will you do the cooking?" Very asked. She hated to cook, preferred to be served.

"You bet," Vikram said.

Very said, "Okay, then. I'm in. Let's do it."

CHAPTER 35

Vikram did not do things on a small scale. If Very hadn't realized this about him before, she surely realized it when the small powerboat that came to retrieve them from the secret cove at ESCAPE turned out merely to serve as an usher. The man operating the powerboat took Very and Vikram to a spot out in the lake where the water was deeper, and where a large tourist ferryboat idled, awaiting their arrival. The man helped Vikram and Very climb the ladder to the big boat, and as if that wasn't terrifying enough, when they set foot on the larger boat, Very saw only a small crew on board. No tourists to be found there. Vikram had chartered a whole freaking *ship* that could hold hundreds of people for the sole purpose of whisking him—and, at the last minute, Very—away from ESCAPE. The ferry would take them to the New York side of Lake Champlain, where, Vikram told Very, a car would be waiting to whisk them to Albany, where they'd get on a plane bound for Vegas.

"Will we be married by an Elvis impersonator?" Very asked him.

"I was thinking more Liberace," Vikram said.

They sat alone together at a window table inside the ferry, which was warmer than the deck outdoors. A candle had been placed on their table, and the gorgeous night view of the lake, along with the ferry's gentle motion, might have been considered romantic. But Vikram was not interested in courting Very at that moment. He was too consumed with planning their wedding from his iPhone—booking flights, and a hotel, and Googling to find the most over-the-top impersonator wedding minister available the next night, and mumbling, "Awesome! Awesome!" at every sequined Liberace impersonator site he found, yet not bothering to share the images with Very.

Frankly, Very wasn't sure she even needed to show up for their wedding. Planning and executing the adventure from a remote ferryboat seemed to be companionship enough for Vikram. She didn't need to be there. The longer she sat in silence watching Vikram, who was tapping away, the more time she had to realize . . .

WHAT THE FUCK HAD SHE DONE?

Very had left ESCAPE with nothing besides her wallet. No luggage. According to Vikram, she didn't need anything but the clothes on her back. That was part of the adventure. Buying all new stuff, starting over. She didn't say goodbye to Jones or Keisha, or even leave them a note saying goodbye and thank you. No time for the niceties, Vikram had said. Very hadn't yet had the courage to call Aunt Esther to tell her not to bother going to ESCAPE tomorrow for Very's graduation, which obviously now would not happen. Nor would the possibility of Very's ever going back to Columbia, or finding Lavinia again, either, so long as Very remained on this boat.

Since Vikram didn't seem to need her participation to arrange their whole future together or whatever, Very left him and walked upstairs to the captain's deck. The ferryboat captain was a real *Aargh!* kind of guy, Very could tell. He wore the blue captain's jacket, and was holding the steering wheel or whatever that thingamajig was as he looked out over the vast expanse of water and charted their destinies, Very surmised.

"Um, excuse me, sir?" Very said to him as she entered the deck.

"Yes, lassie?" the captain said. A real *Aargh!* kind of fellow, just as Very had hoped.

"Do you know where Camp Hoochinoo is?" Very asked.

" 'Course I do. My granddaughter goes there. We're just about to pass it on the port side."

"Huh?"

"Look over to your left."

Very looked over her left shoulder, imagining the right girl over there.

"Someone you're looking for?" Captain *Aargh!* asked. "That's a pretty intent stare you've got going in that direction. Are you sure you're on the right boat?"

"Nope," Very said.

"What's thataway?" The captain gestured port side.

"It's not what," Very said. "It's who. But it's hopeless."

"How do you know? Did you try?"

Very remembered now her first day visiting at Jones's house, when she was ready to bolt from ESCAPE, to break all the rules—when she felt her most defeated. But something about what Jones had said that day had inspired Very to at least try to try. And she had. And it had worked. Kind of. She'd made it through the program. Felt better. Wanted to tackle her problems head-on. Until she'd abruptly thrown in the towel. Because she got scared of something real.

Hello, Fear. Let's meet head-on.

If Very was going to try to try . . . hell, she'd *try*. Not be a mover, or a shaker, or a doer, but a trier. That could be her label. Forget about Very LeFreak. Now she could be Very LeTry. Why not?

Very said, "Do you think the small boat that dropped us off at this boat could be called back into service?"

"You want to go back to the cove where we picked you up?" Captain *Aargh!* asked.

"Not exactly," Very said.

The captain looked doubtful, then seemed to analyze Very's face, as if trying to gauge the seriousness of her intention. Finally he said, "All right. What can I say? I'm a sucker for a pretty girl." He radioed a crew member to report upstairs for a new mission. "But this will cost," the captain told Very.

"Put it on Vikram's tab," Very said. Really, she'd be saving Vikram money with the new navigating coordinates she was about to lay out. The cost of the alimony he'd have to pay her otherwise would be stratospheric. He'd thank her one day for this discounted adventure plan. "And could I ask you another favor?"

"What's that?" Captain *Aargh!* said.

"May I please borrow your phone to send a text message? And could I borrow five dollars?"

"That's two more favors, not one."

Very smiled sweetly. Sincerely sincerely. "Please?"

The captain handed her his phone. He reached for his wallet, but first asked, "When do you plan to pay me back the five dollars?"

"Probably never," Very said.

The captain handed her a five-dollar bill. "I like honesty," he said.

CHAPTER 36

Reliable as always, Lavinia awaited Very on the dock at Camp Hoochie's canoe port. She'd set up a torchlight on the beach behind the dock for the powerboat carrying Very to find her.

But Lavinia didn't seem happy to see Very. She didn't offer to help Very jump from the boat to the dock, she didn't say "hi" or even "bye" to the guy on the powerboat who'd shuttled Very to the dock, and she didn't throw herself into Very's arms and exclaim, "At last, my darling! I knew you'd come for me! I knew that amazing kiss wasn't just my imagination!" Instead, Lavinia glared at the powerboat speeding off into the distance as it left her alone with Very on the dock. She sat down on the dock, her legs dangling over the lake, and crossed her arms over her chest. "What the hell, Very?" she asked.

Very sat herself down next to Lavinia, but not too close—not yet.

"Aren't you happy to see me?"

Lavinia said, "It's midnight. I had to get someone to cover my bunk at the last minute so I could come find you here. I thought you weren't supposed to be sending text messages and stuff like that again until you were officially released from the program. Which, I gather from your text message and sudden arrival here now, did not happen. What now? Have you decided you need to throw an epic party here, too, and you'd like to try to get me fired from my job in the process?"

"I wanted to talk to you," Very said quietly. Humbled. Scared. Had she gone from one bad scenario to an even worse one?

Try to try, she reminded herself.

Lavinia said, "So why all the James Bond action? Sending me a message from a forbidden device, getting dropped off in the middle of the night in the middle of nowhere, all so you could talk to me? Wouldn't a simple phone call have been easier?"

Her tone was angry, but—Very could feel it—there was hope. Very felt an undercurrent from Lavinia messaging Very that despite her hostile affectation, Lavinia was maybe—*maybe*—also a little flattered by the dramatic display of effort.

That was it! *Shazam!* Lavinia had been at the bottom of Pandora's box all along.

Lavinia was hope.

Very said, "What I have to say had to be said in person. And it couldn't wait."

"Why?" Lavinia asked.

Very took a deep breath, then let it out. "I love you, Jennifer."

Very had always imagined that when she finally spoke those

words to the special someone in her life, she'd be looking that person directly in the eyes, perhaps holding her hand. Certainly she wouldn't be sitting next to that person, not touching her, not even looking at her, but looking straight ahead to a lake instead, which wouldn't be so rude as to reflect back rejection.

Very heard Lavinia, and not the lake, answer back, "What about that guy I saw you with the other night? How can you even say such a thing to me when—"

Very interrupted her. "He was a mistake. Vikram was . . . he was the Wizard of Oz. He was a part of the journey to lead me back to what was always there. But in the end, he was a mirage. It's *you* who are the end of the yellow brick road."

Lavinia said, laughing, "Please, stop being so gay. You're making me sick."

Very, too, laughed. She inched her pinkie finger over, and over, until yes, it was touching Lavinia's.

Lavinia let the pinkie-finger action happen, but did not return it, nor look at Very.

"Why me?" Lavinia asked. "Why now?"

Very turned herself to face Lavinia. She reached for Lavinia's whole hand. "You because you are the kindest, most generous person I've ever known. You make me want to try to be a better person. Because there's no one I enjoy being around more than you, even when you're making me pay for rehab with my own money. Because you make pies for people going to flash mobs that you don't approve of but you go along with because you're such a loyal friend. Because you snore so loudly when you sleep it's almost deafening, but you also giggle in your sleep, like you're having the best dream ever; adorable. Because you work so hard, and inspire me to have even a fraction of your dedication. Lavinia . . . you because you're the most beautiful girl I've ever known, inside and outside. You do realize you're totally hot, don't you?"

Lavinia turned now to sit opposite Very. She let Very stroke her hand, but still she did not speak, or look up to meet Very's gaze. Maybe the corners of her mouth curved into an almost-smile. Maybe.

Very continued, "Why now? Because I might be a little bit getting my shit together. It's not about me wanting you to take care of me. I know my life is a mess. I know I made that happen. But I want to straighten things out. On my own. I'm gonna go live at my aunt's again in New Haven. Withdraw from Columbia for the time being. I was in way over my head there. Couldn't handle the academic or financial pressure. I think I'd like to chill for a while, get to know my aunt a little better, maybe try to help her out in her old age, or something? I'll get a job, and work to pay off my debts, and try to take some classes to keep earning credits until I figure out the next step, and try to make my amends, and . . ."

Now Lavinia looked up to meet Very's gaze. She placed her hands on Very's cheeks. "Really?" Lavinia said.

"Yes," Very said. "Really."

"That's a good plan for you."

Oh dear. Very's heart had skipped at Lavinia's touch, but now she realized—Lavinia was only commending her plans. She wasn't giving her heart over to Very.

"I know I'm a total fuck-up," Very ventured. "But if you're taking applications for a girlfriend, I'd like to apply. I'll work really hard, and put in really long hours, and—"

Lavinia shook her head, laughing. Unfortunately, she also returned her hands to her own lap. "I don't think this is such a good idea," she said. "You and me."

"Because of Monster?" Very asked.

"Who?"

"That girl. Whatshername."

"Whatshername's name is Annie. And she's training to be a firefighter, Very. She's going to save people's lives and homes one day. I'd hardly call Annie a monster."

Lavinia was just so impossible. Why couldn't she just admit it already? "But isn't it me you'd rather kiss?" Very demanded.

Lavinia wouldn't answer.

Very pulled the five-dollar bill from her pocket. "I have that five dollars I owe you."

Lavinia reached for it. "Cool—"

Very snapped the five-dollar bill away. "You have to earn it."

"Excuse me?"

"If you can kiss me now, and then tell me it means nothing, and really mean it, I'll give you your five dollars."

"That's not a fair deal."

"Who said anything about fair?"

Lavinia sighed. "You're making this very difficult. But if that's what it takes . . ." She leaned in to Very, but with a confidence that suggested she was going to win this bet.

Not likely.

Very touched her fingertips to either side of Lavinia's face, softly scratching her fingernails along Lavinia's cheekbones. Good grief, even Lavinia's cheeks were perfect. Very turned her head, parted her lips . . . and waited. Lavinia needed to do the work this time.

Lavinia's mouth found hers, and this time it was Very who let it happen. The kiss started delicately, almost politely, but—*aha!*—it was Lavinia's tongue that seemed to want to find Very's, Lavinia's lips that wanted to lull Very's into the most exquisite dance ever, Lavinia's hands that reached to pull Very's face closer to her own, Lavinia who seemed to be sucking the very air from Very's throat.

Their mouths finally disengaged to take a breath.

Lavinia stroked Very's hair back and then rested her forehead against Very's.

"I want my five dollars," Lavinia said.

No way.

Lavinia waited. When Very didn't offer it, Lavinia reached into Very's pocket and plucked the five-dollar bill from it, and then placed it into her own pocket.

"Now the slate is clean." She pressed her lips closer again. "Gawd help me, but you know I can never resist you. You've got the job, Veronica."

CHAPTER 37

Lavinia preferred to play by the rules.

She wasn't going to start apologizing for that now.

In the first place, counselors were not allowed to have overnight guests on camp grounds. Therefore, Lavinia made Very spend the night on the dock, since the dock hovered over the lake, and Lavinia didn't think the camp actually owned that part of the lake, so technically, no rule would be broken if Very camped out there for the night. Mercifully, Lavinia was kind enough to retrieve a sleeping bag from the nearby boathouse for Very to sleep in. Sweetly, the sleeping bag fit two, and Lavinia shared it with Very.

But in the second place, although the moonlight and the lake and the snuggling up in a sleeping bag could be considered conducive to further merrymaking, Lavinia was not a girl who'd go there so soon, even with an official declaration of love from her true love. She'd lock lips with Very, and let Very hold her, and let Very stroke her hair and nuzzle kisses onto her neck, and talk with Very through the night, under the stars, but that's as far as it would go.

"I'm not ready to operate on Very speed," Lavinia told Very before their kissing went too far.

"*I* am not ready for Very speed," Very acknowledged.

She wouldn't mind kissing Lavinia forever and ever. Very couldn't believe how lucky she was, to get to hold this beautiful creature for herself. They didn't spoon-cuddle, but lay through the night face-to-face, breast-to-breast, leg-to-leg, ankles intertwined. All that boner-cuddling before—that had just been a sham. It was Lavinia who was the right fit.

But the fairy-tale night had to end, with dawn rising, and marking the time for the one rule Lavinia was willing to break.

If she drove Very back to ESCAPE, Very would have to check back in through security; there was no safe way to reenter the grounds from the road unnoticed, and of course if Very was noticed, her night away, and all the many violations of ESCAPE policies that had gone along with it, would cause Very to lose her graduation status that day. She'd be letting down Aunt Esther and Keisha. She'd lose her chance to even hope to one day be readmitted to Columbia.

The only solution was for Very to return to ESCAPE the way she'd left it—by boat. And so Lavinia—master camp counselor, many-badged former Girl Scout, Columbia crew girl extraordinaire—canoed Very back to base camp. But Very didn't direct their boat all the way back to the secret cove; she chose a landing spot not quite as far away, at the other end of ESCAPE, so Lavinia would have less paddling back to Camp Hoochie.

They stepped out of the canoe to say their goodbyes, and to share one last kiss.

"Guess what?" Lavinia said, pulling away as Very tried to go in for one last last kiss. "I think you're getting some company today. I forgot to tell you last night with all the other stuff going on. But I got a message from Jean-Wayne. Guess who's checking into ESCAPE as you depart?"

"Beautiful!" Very exclaimed, stretching her arms out in a V-shape.

Very gave her girl one last last last kiss and watched as Lavinia stepped back into the canoe and paddled away.

Very wanted to scream *I LOVE YOU!* to Lavinia riding off into the sunrise, but she also didn't want to wake Jones, whose house was so close to Very's landing point.

Very started the journey back to her cabin, careful not to ruffle bushes or step too hard across the grass. The distance back to her cabin wasn't that far, but it felt like miles, a vast space of land Very had to successfully cross, quietly, without dancing and shouting to the world *My life is a mess and I don't care! I love the best girl in the world! I'm leaving here today to return to freaking New Haven, where I can't wait to bedazzle with my elderly aunt and probably get a job at Target or something! How's that for an Ivy League dropout? Envy my glamorous LeFreak life, why don't you!*

The path was short but felt so long, so Very decided to conquer the distance by planning what she'd do for Jean-Wayne's arrival, to distract her attention away from the fear of being caught. She decided she'd make J.-W. a list of the places where the *Dreams* dropouts had left stashes of green eyeliner. She'd make him a list of the best nights to try for kitchen duty:

Mondays were the worst (mashed potatoes—peeling so many potatoes was hell on the hands); Wednesdays were okay (somehow Hump Day made other kitchen workers more amenable to sing-along dishwashing games); and Saturdays were the best (strawberry shortcake night equaled yummiest leftovers). She'd leave him a needlepoint pattern he could stitch for himself. It would say: *Try to try.*

"Going somewhere?" Jones asked.

Very stopped her delicate tiptoe back to her cabin to see Jones standing in front of her on the path to his house. Geez, it was only, like, six in the morning. Why was he awake? Very noticed the pipe in his mouth. *Oh, that's why.* He was wearing a woman's pink satin robe over his flannel pajama bottoms. That was weird. Very hadn't pegged Jones for that type.

What could she say to him now? She was totally busted.

So Very didn't say anything. She just stood there, like the guilty trespasser she was. But as she stood there, she noticed a woman walking past the window inside Jones's house, wearing nothing but a pink camisole that surely matched Jones's robe. Very almost threw up in her mouth. The camisole was worn by Dr. Killjoy. It and its owner walked up the stairs inside the house and out of Very's—and Jones's—line of vision.

So now who was busted?

Jones looked at Very. Very looked at Jones. Who'd give first?

"Carry on," Jones finally said.

"As you were," Very said.

They nodded to each other, a silent pact acknowledging the sanctity of their secrets.

Very took off in a sprint toward her cabin. Never had she been so excited to return to that dump. It was hard to believe she'd spent nearly a month there, a month of stultifying boredom along with some decent moments, but essentially a time when nothing exciting happened. But then, within the last forty-eight hours, Very had fallen in love with her best friend, broken free from ESCAPE, almost eloped with El Virus, and claimed Lavinia for her own, for real. And when she left ESCAPE today, she'd leave it for a whole new world of trouble.

Perfect.

Very stopped her run, wheezing and aching. She leaned over to rest for a moment and catch her breath. Good Lord, she really needed to try to try to get into better shape. Lavinia had probably paddled herself all the way back to Camp Hoochie by now, and Very could barely manage this short sprint to her cabin.

No matter.

Very stood back up, took a deep breath, and then resumed her run, no matter how much it hurt.

She was halfway there, wherever there was.

ACKNOWLEDGMENTS

This book evolved out of another novel, my first, that I completed in 1996, about an online bon vivant who has to dry out from technology. This was before the proliferation of cell phones, so long ago that people used dial-up to go online. (I just heard Very gasp.) Although that original novel was never published, I'd like to thank all the members of that long-ago writing workshop group in San Francisco who were so instrumental in helping me finish it, especially our great teacher and friend Lewis Buzbee.

Fast-forward to the present, and I cannot extend enough gratitude to the folks who made this book possible: Nancy Hinkel, Allison Wortche, Jennifer Rudolph Walsh, Alicia Gordon, and all their colleagues at Knopf/Random House and WME. Thank you, thank you, thank you. And, as always, great thanks to some amazing writer friends I've been fortunate to call on for support while writing this book: Patricia McCormick, Jaclyn Moriarty, Eva Vives, Libba Bray, Kim Gamble, Anna Fienberg, Melina Marchetta, David Levithan, and Megan McCafferty. Finally, friends and family (you know who you are): ILY.

FROM THE BESTSELLING AUTHORS OF *Nick & Norah's Infinite Playlist* COMES A NEW HE SAID/SHE SAID ROMANCE:

DASH & LILY'S BOOK OF DARES
NOW AVAILABLE!

"I've left some clues for you.
If you want them, turn the page.
If you don't, put the book back on the shelf, please."

So begins the latest whirlwind romance from the bestselling authors of *Nick & Norah's Infinite Playlist*. Lily has left a red notebook full of challenges on a favorite bookstore shelf, waiting for just the right guy to come along and accept its dares. But is Dash that right guy? Or are Dash and Lily only destined to trade dares, dreams, and desires in the notebook they pass back and forth at locations across New York?

Rachel Cohn and David Levithan have written a love story that will have readers perusing bookstore shelves, looking and longing for a love (and a red notebook) of their own.

ALSO BY RACHEL COHN AND DAVID LEVITHAN

NICK & NORAH'S INFINITE PLAYLIST

NICK: "I know this is going to sound strange, but would you mind being my girlfriend for the next five minutes?"
NORAH: I answer his question by putting my hand around his neck and pulling his face down to mine.

An ALA-YALSA Best Book for Young Adults
An ALA-YALSA Top Ten Quick Pick

★ "An emotional, passionate, cathartic, and ultimately hopeful night of wandering, music, and incipient love. . . . Electric, sexy . . . and genuinely poignant."   —*The Bulletin*, Starred

NAOMI AND ELY'S NO KISS LIST

Naomi ♥ Ely.
And she's kinda *in* love with him.
Ely ♥ Naomi.
But he prefers to be *in* love with boys.

An ALA Rainbow List Selection for GLBTQ Content for Youth

"A brilliant tour-de-force—funny, sweet, sly, and sexy."
—*Kirkus Reviews*

"A witty and highly entertaining exploration of love, friendship, and misunderstanding."   —*School Library Journal*